I0669997

Stories They Told Me

Theresa C. Dintino

Wise Strega Books

Stories They Told Me

ISBN 978-19398-12-52-0

Print design by Loose Cannon Ent.
www.loose-cannon.com

To my daughter, Mia
~powerful sage~
Creator of New Stories

Acknowledgments

There are many people whose works have inspired this one. I would especially like to mention Jane Roberts, not only for her work with the Seth material but the full body of her work in which she shares so generously and intimately the insights of her genius mind.

Readers of the text in its various stages include Brian Swimme, Mara Keller, Willow LaMonte, and Linda Eneix. Each of their expertise and input allowed the book to reveal itself on a deeper level. To my sisters, Cecilia, Laura and Maria: companions on the journey. And to Susan, gratitude and prayer.

To Suzanne deVeuve for her inspired painting which graces the cover.

The Winged Goddess of Desire sections from the Zohar and Jewish Midrashim were derived specifically from the following two texts: Barbara Black Koltuv, *The Book of Lilith(Nicholas-Hays Inc. 1986),* and Raphael Patai, *The Hebrew Goddess(Wayne University Press, 1967).*

Specific inspiration for Poetry in text is as follows: *Rachel's Song: The Sea Around Us* by Rachel Carson; *The Sun: The Hidden Heart of the Cosmos* by Brian Swimme; *the birth of life: The Great Cosmic Mother* by Monica Sjöö and Barbara Mor.

Table of Contents

Aureillia's Prophecy

In a world where the Goddess is murdered
These things will come to pass
In ceremonies of death
The flesh of live women will burn
The skies to our north
To thick black smoke will turn
The power of healing forgotten
Blood flows
When in a woman
It should not flow
Mutilation
Knives knowing places
A knife should never know
The power of pleasure forbidden
Women!
To steal your power
This violence upon you they shower
She shall be shattered
Her images smashed and battered
There She lies in many pieces
As worshiping of Her ceases
Fear not, Minoans
Your love for the Goddess is clear
Remember that
Only in a world where the Goddess is murdered
Shall these things come to pass

I was the Prophetess of darkness.
Of these things did I foretell.
I saw my island destroyed. Its people mistreated.
Snake showed me these things.
Filled was I with the pain of the things I did see, and so I learned to dance
the dance of release....

Part I

The Island of Crete 1574 B.C.E.

Chapter 1

The island was scorched with heat. A brazen gold sun. Thick-crowding humidity. Harvest came in slow. The First Fruits celebration happened late.

On Crete we were accustomed to hot weather, yet this was something more. Where we normally enjoyed a cooling-off in the morning and evening, these days began and ended with heat. Sleep was disturbed. Even courts of shade trees and stone benches, usual places of respite, offered little relief. The limestone was heated to the core.

The festival procession was long, originating in the west court and spiraling around and into the Center building, attaining full fruition in the Great Hall where, on the platform at the far end of the room, was an altar. Here, between branches of evergreen and fresh blooms of flowers, we would place all the many first fruits. We, the people of Minoa, were and had been a fortunate community for some time. The offerings were plenty.

This was the first time I was present in the procession as a priestess of the Bird. I was a priestess of the Snake who had transformed into a Bird. At present, I was all there was to my temple. I walked alone, carrying the first cup of harvested barley within a finely crafted golden chalice to present to Her in gratitude and hope for continued prosperity. Lilith, my five-year-old daughter, clapped her hands together gleefully as I walked by. She was standing with her father, Danelle, who lifted her up high to better see.

At the celebration meal after the procession, Thela, my sister, remarked that the wine was especially robust. All surmised that the fruit of the vine must favor the heat. The food, though prepared with great care, was limp with exhaustion. We abandoned ourselves to the wine and took on the dancing with gusto. Hands interlocked, we raised and lowered our arms in rhythm, circling together in the wide forecourt as the day surrendered itself to the night.

Lilith danced until her body collapsed in protest. Danelle carried her to her room in the block that she and I shared with several other women and their young children. I joined him, eager to change out of ritual attire. After settling Lilith in for the night, we started back to the celebration. When we reached the place in the path that splits one way toward the Center and the other way to the sea, Danelle paused and, pointing in the direction of the sea, said, "Shall we?"

I nodded in agreement, delighted to abandon further festivities. The path ended on a wide, sandy beach lit by the full harvest moon. Scattered about were many others who had slipped away from the group as well. From where we stood, we could see the marina and the tall masts of ships docked overnight. From the hill beyond came the muffled sound of celebration. Danelle grasped my hand and, together, we walked away from it.

The sea approached the land in hard-pounding waves that ambled toward us as we walked along the shore. So many times had we walked this beach together, shared ourselves to the sound of its constant pulsing. The sea was a part of our beings; the essence of our connection.

I knew Danelle at the beach as different from Danelle in our village of Knossos, Danelle at the temple, Danelle as the father of my child. Danelle at the beach, with white, salt-stained skin whose sandy legs and feet moved against mine, was playful and passionate, windblown and sun-browned, reaching into the depths of my being. Danelle at the beach was mine alone.

I spread my arms wide to the cool wind the waves created and said, "Only to cool off. I have been hot since I awoke."

Danelle stopped walking and considered me, hands on his hips, a crafty smile on his face. He arched his eyebrows slightly and let out a snicker before grabbing me into his arms and running to the water, where he threw me directly into the crashing waves. The shock of sudden water left me gasping for breath. I arose and attempted to orient myself through the strands of hair that clung to my face, when Danelle grabbed me yet again and released me into the crest of a breaking wave. The wave's power was so fierce it dragged me against my will toward the shore. I could hear Danelle laughing as I was left crawling in the sand. It was a mean, satisfied laugh, which I could not allow.

I raced toward him, intending to submerge him. He escaped me, diving into the water and reappearing behind me. I pulled his face to me and kissed him long and lingering on the mouth, weakening him just enough to get a firm grip on the back of his neck and force him under the water. He struggled but, in spite of his best efforts, could not overpower me. I allowed him up for a bit of air before pushing him back under the waves. After several times, he held his hands up in surrender. "Aureillia," he cried, "Stop. I need air."

"Tell me why I should?" I said, gripping his neck and holding his face close to the water.

"Because I'm nice," he sputtered. "I'm sweet. I'm...I'm Danelle!"

"Nice? Sweet? You threw me into the water."

"You said you were hot."

"You threw me in twice!"

I forced his head back under but this time I went with him and, wrapping my arms around him pulled him into me. I could feel the smile forming on his lips as I covered them with mine. We came up for air together. I held his head within my hands, my fingers moving through his short, half-wet hair and studied his face, the wise lines curving around his mouth. "I suppose I forgive you," I said.

"Forgive me?" he laughed, lifting my skirt, his hands upon my thighs, tickling me with pleasure. I felt the descending within, the quick rush of blood, the heat of desire between my legs. "You should be thanking me," he said, moving his thickening upon me. "I helped you cool off."

"Thanking you?" I said.

"Shhh," he said, covering my speaking mouth with his. Our tongues met as he entered me, slowly. My legs, welcoming him—opened—took him in to the deeper, where I pleasured myself upon the length of him, the inside of me expanding, swelling with delight to his presence. The water crashed over us as I demanded more from him, its white foam sparkling in the moon's light as he surrendered himself to me. I gasped in completion and nuzzled my face into the well-known crook of his neck and shoulder. "Aureillia," he whispered. Familiarity is a gift.

Each time we shared each other was but a continuation of the time before, an ongoing dialogue between our beings. We knew each other so intimately, it was a returning, a welcome home.

After, we lay in the sand looking up at the moon. "Do you see the shadows on the moon?" I asked.

"Yes," he answered.

"Even She has areas of darkness," I said.

Danelle raised himself up on his elbow and looked into my face. "Is that what it feels like?" he asked. "Areas of darkness?"

"Places where no light enters. A heavy sponge. Dense patches of fog. Yes. Don't you have any?"

"I am sure that I do. I simply have not yet encountered them." He looked back at the moon, so bright in spite of Her darkness. His hair, silhouetted against it, stood up around his face which, though shadowed, I could see had become serious. "Aureillia," he said, "I've been wondering. Do you suppose it at all matters who it is that stabbed you?"

"What?" I cried. "Stabbed me when?"

"In your final vision. It seems odd to me that you saw yourself stabbed, but you do not know who it is that stabbed you."

"What would ever cause you to think of such a thing?" I stood and began to wring the water out of my dress. I twisted and squeezed, hurried and impatient.

"How is it," Danelle continued, brushing sand off my back, trying to be helpful, "that you walk around with this knowing. You never speak of it; we never speak of it. How difficult it must be for you."

"Stop!" I said, suddenly, pushing him away.

"What is it?" he asked.

"I wish not to speak of this," I said, pulling my dress down over my head. "Stop this now. I do not want it now."

He nodded his head slowly, observing me with concern. "I'm sorry, Aureillia," he said. "I did not mean to upset you so."

"No. It's just...I'm simply exhausted from the day. All this heat." I released a deep sigh. "Come, let's go," I said, taking his hand into mine.

We walked back to Knossos in silence.

Chapter 2

"He is right," Helena said when I told her of the happening on the beach. We were sitting on pillows, facing each other in her private consulting room in the temple of the Butterfly within the Center.

The Center building was the center of activity, the center of the community. Here were the temples: temple of the Snake, Butterfly, and Bee; temples of Male and Female Being. Here were the healers, the artists, administrative councils, storage rooms. Here is where the festivals happened; Snake Goddess festivals, festivals of the Bees and Bull leaping.

Since there was not yet a temple of the Bird on Crete, it was my responsibility to create one. As I did, I was temporarily under the tutelage of the temple of the Butterfly. Helena, the leader, was mentoring me by passing to me certain teachings of the Butterfly that would be useful in my work as a Bird.

Helena's consulting room consisted of one wall of stone behind me. The other three were partitions of yellow silk. On either end of the long silk wall across from me stood a large labrys, or double axe, upon a tall wooden handle. The labrys's wide, arcing wings cut into the temple air, representations of the Butterfly Goddess.

"That's it! It is exactly this which has been bothering you. You have not yet completed that vision."

Helena was referring to a vision I'd had as a Snake priestess in which I had seen myself and my then-mentor, Barbara, living again in another time, in what seemed to be the future. In this village, in a place called the hills of Judah, there was a series of underground chambers where we secretly worshiped the Goddess. In my final vision, I had seen myself murdered, stabbed in the back in that place, in those caves.

"That cannot be true," I said. "That vision served its purpose. I saw what I was suppose to see at the time. It is over, finished. I do not wish to return to any of that."

"You are mistaken, Aureillia. Danelle is right." She was becoming excited. She stood up and began thinking on her feet, walking back and forth. Her movements caused the wall behind her to sway, moving once forward into the labryses, once back away from them. Her, long, loose-fitting dress flapped about as well, its wide arcing sleeves fluttering. Her excitement only added to my sense of agitation. "You must turn around," she said. "You must face whomever it is that is stabbing you."

"Ridiculous," I said, pulling my knees up into my chest. "Why should that matter?"

"Because you already know who it is," she said. She came and knelt down beside me. I looked down at the floor and blinked hard. "You are simply unwilling to accept it," she said, quietly, her dark hands upon my knees. "It is this—this truth you are unwilling to accept. It is this which is causing you pain."

"You do not know what you are talking about," I said, spitting venom.

"You are quite right," she said, standing up and backing a safe distance away from me. "But you do. You know what I'm talking about. You know what I'm saying is true." I said nothing, but turned my head to the side, still holding my knees into my chest. "Turn around, Aureillia. Look into his eyes. Turn around and face him."

She walked out of the room. I listened to her sandals slap against the bottoms of her feet. How I hated her at that moment.

Surrounding the Center were blocks of rooms where residents of Knossos lived together, groves of cultivated trees and patches of intentionally planted crops. Beyond these were forests of trees: cypress, pine, oak. To these trees I went often, in retreat. As now, I emerged from the Center into the shocking bright light of midday Knossos and followed the well-worn trail into the trees. Alternating shades of darkness and light flashed almost wildly around me as I pushed deeper into the thickness of the forest. Birds chirped and went about their lives above me. The air became cooler, the smell thickened. Of course, Helena was right. She was exactly right. I knew I had not fully processed that particular vision. At the time I received it, even to Barbara it had seemed odd. When I first told her of the vision, she scrunched her nose up and shook her head. "Aureillia," she asked, "Who is it that is stabbing you?"

"I don't know," I replied. "I cannot see him."

"Why not?" she asked. "You do not have one singular perspective in this vision. You are an observer of events as they happen. You see us. You see our faces. You see yourself as other. How is it that you cannot see who it is that is stabbing you?"

"I can see his arm," I said. "It is this which makes me positive that it is a man. It is most certainly the arm of a man."

"Follow that arm," she said. "Follow that arm back to the face."

"No," I said, shaking my head. "I cannot, I tell you. It is all darkness."

A look of alarm crossed her face. I saw it but chose to ignore it. "Not important for now, I suppose," she said, shaking the concern away, but her hands were moving, one tapping rhythmically upon the other as she pursed her lips and looked at the wall behind me.

I took the comfort of the lie. I knew it then. It was evident from the darkness; a black veil closing over even the possibility of revelation. I knew it was odd, but I did not care. I could handle no more. I had felt it in all of my being.

Here, years later, it wished to return. Now that I'd had time to rest, to recover, it was ready to finally reveal itself to me. I did not want it to. I wished to stop it. To say 'no' to it once again. I knew, however, following the dirt trail as it wound itself back toward Knossos, that it was already too late.

To the people of our community, the community of Minoa, Danelle was a much-beloved artist. He spent his time carving miniature images onto semiprecious stones. He had developed the gift of creating individual sealstones for people upon their request. Most ended up proudly displaying them as a pendant hanging from a cord around their neck. The images he created resonated with such insight and intimate detail about the requesting person that some attributed to him the gift of divination and oracular sight. Danelle, however, rejected this title.

"You seem chilled," he said one evening as we stood in the forecourt of the Center building watching Lilith, our daughter, play with her friends.

"Yes, I am. A bit," I answered, tugging at my shawl. "Come, sit beside me." I sat upon a bench and pulled him down close to me.

"Are you ill?" he asked, leaning in toward me. Age on Danelle's face revealed itself in elegant lines around his eyes and mouth. His skin, with the years, had grown taut, fitting more closely around his features, giving him an even more defined look, showing better his blue eyes. His hair, instead of whitening, had darkened but still shone golden in the sunlight. The work he did had caused his posture to become slightly stooped.

"It is possible that I am ill," I answered.

"Is it the venom? Has the venom returned?"

"I do not believe that it is the venom," I said, hoping to ease some of the worry that had come into his face. Within the body of a Snake priestess, the venom that remained could, at any time, become toxic. We had both seen this happen with Barbara and knew the same fate might be awaiting me.

"What is it then?"

"I am not sure," I said. I leaned into his arm, which was wrapped around me. The night air was cool and permeated with the presence of flowers that only reveal themselves in darkness.

"Danelle," I said, "you know that I am ever so grateful to you for everything that you have done for me?"

"Why do you say such a thing?"

"Do you know it?" I asked. "Do you know that you are my dearest friend?"

"Aureillia, why are you speaking in this manner?"

"Only to answer, please, Danelle."

"Yes, I know," he replied, squeezing my hand firmly within his. "We've been friends forever. Even when we were that age," he said, pointing to Lilith and her playmates, "you were my favorite person."

I smiled, remembering our childhood days together. He was always a bit older. A bit more mature. A guardian and protector while at the same time deeply respectful. "If only it could stay that way."

"I see no reason it should not."

I took his large, fine hand into mine, rubbed my cheek upon it and enjoyed his smell. I knew that Danelle had given me all the patience that he had within him to offer already in my time as a Snake priestess. Though he was generous and kind and may have been able to find within himself more, I dared not ask it of him.

Because of this, I tried with all my being to settle my feelings about my vision on my own. I sat extended silent time. I prayed for help. I took long sojourns to mountain sanctuaries. I even let Helena lead me on guided journeys back to the place of the vision. Yet, whenever it came to the time to turn around and look, I could not.

One day, after another exhausting try, Helena came and sat beside me. "There is a place," she said, "one place that I know of. In this place it is said no one can resist visions, no matter how hard they fight. Go. You must go. You must take him with you."

Chapter 3

I requested space for two on the ship that regularly sails to the healing temples of Malta. I asked Danelle to accompany me there. He agreed.

Unlike other sea voyages, one requested journey to the healing temples of Malta from the elders. We departed on a special boat with other pilgrims. Midway through the journey we were served a drink to help with seasickness from the large waves we had encountered. The drink relaxed me so, I fell into a deep slumber and was surprised to find when I awoke that we had arrived.

Priestesses were there to meet the boat and any pilgrims that might be on it. They led us to a cool stream full of separate pools in which to bathe. The priestess who attended to me was a young woman whose hair hung in many braids around her face. She became alarmed upon seeing the many bite marks on my arms.

"I am a priestess of the Snake," I said. "It is not harmful to others."

She studied the bites for some time. Her tight fitting necklace of obsidian brought forth the deepest hue of her black skin.

"I must go for something. I will soon return," she said, leaving the water and walking to a stone building beside the stream.

I submerged myself into the refreshing water, my skin absorbing it eagerly after all those many days of salt air. The priestess returned with a clay vessel in her hands.

She guided me out of the water to sit upon a woven mat resting on plush grass. Taking one of my arms into hers, she began to rub the substance from within the clay vessel onto one of my bite marks. It was hot oil, and stung. I gasped and pulled my arm away.

"This is fighting herb," she said. "It is good ally for snake bites. It can bite back."

I gave her back my arm. She continued rubbing the oil into each bite in slow, circular motions. Through the bite, Snake passes sacred teachings to Her chosen priestesses in the form of visions and voices. The information I had processed in my time as a Snake priestess had been particularly difficult. With each mark she attended to, I received a memory of the vision to which it belonged. This surprised me; I had not realized I was still this intimate with Snake.

"These bite marks are very dark," she said. "They do not normally remain this strong. It is clear to me the snakes have caused you great sorrow and that you hold to their memory still."

"It is true that they have caused me much distress," I responded. "Do you believe the memory can be somehow reduced?"

"If you could find a way to better integrate the teachings, these scars and yes, your pain would be less." She lifted an armband up out of the pile of my belongings that I had removed in order to bathe. "The first thing you must do is stop wearing these," she said. "One can integrate nothing fully if one does not accept who she is."

"I wear them for others as well," I said, panic overtaking me. I had not been without my armbands since I had become full priestess. "It seems to make them uncomfortable."

"That is none of your concern." She placed the armband back onto the pile. Its gold glimmered against the sun. "You may do as you wish, but you must know, healing can only begin when we are willing to tell the truth, regardless of how it makes others feel."

Being clean made me aware of a feeling of exhaustion, which I assumed to be from the boat ride. She gave me a clean, sleeveless, white robe to wear and led me to a small hut of woven grasses. Inside was a low bed covered with a blanket into which I crawled, falling immediately into slumber.

I awoke to the bright light of the sun breaking through the weaving of the roof. It was suffocatingly hot. I sat up and rubbed my fingers against the protruding bite marks along the insides of my arms. My armbands—golden twisting snakes with a head on each end—sat upon the robe in the corner of my hut. I put the robe on, but left the armbands there.

This hut, I observed as I emerged from it, was one of many scattered on a hill overlooking a shoreline with a long, white beach. From the ledge upon which I stood, I could see Danelle on the beach below, crouching in the sand, looking at something. The bright blue water rolled gently toward and away from him, its white edging leaving part of itself behind with each inward stroke. When I approached him, I saw that it was a starfish he was observing, poking at it with a stick, occupied with its movement. He stood to greet me. He looked rested. His face was shaven smooth and his eyes were clear. I saw him notice my arms.

"I have been advised not to wear my armbands," I said.

"Have you?"

The armbands had protected the skin they covered from the sun, creating white rings underneath, making the bite marks, for the present, even more noticeable. "It is most difficult," I said, holding my bare arms into my body.

"Yes," he said. "I should think it would be." He took one of my arms into his hand and traced the inside of it with his other hand, passing back and forth over the bite marks, the soft, vulnerable skin around them with his fingertips. "You need not hide them from me," he said. "I know who you are."

I smiled at his perceptiveness. "Let's go find some food," I said. "I'm hungry."

There were only a few active temples on Malta at this time. All others had ceased functioning long ago. Malta had not maintained a steady population for some time. There were settlements of people, separate from the temple priestesses, scattered about. It had been difficult for these settlements to grow and develop into villages, because of the presence of the rootless people who roamed the sea, often pillaging the island which, with its central location and lack of strong center, was too readily available. The priestesses and operating temples they left alone. They did not consider them to be a threat and even visited them for advise and prophecy, which made some of the priestesses uncomfortable. These people were a different breed. The priestesses did not agree with many of their actions and yet, felt disinclined to send them away.

We were told, however, to take great care when wandering about the island on our own and exploring the temples no longer in use. This made me think of Hypia, Danelle's mother, whose passion had always been to preserve the ways of Minoa, our society. She had recognized it early. There was a fire spreading across the lands. One that included aggression, plundering, and disrespect for the Goddess. This fire I had witnessed burning out of control in my visions. It saddened me to encounter it once again, here.

After eating we were led to the Tarxien, the active above-ground temple complex. It was a rounded, expanding building with a flat roof covering its immense sprawl. The front was a series of lintel designs—two standing stones crossed by a third stone at the top. On either side of these were stone walls that opened into a wide half circle. The arcs of the curved walls stretched apart like two engulfing legs, pulling us in.

The central door had a large boulder pushed into it over which one had to climb to enter. At this boulder, we were met by a priestess who informed us that here we would make our request to the Goddess. At night we would sleep in the underground temple, the hypogeum, awaiting a response.

"You should know," the priestess said, "if you make a request of the Goddess in the Tarxien, you are required to remain on Malta, returning to the hypogeum each night thereafter, until you have received your response."

I looked at Danelle, who suddenly seemed very tall, and then at the priestess. "I agree," I said, still looking at him, this person familiar yet unfamiliar, all at once possessing the qualities of a stranger.

She looked at Danelle. He turned to face me. Looking into my eyes, he said, "I agree."

She waved us inside. We lingered, looking at each other. The wind blew, carrying the scent of Jasmia. I gasped at the feeling of loss it contained.

"You first," Danelle said, indicating that I should climb up the large rock in front of me and enter what appeared to be a very dark tunnel first.

I lifted my robe and climbed up the stone. Once on top, I put my head into the opening. Its damp, lightlessness gave me a sudden chill. "It is very dark," I said, turning around from within the darkness and facing him.

"Yes," he said. He was smiling.

I sat back and regarded him.

"What is it?" he asked.

"You're smiling," I said. "I had not realized that your smile had gone." The sun was shining on him, making him look bright and joyful, reminding me of the boy Danelle I had known. I reached out to him and touched his glowing face. "Are you sure?" I asked.

"Sure about what?"

"This," I said, indicating the temple. "Making a request. The commitment."

"Isn't this why we came?" A line was growing behind him. He turned around and looked at it. "I suppose we must," he said. "Go on. I won't be far behind you."

I turned and began to crawl through the tunnel of stone. It was very long and became tighter the farther I crawled. In the center of my womb sat the seed of dread. I knew neither Danelle nor I would go back on a commitment made to the Goddess. There was a large part of me that resisted what I was about to do. In the darkness, this part threatened to overwhelm me. There was, however, only one way to go, and so I moved in a forward direction, feeling my way along cool, moist rock until the air finally lightened into the other side.

I crawled down the ledge into a large round room with many people in it. There were several altars against the walls covered with offerings. Though it was a relief to be out of the tunnel, there was something disquieting about this room as well. The rounded red walls seemed to lean in, creating a thick pressure. I found it difficult to breathe. Yellow light filtered in from the other end. I took Danelle's hand and walked toward it. It was coming from a doorway that opened into an open-air, circular court surrounded by yet more temples and shrine rooms. This was a large temple complex indeed. The court was full of benches, libation bowls, and many sculpted figures. I relished the blue sky above me and breathed in the fresh air. There was a tall, flat standing stone with an intricate dual spiral design carved onto it. I indicated to Danelle that I would be making my request here. He motioned to me that he was going back within, to the dense red room we had only just left. Then he kissed me with a long and pressing urgency. I leaned into the urgency, grabbing him almost greedily before setting him free.

I knew well my request. I had known it before I left Crete. I stated it here, in the open air court of this temple, before this tall, receptive stone. The spirals were interlocking and, at the same time, independent of one another. The eye could not see where one ended and the other began, though it tried, moving over the curving, connecting arcs. I wondered what it was that Danelle would request.

At night a priestess led us into the hypogeum—the large group of moon-shaped chambers dug into Her depths. We followed the bowl of fire she held in her hands, descending deeper and deeper into Her womb tomb. The moment we entered this space, I became aware of Her presence: a deep, dark energy, the flow of moisture, an inner welling. The deeper we descended, the stronger it became. We passed through many interconnecting rounded chambers. Many of the chambers were at different levels, connected sometimes by polished steps, other times by steep, wooden ramps. The atmosphere was cool but thick with a dampness that enveloped the body in a blanket of sticky dew. The bowl of burning light made uneven flashes upon the glistening stone walls surrounding us.

The priestess led us into a large oval hall with a high, vaulted ceiling painted with a red, curling pattern. Many pilgrims were lying on mats upon the floor. She motioned to two unoccupied mats with folded blankets beside them. The far end of the room had a carved lintel design that created three mock doorways reminiscent of the design in the Tarxien building above. The work was stunningly exact, with a fine polished smoothness.

I sat on my mat looking at this image, this mystery evoked, carved into this stone wall. Doorways to where? I wondered. Were these only false passageways or were they something more? The priestess walked away taking her light with her. In the blackness, I unfolded my blanket and pulled it up over myself. There we slept, returning night after night, awaiting a response from the Goddess as we had promised we would.

During the days, we roamed the island exploring the remains of abandoned temples and following dirt pathways that led to temple centers whose roofs had fallen in on them. Unlike Knossos, which was defined by sharp angles and straight lines, here on Malta, everything was rounded. The temples were big bellies and breasts bulging with Her presence. There were sculptures of large, rounded women and ripe, ready eggs. Spirals were omnipresent. It gave a feeling of comfort, this roundness. A feeling of being embraced, enveloped, and cradled.

Inside one of the temples, Danelle turned to me and said, "Why is it that certain places have more power? There's a force here in this Island. The hypogeum," he said, his eyes widening at the wonder of that place.

"Yes, I feel it as well," I said. "The presence of the Goddess is very strong here."

"Why would She be more present in one place than in another?" He looked around himself, wondering. The plaster had worn off the interior of the temple, exposing the many limestone slabs that had been put together to create the walls. "The air is thick with something—an energy." He walked over to the wall and moved his hand in large circles upon one of the stones. He put his ear against it. "Do you suppose," he asked, "the Serpent of Fire is also found in certain places? In certain stones?"

"What an intriguing thought," I said.

"Remember when our serpents joined, when you could see them joining? How we both felt the combining of our energy, the creating of a new serpent, how that made us both feel more power?"

"Yes, I remember."

"Do you suppose there is a Serpent of Fire in plants and trees, indeed in flowers, the ground, the rocks, which our serpents join with, making them pulse stronger?"

I thought about caves, certain sacred trees, the water, the circle of standing stones, all the places in which we knew the Goddess to reside. "It must be so," I said.

Danelle spread his arms out their entire width and leaned against one of the stones. They did not reach either end. "Such enormous stones," he said. He rubbed the rock with the open palms of both hands up and down rapidly, repeatedly, then he held them a distance away from it and made as though to push them toward the stone.

"Aureillia, come," he whispered. The robe the priestesses had given him to wear looked strange on him. Danelle did not ordinarily wear robes. Unlike most other men on Crete, he preferred to wear shirts with shorts or skirts. This, as well as his unusually light hair which he kept short made him stand out.

I came and stood next to him.

"Do as I have done. Rub your hands up and down upon the stone until they feel warm, then hold them a distance away from it."

I did as he said. I rubbed both of my hands over the stone until they felt warm, then I held them away. There was the feeling of something pushing against them. As though there was something between the rock and my hands.

"Oh my," I said. "Is that the Serpent?"

I looked at Danelle. He raised his eyebrows and smiled before pulling me into him.

* * *

"There is great power in the stones," the priestess answered when we asked her. Their force is enhanced through chanting, praying, sleeping, ritual, and drumming.

All these things add to their strength. Our foremothers chose these stones because of their power. The Goddess led them to them."

"But what is this power?" I asked.

"The Goddess," she said. "The Goddess evoked."

"Why here more than in other places?"

"Belief," she said. "Belief in Her. Here belief in the Goddess is strong and has been for a very long time. She pulses strong here because we invite Her. You invite Her. All who travel here invite Her. Here, She is most welcome."

I thought of my prophecies. "Why would She not be welcome in other places?"

"The Goddess is challenging. She is fiery. She is truth. Some wish to avoid Her."

"Avoid Her?" Danelle laughed. "Of course there is no avoiding Her."

"Of course," the priestess said, looking at him.

Chapter 4

Deep within the Tarxien, in a shrine room on the other side of the open air court was an altar to the Goddess with large, stone pillars on either side of it. These pillars were tall, reaching almost to the roof of the shrine. Lamps were lit above this altar so that one could clearly see that the pillars had been meticulously carved into the form of the male sacred limb.

We had wandered in here quite by accident. When I noticed the pillars' distinctiveness, I turned to say something to Danelle but he was not there. I was sure he had followed me in, and so was confused by his sudden absence.

I searched through the other rooms of the temple, yet found him nowhere within. Finally I exited the Tarxien and saw him sitting in the grove of trees beyond the front court. He sat with his arms upon his upraised knees. I knew this posture well. It meant he was bothered and was thinking. I came to be seated beside him but did not say anything. He had a long piece of grass in his mouth which he took bites of and chewed slowly.

I lie down on my side facing the Tarxien, watching the pilgrims come and go.

"Tell me about the men in your visions, Aureillia," he finally said. "Are they anything besides cruel?"

I sat up and observed him. His eyebrows were pushing toward each other, making him look sad. His short hair stood up a bit on his head in the front as though pushed there in agitation.

"I have never considered the matter," I said. "Why is it that you wish to know?"

"I need to know, Aureillia. Is there not some other quality about them that you can tell me of?"

I could see that he was very serious, and so I forced myself to think about the men in my visions. It was very distasteful, and I did not wish to do it—but for Danelle I would. For him, I did things I would ordinarily refuse.

"Angry," I said, "They seem angry. Scared. Yes. Rather fearful. That's it. It's odd," I said. "They seem fearful of the very women they are cruel to."

"What about admirable things? Are there not admirable things that you can name? Are you unable to see anything likable?"

"Hmmmmmm. Well," I said. I tried. I sat there and I tried to see admirable, likable. I looked into my visions, even the ones hardest to look at. "No, Danelle," I said. "It would be telling a lie to say that I see anything admirable or likable, but that does not mean there is not any. It simply means I am unable to see beyond their cruelty."

"You are surely right," he said. "There is probably nothing likable." He threw the piece of grass down to the ground and dropped his knees into a cross-legged position. He was wearing his own clothes today. Shirt tucked into long shorts. I said nothing. I did not understand why he was asking, and I knew I had not given him the answer he wished for.

"The priestesses here tell me there is a worm within me, eating me slowly from the inside out," Danelle said.

"A worm?"

"Yes. Something small but festering," he said. "I know it to be true and I know it has something to do with this."

"Danelle," I said, "You are nothing like those men in my visions." I put my hand upon his arm. He pulled it away and looked at me, cross.

"They tell me it will become a dragon. The worm will turn into a dragon before I am well."

"Oh my," I said.

* * *

There are moments in a life that are defining moments. Moments that one can point to and name. Moments that act as a dividing line for a before and an after. This was one of those moments.

I entered the hypogeum, like all other nights. I followed the priestess holding the bowl of fire, watching the light flicker upon the dark stone walls like every other night. I lay down upon my woven mat and fell into a deep sleep, but this night, unlike all the other nights, the answer came.

I awoke to a room that was palpably different. The walls, ordinarily hard and cavelike, were more rounded and concave, possessing a touchable, porous depth—they were almost spongy. This spongy darkness was alive and pulsing, as though moving, swaying. The mock lintel doorways glowed, as though lit up from behind. It was a faint light coming through the darkness in a swirling motion. I walked to them. All three of them were beckoning. I could have walked into any one of them. For a moment I was confused: Which to enter? They were all pulsing equal attraction. I closed my eyes, asked for guidance. The one on the right reached its arms out and drew my being to it. As I stood in front of it. I could feel a changing, my being becoming more particlelike—a feeling of dissipation, dissolution. When I felt myself to be scattered about completely, I passed through.

Once through, my being becomes again stable. Only I am in a different place, in the underground caverns, in the village in the place called the hills of Judah. There is terror, widespread panic. People from the village above are running into the caverns—screaming, forcing past me. Their cold hands push fearful against me. I am knocked into the wall, into other people. I continue my way toward the shrine, where I know I will find Barbara. When I arrive at the shrine, I stand in the doorway. People continue to crowd behind me as I watch Barbara break the heads and arms off the sculptures of the Snake Goddesses, removing their power. Her hands move in quick, fragmented movements as she tries to accomplish this task efficiently. I look into the hallway and see them coming: The men with the swords.

"Hurry," I call to Barbara. "They are coming."

She looks up at me and nods, then resumes her work, moving faster, as she places the broken pieces into their storage place behind the altar.

I look back to the hall and see one of the men coming toward me. I run down deeper into the chamber. He grabs at me but only gets a handful of my shawl, which I let go of and continue running. When I reach the level of the overhang—a long balcony overlooking the large shrine room below—I see that the stairs down are blocked, full of fleeing people. I run toward the overhang, knowing there is no escape. He catches up to me. He is right behind me. I know. I feel him there. A dark, penetrating presence. I know what is to come next, what always comes next. And then I do it. I turn and face him. A rock falls hard into my chest when I allow myself to finally see him, to look into the face of Danelle. I try to look into his eyes, but they are not his eyes, they are vacant, clouded over, frightful eyes. With these eyes, I know, he cannot see me. In his face is rage and hate. This rage and hate from his being toward mine is so strong it startles me. My body fills with an inner scream, which I stifle. Within me I hear it, a muffled wail. My arms, which long to throw themselves up high into the air in grief, I restrict. Instead I cover my eyes and turn myself around in surrender.

I returned to the dark silence of the hypogeum. The cave walls were once again cave walls. Cold hard stone. Danelle was sleeping. I approached a priestess with a light in the next room and asked to be escorted out. The sun was only beginning to emerge. I sat on the hill outside the hypogeum watching the scenery return, the faint outline of the sea becoming a crisp focused image; the trees around me transforming from looming shadows into well-defined trunks with stretching branches, the ground beneath me, the air about me, changing into their daytime form.

I was not surprised. I had guessed for some time that it was him. Though I had guessed, I had not allowed myself to fully receive that knowing. Now, I sat with it, no longer a mystery or a suspicion to avoid but a clear answer living within me. What I had not expected—the thing which had surprised me—was the hate. All the hate I had felt from him toward me. It was this which caused my heart to sit heavily upon my stomach.

I waited for him. I sat there and waited for him to come out of the hypogeum. When he finally did come out, I stood and looked directly at him. There was no sense in trying to conceal it.

"You've received your answer," he said, his shorts and shirt crumpled from sleep.

"Yes."

"Tell me."

"No. Not yet."

"You must," he said, his voice rising in anger. "No more secrets, Aureillia. I can tolerate no more secrets between us."

"You are right," I said. "I must tell you. That I understand. I only wish to wait until you have received your answer. Please," I said, "grant me this small delay."

He eyed me curiously, anxiously, his hands upon his hips for some time before nodding his head in agreement.

I was relieved to find that his presence did not bother me as I had thought it would. Helena was right, allowing myself to open to the teaching had offered me relief. Instead, what arose within me were feelings of fear and panic for Danelle—a will to protect him. Looking at him then, standing on the hill outside the hypogeum, all blue sky and clear air, he seemed too wide open, too vulnerable. All at once, I understood that I would lose Danelle to this discovery.

The day became a day of mourning for me. I acted toward Danelle in a way I never had before. I held tight to his presence, never leaving his side—and he tolerated it. Though I knew he wished to, he never requested again that I reveal to him my vision. In spite of the fact that I acted in a way strange for me, he did not ask that I explain my behavior. Danelle is the biggest person I have ever known.

The next morning, it was I who found Danelle outside the hypogeum, his head buried in his hands. I knelt beside him.

"How could I have been so blind?" he asked, the turbulence of a wild sea was in his eyes. "You and Barbara and a third person, a man. How could I not have seen? Barbara knew," he continued, brushing his hair back off his forehead so that it stood up in front. "She told me, so long ago. She said, She will find a way to forgive you. Forgiving others is the easy part. It is in forgiving ourselves that we become stuck, muddled up'. I thought she was delirious. I thought the venom had taken her mind! A curse on that, Aureillia!" he said. "A curse on this island. A curse on you and your visions." He stood and began to walk away.

"Danelle, wait," I said, following after him. "We can find a way through this. I am still full of love for you."

"Then you are nothing but a fool," he said. His words were harsh and cutting. I backed away in pain. "You must not follow me," he said, making an effort to temper his voice. "I am full of rage. You must not be near me now."

I nodded my head and held myself still as he walked away. I returned to the docks and booked passage on the next ship sailing to Crete.

* * *

On the morning I was to leave, as I stood on the shore waiting to board the ship, Danelle approached me. I had not seen him since that morning outside the hypogeum. He looked pale and drawn. He allowed me to embrace him.

"It would have been unfair not to say good-bye," he said. His body was trembling. I held him near.

"I wish you peace in this journey," I said.

"Aureillia," he whispered, holding me.

I took his face into my hands and kissed first his forehead, then either cheek. "You know where I shall be," I said. "And I shall be there, waiting. As long as it takes, Danelle. As long as it takes."

Part II

Aureillia's Prophecy

From Arcadia they will come to destroy us
After a fine, white, all-consuming ash
Falls from the skies everywhere above us
Covering suffocating plants and grass
After giant waves crash over our beaches
The force of Her water pounding far away reaches
When we have been devastated by earthquakes
And have not food ourselves to take
As our buildings lie in rubble around us
Those who now covet our most sacred labrys
Shall come in bands and hoards
And with their knives and swinging swords
Take Knossos – alas, our entire island
Minoan blood staining their hands.

Chapter 5

Aureillia

I was delighted to see Lilith's curly head bobbing toward me as I walked up the wooded hill toward the block of rooms we shared with a group of other women and their children. All through the trip my arms continued to reach for her, though she was not there. My mind continued to observe a schedule of care for her, my very being noticed her absence in an all-around way, as though it were missing a part of itself.

I lifted her up and pulled her in. Her buoyant body wrapped about me; warm arms around my neck, strong legs circling my waist. "Oh, Mother," she said, "I've waited such a long time for your return."

"Yes, it has been a long time," I said, burying my face in her hair.

"Danelle?" Hypia asked, for she had been out wandering with Lilith.

"Danelle has not returned with me," I said.

"Where did he go?" Lilith asked.

"He decided to stay on longer," I said to her.

"I have never known Danelle to be a traveler," Hypia said. On her face was the same expression as had been on the faces of the people at the marina who had asked about Danelle: surprise and disbelief.

I looked at Hypia but did not answer her. Instead I kissed Lilith on the forehead and set her down.

"We can talk more later," Hypia said, remembering Lilith.

"Yes," I said. "As for now, you two must tell me about everything that happened while I was gone." I took Lilith's hand and allowed her to lead the way back to our block, listening as the stories poured out of her.

* * *

After a few days, I went to Danelle's workshop in the Center building. It is remarkable how a room and the things in it, especially a workshop, absorb the essence of the person who inhabits it. Danelle's presence was everywhere in this room. I noticed it the moment I entered; a tall integrity, a generous grace. I sat at his work table for some time absorbing it.

I had never been in Knossos without Danelle. From my youngest years, he had always been here, as steady and constant as the hills. It was a strange, almost foreign place without him. A place I needed to come to know.

Scattered across his table were pieces he had been working on before he left, some still under enlarging glasses, half-finished. I began to examine them and was taken aback by what I saw. They were all depictions of men killing birds. All different kinds of men. All different kinds of birds. Some were shot in flight with arrows, others in the ground stabbed with swords.

The birds all had breasts.

I sat looking at them, rubbing my hands against the insides of my arms and shivering. I had never known Danelle to create anything like these. A cool breeze passed over me from the open window behind me. I walked over and closed it, making it very quiet within. *Men Killing birds? Before we left? Before Malta?* I shook the questions away, returned to the table and gathered the pieces into a box, which I placed on one of his shelves. I wiped the table top with a piece of soft wool and swept the floor clean of all the sand that had come in through the window in his absence. When the room was neat and orderly, I gathered the few things I knew to be most dear to him and left, securing the door behind myself.

* * *

It was strange, starting a temple. What did I have to offer that was different from other temples? What would my interactions with others be like? In what way would I serve? What did I know of birds?

"Learn as you go," Helena would say, when I became anxious. "Your temple shall grow, evolve, as all temples do, out of a need in the community. The community shall dictate your work. Trust in that."

"When will they dictate? How shall I know?"

"Hush," Helena would say, seeing my fretting. "You will see. It will happen."

Helena was a very balanced woman. Her voice remained level even if the subject about which she spoke excited or angered her. She possessed always the same level of steadiness and calm, confidently managing difficult situations. While I admired this trait, at the same time it infuriated me because I did not possess such grace. I was always flitting and flapping about. Often was I made restless by things within me bubbling over, making it impossible for me to remain calm. I mentioned this to her one day.

"Of course, it is so," she responded. "For I am butterfly and you are bird." I was filled with the image of the butterfly, floating almost effortlessly upon currents of warm air.

"How can I cultivate this trait?" I asked her. "This steadiness?"

"It is quite possible that you cannot," she said. "Bird can never be butterfly. Rather, you must strive to be the best bird you can be. As you admire in me my steadiness, Aureillia, so it is that I admire in you your passion. Passion is fire. Only fire can change things. It is the Goddess' tool for transformation. This you possess. It is a great gift."

* * *

At the present, my temple of the Bird was a small room below the temple of the Butterfly, on the bottom floor of the Center. It was a cavelike room with one small window high up in the west wall. A Center artist had painted the wall across from the window with white feathers on a black background. The feathers lay lengthwise on the wall, every other one facing the opposite direction, as though they were descending through a black sky. When the light came through the high window and moved upon them, it gave a feeling of fluttering, of flight. One could almost feel them lifting in a gentle breeze, their whiteness lighting an otherwise dark room.

The bench altar I had placed on the south wall. Upon it were clay eggs painted the same white-on-black design, a bird's nest and some offerings of shells and stones. The floor was covered with woven mats, and there were several pillows spread about.

It seemed odd to think that everything I knew of birds I had learned from Barbara, who had been my mentor as a priestess of the Snake. Before she had been a priestess of the Snake, Barbara had been a bird observer—a person engaged in watching and identifying the patterns and behavior of birds.

Helena was not Barbara. I had to keep reminding myself of this when I, quite unfairly, found her sorely lacking. Ours was a much more formal relationship. It did not have the intense emotional element that Barbara and I had shared. Comparing anyone to Barbara was grossly unfair. I knew this, yet I searched for her in others still.

The realm of the Butterfly was the realm of return, rebirth, and regeneration. The temple of the Butterfly assisted people through difficult transitions. Leaving the physical form was one of these transitions. The temple of the Butterfly served the community most in this capacity. There are, however, many other transitions one must pass through within one's journey through life, and this temple concerned itself with those as well.

The symbol of the Butterfly and Her temple is the symbol of the double axe—the labrys. Like the butterfly, the labrys has two wings that open gracefully on either side. The labrys is the symbol of the lifeforce, the open-winged Goddess within. "It is also a symbol of infinity," Helena said. "The never-ending flow of life and Her mysteries. There is one other teaching of the labrys I must pass to you, for it is my feeling that it will be important for you in your work with the birds as well. The labrys is a symbol of connectedness, of union, of the oneness of all things. As the Goddess has many different manifestations, yet we know Her to be One, so it is true for all of life. Though it has many different shapes and forms, all life is one. Often it is that things appear to be separate, but they are not. Though this is a very difficult teaching, it is also a very important one—for it is this teaching we need to remember when trying to understand and get through the most difficult of situations. You, Aureillia, were snake; now you have become bird. This may seem to you to be two separate things, but it is not. Never could you be one without the other. They are but two parts of one whole. Try to keep this in mind as you make your way."

When my niece, Leida, was but a girl, she too had heard the call of the Snake. Her mother, dear Thela, after having witnessed my experience, encountered much resistance to the thought of her daughter becoming a priestess of the Snake.

Leida, perceiving this fear within her mother, had tried to ignore the call.

Because of this, her entrance into the temple had been stalled. The delay had been costly. By the time she finally did enter the temple, her intended mentor was unavailable. She had been assigned an alternate mentor, who turned out to be a poor match. Frustrated, Leida had rejected the alternate and was waiting for her original mentor to become available again.

Thela was tormented. She was aware that she had caused the delay and felt responsible for Leida's current condition, one full of resentment and anger. Leida also had an abnormal fear of the snakes. Sometimes it seemed to me she would never come to terms with it.

I had approached the temple of the Snake Goddess many times to try to discuss this matter with them. I was told repeatedly that the leader of the temple would come and speak to me. She never did.

One day, after my return, tired of waiting, I entered the temple unannounced and approached her.

"Why do you not come and speak to me when you tell me you shall?" I asked, angry.

I had interrupted. By entering unannounced, I was breaking one of the main rules of the temple. The red-and-black mottled snakeskin design painted onto the walls left me dizzy with anxiety. The dense smell rose from the snake pit below, nauseating me.

She was engaged in an instruction with her apprentice. The apprentice lay unclothed upon a woven mat on the floor. The leader knelt beside her, readjusting the lengthened body of a snake upon her. Feeling the snake's skin against her own is one of the ways in which a Snake priestess becomes accustomed to the snake. Seeing this recalled to me instantly the feel of the coarse snakeskin upon my own—the tiny hardened scales, opening and closing in movement; the heavy spiraling weight pressing. I drew in a breath, hugged my arms close to my chest and tried to remain focused on my reason for coming.

"There is no reason for me to discuss the matters of this temple with you," she said, rising and addressing me directly. The snake slithered up the apprentice's body. She glanced down at it.

"This is my niece we are speaking about."

"You, Aureillia, are no longer a Snake priestess."

"I am a Snake priestess. A Snake priestess I shall always be."

"You are now a priestess of the Bird. What you do no longer concerns us here."

I flew into a fury. "I gave this temple my youth," I said. "Indeed, my health! How dare you tell me I have no business here!" The anger had caused my voice to become loud. It pounded through the temple where silence was rigidly observed. She reached down and lifted the snake off of her apprentice. It writhed in her hands. The apprentice sat up, watching us, wide-eyed.

"The girl is the daughter of my sister," I said. "My sister! That is reason enough."

"You never did fit in here," she said, lowering her voice, even in her anger. "You were always too loud. You always demanded extra space."

"Do not disgrace this temple by denying the function I performed as one of its priestesses."

"Your work is finished here, Aureillia. Return to your birds."

I flew out of the temple, flapping my wings desperately in confusion. How could I ever help Leida? What would become of her?

Chapter 6

Danelle

Here the quarters are made of straw. Tall grasses woven together into round huts, huts clustered together forming circles, circles forming a village. Here, more sun, less food. A much less certain existence.

I sailed here from Malta with the weight of abandonment upon me. I sailed the long journey here hoping for something so different there would be nothing to make me remember. I was not disappointed.

In a small, empty hut separated out from other villagers, I made my home. Probably the previous home of a person who, due to illness or some other reason, had been excluded from the community. This small, isolated hut on a cliff overlooking the sea, removed from the village by a long, winding trail, met my needs perfectly.

Within me was an emptiness—a numbness—a distance from myself I had not before known. There was also a great desire to not think.

The hands, forever busy, longed to work. I tried to keep them still, but it was not possible. Slowly, I allowed myself to draw. The drawing led to carving into and upon anything I could find; mostly wood, some old gourds, and small flattened stones. This was my gift, as much a part of me as my hands or my voice. Always it welled up within me, requiring release. It mattered not in what form, only to express the energy that becomes present. Always I had my work. When things occurred that were trying, it was the work I turned to and the work was always there.

Now, again it was here—a faithful companion—yet there was within me a large desire to reject it. This I did not understand. I did observe, however, that though I could not name it, it was this same thing that allowed me to continue to work when my eyes burned hot as red coals, that very same thing which now allowed me to reject my hands.

My hands, the instruments of my work, which I had always cared for diligently, I began to ignore. Because the work is hard on them, I had always protected them, soaking them in the circling waters after which I would rub oils and herbs into them. They responded well to my efforts, remaining soft and supple, free of pain.

Now I did none of those things. Instead, I chose to ignore them. Where before was the desire to nurture and care for them, now was within me the will to hurt them. I allowed them to become callused and hard, full of small cuts, which, because I did not look after them, became large. The work itself hurt; each half-healed cut reopening, bleeding. Illness began to settle into them, causing them to sting and ache. I cared not. Rather I found satisfaction in their condition.

My hair, which I had always kept short, I allowed to grow. It hung into my eyes and down upon my shoulders. My face, too, became covered with hair.

It was the hunger, however, the empty and turning stomach that I could not tolerate. In Minoa, food is everywhere abundant. A lack of food is unknown to Minoans. Here, for the first time, I had come to know hunger. I cared not for it. I fed myself with roots and berries, greens and nuts I found on my own, but still my stomach sunk into my back, and there was a constant burning at the back of my throat. The land was different here than on Crete. Many of the plants I did not recognize, many of the berries I could not identify. Here, where less cultivation of Her soil was carried out, and the land was hotter, even scorched, food was scarce. These people were a pastoral people, living in small groups in modest accommodations, tending to their herds of sheep and cattle, growing only small crops of food. What was grown was closely guarded. I was accustomed to groves of trees overflowing with Her bounty of ripe, juicy fruit, to eating in a central dining room—grains ground and baked into sweet cakes, cooked mutton, and cured cheeses. I could have fished or hunted, but I did not want to interfere with the local hunters and fishing people. I did not want to offend. Though they had not welcomed me into their village, they did not seem to mind my presence, being always polite and cordial when passing near me. It was clear, at all times however, that I was an outsider, and an outsider I was to remain.

I did not have the patience to tolerate hunger and I could find no reason why I should. I knew of other ways to acquire food. I had observed the rhythm of the days in which they set up market with the neighboring villages. I began to take my work to market. There I traded it for food and other things I required. With it, I fed myself well.

Not long after that, the people of the village began to come to me, making requests for personalized stones. My being perked up in response. I was surprised by this place within me needy for others. It was this, this needy part within me, which allowed me to continue, to open the door when there was a humble knock on it, this same part within me, eager and excited, that would welcome the person in, sit in their presence, attempt to speak to them, stumbling over mixed tongues—to try to feel their essence—that I may indeed carve them a stone. They knew more of my language than I of theirs, having had more contact with Minoans than I had with Libyans. With repeated visits, however, I was learning more.

While I allowed myself these interactions, at the same time, I begrudged myself the pleasure I derived from them. I observed this in myself, this will to deny myself pleasure. I watched it, as though observing other. I was a man observing himself, other inside his own being—a person questioning his own urges and choices. Never before had I stood outside myself in this fashion. Never before had I experienced the feeling of two inside one. I barely recognized myself but for the work. Ah, the work. Always the work.

From the cliff overlooking the water, I had a perfect view of the small, secluded cove from which many of the villagers departed each morning in fishing boats. Before the sun's return, I would hear them pushing off. Through the early hours, I would watch their small boats out in the distant water making the morning rounds, returning midmorning with full nets and traps. Upon their return they would start a large fire. There, on the beach they would clean, cut, and cook the day's catch. The smell would rise up to me, filling me with desire. Though I had acquired much with my work at market, I had not yet acquired fresh fish. I would observe as they ate their share and then brought the rest up to the village.

In the afternoon, they would return to the cove to prepare the traps and nets for the next day's journey. There were often children who would accompany them back to the cove to play in the shallow waters and run around the beach as they worked. These scenes, the sound of children playing, were achingly familiar.

It was only when I wanted to take care of my hands again that I was able to see how terribly I had been treating them. Sorrow overtook me. I went to the water. I soaked them within Her. I begged for forgiveness, spreading oil upon them, whispering blessings. I refused to work until they were well again. As strong as the desire was to hurt myself, the desire to care for myself proved stronger. I was grateful for that. She healed them, restoring their former smoothness so well that forgetting the pain I had inflicted was easy. I removed the hair on my face in acknowledgement of Her forgiveness. The hair on my head I tied back with a cord, showing my respect. I continued to allow it to grow, however, as a way of observing the time that was passing; the time I was spending here in Libya, the time away from Minoa.

* * *

When Rodin came to see me, it was clear right away that he had come for a reason other than to make a request.

"You are Minoan," he said at once when he saw me. "I had not been informed that you were Minoan."

"Is it so evident?"

"Quite."

It was true. Being here in Libya had made me realize just how Minoan I was. No one had ever said it to me with such confidence. I liked his confidence. I crossed my arms in front of my chest and watched him looking over my living quarters, my work. His curiosity produced in him no shame. He held his hands together behind his back, observing my engravings and sculptures as well as my belongings with equal interest. His hair hung in long rolls of curls around his face and down onto his neck. He was short in height, yet possessed a thickness of build. His being seemed to pulse with strength. His flesh bulged into tight rounded curves upon his arms, chest, and legs, giving his dark skin a polished look. He wore no shirt; a red, woven skirt around his waist with openings on either side, leather sandals, and a necklace of obsidian and jade. There were red triangular markings on his upper left arm and right cheek. I was only just learning the language of the markings these people wore. The sacred triangle I knew to indicate importance but what kind of importance I did not yet know.

"What is it that you run from?" he asked, with his back facing me.

I said nothing.

"It is clear that you have a great gift. People use their gifts in Minoa." He approached me as he said this. There was a great difference in our height. I looked down at him. Among the local people I was extremely tall. Always I have been a person of great height, but among these people it seemed ridiculously evident.

"Do sit down, please," he said. "Your height has me at a great disadvantage."

I obliged myself to him and sat down upon the small wooden bench I had carved.

He observed me for a while sitting there before he turned away and began to explore my quarters again. "There is great sadness, it is clear," he said. "Perhaps some time you will find your way to telling me about it?" He looked at me, his eyebrows arched into a question.

"Perhaps."

"Hmmmmmm, but not now?"

"Not now."

"You see, the problem is," he said, rather smiling and enunciating his words. He had a supreme command of the Minoan language, an accent almost undetectable. His lips were wide and moved with ease and great deliberation over large, white teeth, over foreign words. Though I wished desperately not to like him, I was already feeling toward him a fondness. "You cannot stay here. I am the oracle here," he said, moving his hands in gesture toward himself. "How is it that your community does without you?"

"I am an artist, not an oracle," I said. "Minoa has no shortage of artists."

"My dear man, you are quite mistaken," he said. "Is that what this is about?"

"This is about nothing," I said, irritation settling in my back, at the place between my shoulders. "I needed time alone. It is true. It has nothing to do with my work. If I am bothering you and your community, I shall take my leave."

"Yet, you give counsel," he said, leaning in toward me, hands behind his back.

"I do not 'give counsel'. I needed some food. I was hungry. I traded some of my work for food. I did not ask that they come to me. They come to me on their own."

"Even so, counsel you gave."

"No, not counsel. Engraved objects. Personalized signature stones."

"How is it that it is clear to all but you that you are giving counsel. Do you not understand that oracles and seekers are but two halves of one whole? Seekers come because you offer. If you were not an oracle, you would have nothing to give."

"I do not understand you."

"I see that you choose not to. However, it is I who am in error. I understand now that you are an oracle seeking oracle."

"I am a man who happens to carve who needs time to himself to think."

"Yes. Yes," he said, but it was clear he was placing little worth on my words.

"This bird-woman," he said, lifting one of the many engravings of Aureillia, "it concerns her, doesn't it?"

"You are correct," I said. "However, that conclusion is not difficult to arrive at." My being flushed in recognition of the vast amount of engravings there were of Aureillia.

"That is true," he said, looking at me out of the corner of one eye. "Why is it that you wish to deny your gift?"

"Look here," I said, standing up, fury ran fierce within me, pulsing through my arms and legs. "I do not wish to deny my gift. I have not been initiated into the oracular role. I have apprenticed as an artist. An artist is what I am."

"Birth is initiation enough," he sang, rather chanted under his breath. "Your name?" he asked, again not looking at me but tilting his head to one side toward me, as a bird.

"Danelle."

"My dear Danelle," he said, letting my name linger and roll gracefully across his tongue and through his teeth. "Birth itself is an initiation. Either you are born with a gift or not. You can go through any number of initiations, but if you are not born with a gift, you shall not possess it. You are your gift. Your gift is you. You possess it because you are it. It is not something acquired through ritual. It is in this way that Minoans lean too far in the ways of others. We respect you for so much. Your community we hold in the highest regard, except for this very matter. On this matter, we vehemently disagree," he said, with much passion. He was absorbing to watch. His gift for speech mesmerized. I had been so completely captured by his words, I had quite forgotten myself.

"This woman, she is of course, a priestess," he said. "This I can determine from her attire."

"Please, do not speak of her," I said.

"You do not trust me. That is clear. Why should you? I shall think upon it. I shall return only when you are sure you can trust me. None of it is any good if you do not trust me." He tipped his head again to one side. "Your father is a priest?" he said, as though I had said it to him and he were merely repeating it.

"You are surrounded by the initiated, yet you remain a virgin," he said. "This would account for the pure, rather clean feeling I am getting from you. No. No. The fault is not with them. They see you. It is you who do not see yourself." He was shaking his head at the information he seemed to be receiving from someone or something other than myself. He sighed deeply. "I am a busy man. You promise me much work. Alas, just when the path looks straight, it curves suddenly. Danelle. It is a good name. I am Rodin."

I nodded to him in acknowledgement of his offering me his name.

"Burn this," he said, handing me some short bundles of thick grass. "Burn this and breathe it in deeply as you burn it. As you breathe it, think of her—the light?"

"Aureillia."

"Yes, the one of the light. You do deserve her, you know," he said. "You are more than worthy."

Chapter 7

Aureillia

The time had come, I knew. It had become necessary for me to learn more about eagles. I was still identified with owl. Owl was my familiar. Owl had been present at my birth. Before my initiation into the temple of the Bird Goddess, I had assumed, as a priestess of the Bird, I would become owl. I had been mistaken. In my initiation, I learned, I was to be eagle.

Still, I thought of myself as owl. Owl with her silent night flight. Owl with her two-sided hearing. Owl with her possession of inner depth—a keeper of secrets.

Eagle is a bird of the day! That alone gave me pause. To be out in the open. Exposed! Hunting in broad daylight. Why, that's a whole different hunt. After having identified with owl for so long, eagle seemed almost flamboyant.

The best way to become familiar with a creature is to find one and observe it. So it was that I set out wandering the bird trails I had walked so long ago in my youth with Barbara, searching for eagles.

Often I took Lilith with me on my explorations. The trips were slower with her stopping to look at every flower, touching gently their colored petals, smelling, sometimes crushing them quite by mistake.

Since her early childhood, Lilith had loved to swim with the dolphins. On clear mornings or early evenings we would go. I would stand in the shallow water watching them, their sleek gray bodies swimming around her as she squealed in glee. They had a special call for her; we knew it as Lilith's call. We knew each of them intimately as well, not only by the names we had given them but by their own individual calls. They would welcome her into their pod and take her with them, out into the deeper water where I could no longer see her. I would sit on the beach and wait for her to emerge finally from the shallow water, refreshed and filled full for the day.

Lilith understood the language of the dolphins; a gift I had passed inadvertently to her through the venom that had remained in my blood during the time she grew within me. When she was very young it became apparent that the venom within, combined with total submersion in water, enabled her to transmute a language previously unknown. I too possessed this ability. Of late, however, the dolphins were only interested in Lilith. They made this perfectly clear by remaining silent when I was in the water with her. She did not want to be with them in silence.

I began to wait for her on shore. I knew they were telling her stories, filling her full of times and places far removed from here. Though I wanted to, I did not ask her to tell me what they told her. I waited for her to tell me on her own. But she never did. Though she was a very talkative child, she rarely spoke about her time with the dolphins. That should have been my first clue.

Lilith was bright. It was clear that I would not need to nurture her ability to think about and understand the world —but her soul, her soul needed protection. I could sense it. It was an in-the-womb feeling. She had weak filters. Because she appeared strong and confident on the outside I had need to remind myself of her underlying vulnerability. My work at the temple was consuming, but I made a firm commitment to fence it in with clear boundaries, leaving myself plenty of time for my daughter.

Because she seemed to absorb the energy of others easily, I made sure we had plenty of time alone together. I knew that if she came to know and recognize her own energy, she would slowly begin to be able to tell the difference between hers and that of others. This is a vital teaching, one my mother had schooled me in well. To know and recognize one's own energy essence, so that you are able to determine when the energy of another has gotten inside you is an essential skill. It helps one to maintain balance in unbalanced situations and allows a person to understand the messages from within that are crucial to making choices as an adult.

She had been growing, leaving the dependency of infancy behind. Now, her body stretched itself into the elasticity of a girl's. Her walk became more relaxed, hips sliding back and forth, back straight, chest proud. Her hair was thick black locks that sprouted gleefully upon her head, cascading vibrance down her back. Her eyes sparked with light when she smiled or became excited. Her face was the perfection that is a girl's face; round and smooth and full of pure wonder.

She spent her days with friends from the block we lived in much like I had as a girl, running through Knossos, skipping along the beaches, exploring the forest trees. Often, however, I would notice her off to the side, alone, immersed in her own thoughts. Things which she did not speak of consumed her. Of course, I was always watching, looking for signs of the venom—the venom I had passed to her, from my blood into hers. I was always on the lookout for other ways it might be affecting her. I had been careless with my body before I conceived her, and forgiving myself had been difficult. Though I tried not to think of it, it was always there, nagging at me—the wondering, the worrying. We visited a Center herbalist regularly who was working with us to help strengthen Lilith's body with tonics. Still I waited; for what, I did not know.

Though the days Lilith accompanied me on my search for eagles were slower days, I noticed that they were also the days in which I would discover more. Being forced to stand still and wait for her enabled me to see things I might not have noticed otherwise. And her observations, made from such an unassuming place, directed my attention toward the things I would have easily passed by.

Being a bird of the day, eagles were ever so much easier to find than owls. We had located a pair of Golden eagles and returned to them often to observe. There was a certain hill we could climb that led to a ledge directly overlooking the two eagles and their perches in a nearby pine tree.

Unlike owl, eagle is a nest builder, often returning to the same nest each year at mating season, adding on and rebuilding before settling into it once again to bring forth young. Eagle nests become enormous; trees sometimes bend under their weight.

The flight of the eagle is truly magnificent. They have the ability to gather the air around them in such a way that allows them to lift high and higher still. There they soar—wings wide, gliding effortlessly—watching the world below with sharp, focused eyes.

Seeing them fly within this circle of hills, traversing this wide canyon with ease, gave the landscape a depth I had not before perceived.

Since it was mating season, we were able to observe the most splendid of all— the eagle's 'sky dance'. As the eagles soar together, the female descends to a place below the male. Suddenly she flips over onto her back, he grabs her talons within his, and they tumble and spin, connected, through the air toward the earth, releasing each other only in time to regain flight.

Over and over again they would perform this dance. I observed in wonder as they spiraled in abandon together through the bright blue sky, both trusting that, at the right moment, they would disconnect; save themselves.

One day, sitting on the tall ledge observing them, Lilith said, "Why is it that the eyes of the owl are different?"

"Different?" I said. "In what way different? I suppose they are bigger."

"No. No. Not that," she said, "Close together, both in front, like ours."

I thought of the owl's strong eyes piercing me with a question as she looked at me. "It is true," I said, "most other birds' eyes are on either side of their heads."

"Like the eagle," she said.

"Like the eagle," I repeated, "Lilith, you are right."

"Yes, mother, but why?"

"Why indeed?"

"Why Mother?"

"I had not though of it," I said, "but it is true. Most birds' eyes are on the sides of their heads, I suppose to see better to the sides than in front. But why do they need to see better on the side rather than the front? That is the question."

"And why must owl see to the front?" Lilith asked.

"Yes, why?" I asked. "I think we shall discover the answer to that question together," I said. "But more important is this whole idea of contrast."

"What is contrast?"

"Comparing one thing to another to better understand both."

"What is it that you wish to contrast?"

"Owl and eagle."

"Owl and eagle? Oh yes, may we please, together?"

"Of course, yes. Perhaps we should first start with the eyes as you suggested."

"Yes, Yes. I've got another one," Lilith said. She was jumping up and down, her curls jumped with her, landing only with a momentary delay. "Right now, mother, may I start right now?"

"Go ahead."

"Night time hunter. Day time hunter," she said.

"It is so," I said.

"Bigger head, owl," Lilith continued.

"Eagles soar, fly higher," I said.

"Eagle, day time owl?" Lilith said, looking at me, her face squeezed tight into a question.

We began to keep a list in my room. Large and spreading across one whole wall. On one side I wrote **EAGLE**, on the other side I wrote **OWL**. Beneath we would write our observations of the two. Anyone with insight was welcome to contribute. It became quite like a running dialogue on my wall. Each time I entered my room, the first thing I would do was to check the wall for new comments.

Eagle	**Owl**
Lives high, need to go up, up, up to find an eagle (Lilith)	*Bigger head (Lilith)*
Less able to camouflage (Aureillia)	*Master of camouflage (Aureillia)*
Eagle – exposing truths (Aureillia)	*Owl – secrets (Aureillia)*
Daytime owl (Lilith)	*Night-time eagle (Lilith)*

* * *

Danelle's absence was trying. The community was not making it any easier. I had thought the longer I remained among them, the more I would be allowed back in. Unfortunately, the opposite had proven true. It felt as though I were being pushed away a little more all the time. I was not sure why. There was a cool, reserved atmosphere toward me.

Because of the message of my prophecies, many people in the community harbored resentment toward me. This had been a hard hurt at first but I had become accustomed to it. Now, it seemed to have transformed into something other, something more aggressive and hurtful.

Since I had not been able to effect a change for Leida with my communications at the Snake temple, I decided to try to help her through this on my own. We would meet and walk together. We would talk about the snakes. I was hoping to dispel some of her fears about them by telling her some of the things Barbara had taught me when I was first getting accustomed to them. That, however, had been very long ago and I found myself creating most of the information.

Leida possessed much more knowledge than I did when I was her age. She was continually surprising me with the things she shared with me. Though the process was slow, she did seem to be responding to my efforts, opening up a little more with each day.

Unlike most of the women on Crete, Leida dressed in dark colors—browns and blacks—and she wore her hair always down. It was thick, deep, red curls, which, when the wind blew, became bushy, standing up and out on her head. Still, she did not tie it back. She smelled of the fields of drying sage and had a full physique—voluptuous and round. She spent much time alone and seemed to prefer it that way. Her relationship with her mother was often strained. She seemed to resent Thela's worrying over her.

One day I led her to the very place on the beach where I had finally overcome my fear of the snakes. I told her how Barbara had led me here and had me close my eyes and feel my power by recognizing within myself a power that matched that of Mother Sea. "Once I was able to recognize my power," I said, "I was no longer afraid of the snakes. Fear diminishes power. One must own her power entirely if she is to work with the snakes."

"I too use the sound of Mother Sea to find my power," Leida said. She sat down, crossed her legs beneath her, and closed her eyes. I sat watching her, surprised since it appeared as though she were working with the Serpent of Fire, a secret teaching I did not think she had yet encountered. She sat like that for some time, breathing. The waves moved in and out, gradually making their way closer to us. After a time, she began to rock and speak, "The community will turn against you," she said, her voice low and unfamiliar, "But it will force you to discover the truth."

"The truth?" I said. "What truth?"

"The truth you now seek," she said. She was in trance, her eyelids fluttering, "Snake is not through with you. Snakes desires that you see more."

"Leida, how is it that you are receiving snake wisdom without the presence of the venom?"

"My mother's hesitation has served a purpose," she said. "The snake speaks to me though I am not initiated. Though I have not received Her sacred bite."

"Why?"

"To show us that snake wisdom is available everywhere, not only in the temple of the Snake, not only through Her bite."

"Everywhere?"

"In every drop of rain is She found. In each grain of sand; Her wisdom is ever-present." She began to shake, her body jerking involuntarily in movements I knew to be dangerous.

"Leida, come back now," I said, my voice firm and low. Her breathing changed. Her body relaxed, each part descending, sitting a little more heavily upon the sand, as she came back to being Leida sitting with Aureillia on the beach. She opened her eyes.

I took the end of my dress, wet it with Mother Sea, and wiped her face with it. A beautiful face with pointed features, and large, dark eyebrows. A face so like Thela's, save for the anger. In Thela's face, anger was not found. Leida's resonated with it. I dabbed around her nose, her forehead. "Leida," I asked gently, "have you been experiencing this often?"

She nodded her head and pursed her lips. "Others will not listen to me because I am not initiated. And yet I hear voices. I see visions. What do you say to that, Aunt Aureillia?" Anger rose in her voice. "What do you say to that?"

"I say it is wonderful."

"You do?" she said, observing me in disbelief.

"This is not a cause for sorrow," I said. "This is a cause for great joy."

"How is it that you say such a thing?" she said, challenging. "It is over this very issue that I argued with my mentor. It is for this very reason that I rejected her, that I am not yet full priestess. To not be able to use the gifts the Goddess has given you, this is cause for the greatest sorrow."

"How long have you been experiencing this?"

"For close to one year," she said. "Since the time that I would have become full priestess, had I not been delayed."

"Is it so?"

"Yes," she said. "For this reason it seemed important to me."

"Besides your mentor, did you tell any other?"

"No. There was no one I could trust—or who would understand, or so I thought, until I saw you fight for me at the temple."

"You saw that?"

Her cheeks reddened, yet she continued to look directly at me, her brown eyes piercing. "I wanted to see what you would say to them. I wanted to know how they would respond." As she spoke I was able to finally feel her power; the well of hidden power behind the hardness. Leida was not angry, she was hurt—suffering the pain of not being heard.

"Tell me how your mentor responded to this information."

"She said it could not be true. She said I must not speak of it."

"I do not know what has happened to that temple," I said. "The behavior of the priestesses is truly frightening."

"The work has become most difficult for them," she said, looking out toward the sea now.

"Difficult? In what way difficult?"

"Forgive me, Aunt Aureillia, but there are things that you do not know." She dug her toes into the sand. "I would like to be honest with you now, if you would so allow me."

"Yes," I said, "Do tell."

"Their work has become most difficult because of your prophecies."

"How is that possible?"

"They have people, many people, who come to them, more and more all the time who say they need to discuss your prophecy. It is a burden they know not how to deal with."

"Oh my," I said.

"There are those who think," she said, glancing at me to see how I was taking all of this, "that these people should be sent to you."

"To me?"

"They say," she said, straightening her back up tall toward the sky. "We have work enough. She has a whole temple and no work."

I was trying to keep up with her but she was speaking so fast, as though releasing something that had been locked inside her for a long time. "I was thinking, Aunt Aureillia, perhaps you should teach them the dance."

"The dance?"

"The dance. Your dance. The dance of release. You see," she continued, anxiously, "I have observed these people, as I once observed you. It seems to have gotten inside of them, as it did you."

"You were but a girl, Leida."

"Yes. I saw it even then, how it had gotten inside you. How you held it there, carrying it within you. But when I see you dance, when I watch you, when I see all those things leaving you, when I see you becoming Aureillia again, the greatest joy fills me."

"You watch me dance, even now?" I asked.

She looked toward the sand and nodded her head.

I stood up and brushed the sand off my dress. I patted my hair into place, took a deep breath and straightened my back, making myself taller. I tried to behave in a ceremonial manner. I extended my hands out to Leida. She put hers within them and let me help her rise to standing. I straightened her dress, brushing the sand from it and pushed her hair away from her face, placing it in back of her shoulders.

Her eyes looked up into my face with hope, wonder, and fear all mixed together. I lifted my arms out in front of me so that my hands stood over each of her shoulders in sacred gesture. "Leida, daughter of Thela," I said, "The Bird Goddess desires you as one of Her priestesses."

Her face turned to pure golden light, glowing as I had never before seen it. "Oh, Aunt Aureillia, me work with you?"

"You are snake becoming bird," I said, trying to contain my glee and remain formal. "You understand the work that must be done. It is with the greatest reverence and respect that I ask. Do you consent?"

"I would be most greatly honored," she said, remembering ceremony and bowing to me.

I tapped her on the shoulders three times and bowed back to her. "Initiation begins now," I said.

She looked at me anxiously.

"You know the dance?" I asked.
"Yes," she said.
"Dance for me then."

Chapter 8

Danelle

I did as he said. I burned the bundles of grass. One evening I dug a small hole into the floor of my hut, built a fire, and put the bundles in it. They possessed a strong, pungent smell, which, when I breathed it in deeply, caused me to cough. The smoke within made me feel uneasy. I stood to walk off the uneasy feeling but became dizzy and had to sit back down. Sitting, I became agitated. Then I remembered what he had said. "Think of her," he had said. I, however, do not think. I draw. And so I drew: I painted, I carved, into wood, into clay, onto papyrus. The images poured out of me with no space between them. One led immediately to the next, sometimes even pushing one aside before it had reached completion to begin yet another.

The images I created shocked and frightened me. I drew them nonetheless. When I felt too terrified, I burned more grass and created more. I did this until the grass was all burned and I could draw no more.

My floor was covered with drawings, paintings, sketches and carvings, all depictions of the same thing. My floor was covered with images of men, different men, all kinds of men, all doing the same thing in many different ways. My floor was covered with images of men and birds—all kinds of birds. They were all images of men killing birds.

* * *

"You have done well with the weed, my friend," Rodin's voice said, waking me from slumber.

When I opened my eyes, I knew not where I was. It took me some time to realize that I had fallen asleep on the floor of my quarters. I sat up. It was only then that I became aware of all the horrifying images I had created surrounding me. I stood up and began to back away from them. My feet landed upon some, breaking them with loud snapping noises underneath me. I took my hands to my face to wipe the sleep out of my eyes and was alarmed to see them stained red. My body shook. I began to wail. It was a wail I did not recognize —a sound foreign and unknown—coming from deep within me.

Rodin took me by the arm, led me to the stream down the hill below my quarters and placed my hands within it.

"Hush, now," he said, in a calm, soothing voice as he rubbed dirt within them to clean them. "It is only ocher," he whispered. "Only something you have been painting with. It is nothing more than that."

When he had finished cleaning my hands, I filled them with cool water and rinsed my face several times. He squatted behind me, placed his hands on either side of my head and turned it toward the sun. "Close your eyes," he said. "Close your eyes and look up into the sun." He lifted the hair off my forehead so that the sun met the place on my forehead between my eyes. A warm red light began to grow in that place until it turned into a circle radiating white and yellow rays around it. With each breath I took, I felt my body relaxing into that light. There was a sensation of something drying, a clearing. The wheel began to spin, gathering more colors within it as it moved, bright lines of reds, greens, and blues. I sat with the spinning. Water released from my eyes in long, slow streams.

Rodin removed his hands from my forehead. I opened my eyes. He sat down beside me, close, so that our arms almost met. I did not move away from him. I found his presence intensely comforting. My being spilled open.

"What is it," I said, "that could lead a man to murder a woman, but more than murder her, to hate her with all of his being? How could I? How could I hate her with such ferocity?"

Rodin, unmoved, remained seated where he was, looking not at me but forward, moving a piece of grass around in his mouth. "I cannot answer that question," he finally said, "but I would be most interested to know the answer once you discover it."

"You anger me," I said, pushing myself away from him and facing him head on. "Why is it that you anger me so?"

He again remained where he was, still looking forward. "You are not accustomed to being in the position of seeker," he said. He removed the piece of grass from his mouth, threw it into the water and turned to face me. "It is frustrating to fumble around in the dark when it appears another near you holds a lamp. You may rest assured, however, I know not the answer to your question. Even if I did, it would serve you no purpose for me to tell you. Questions can only be answered by those who do the questioning. Come," he said, standing up and extending his hand to me. "We must build a large fire. I will need your help."

We walked together to the wooded area beyond the stream and began to gather wood, carrying it back to the hearth outside my quarters. We carried wood until my arms ached with weight. Then we built a large fire. A fire taller than I. When the flames began to grow long, yellow tongues, Rodin asked me to gather all the drawings, carvings, and paintings the grasses had helped me to create. When I had gathered them all into piles around him, he began to throw them into the fire. The ones of clay he had to break into pieces. He did this, sometimes with his foot, other times over his knee or with a large stone.

"You must take the greatest care with images such as these," he said. "When they appear to you, you must express them, you must look at them, you must try to determine their significance, but you must then destroy them, lest you infect others with them. What is seen with the eyes has great power, more power than we realize."

I watched him throwing them into the flames, their shapes melting and contorting in the heat, the redness bubbling up, evaporating, the wood becoming fire, the papyrus curling, curling, curling before turning to ash and lifting toward the sky.

"Please," Rodin said, turning toward me, "return to your quarters and be sure that you have not overlooked any."

I returned with several small pieces I had sketched before, without the help of the grass. These images had been haunting me for some time. I did not tell this to Rodin.

He looked down at them, scowling and shaking his head. "How is it," he asked, "that these images came to be part of your soul material? You are not a man of the sea. Minoans have done well protecting their people from even the knowledge of such horror."

"Aureillia's prophecies," I said, only then realizing the truth of that statement.

"She is a prophetess?" he asked. Perspiration beaded up and dripped from his forehead down onto his face from the heat of the fire.

"She is a Snake priestess who foretold of darkness."

"I see."

"I killed her."

"How is it that you killed her if she indeed lives?"

"Not now. In the future. In the future I am a horrible man who murders her. She saw it. I saw it. We both know. I killed her."

"Correction. You might kill her."

"No. I did. I do. I mean," I shook my head in confusion. "I will. I saw myself killing her," I said, sitting down on a log.

"Do not be fooled by the illusion of time and permanence," Rodin said.

"I do not follow," I said, looking at him. His calmness in the face of my terrifying confession reassured me, eased my discomfort. The sun was shining behind him so that I needed to hold my hand over my eyes to see him, giving him a dark, shadowlike appearance.

"I see that," he said, throwing the last of the pictures into the fire. "We shall come to it."

He came and sat beside me, wiping the moisture from his face with a cloth that hung down from his belt.

"It is too soon to speak of such matters" he said, "however, for the present, to settle your mind, for this is distressing information to carry with you, you must understand one thing. You may one day murder Aureillia. But you also may not. The things that she saw, the things that you saw, are only possibilities. You must know that the choice is always yours to make. Remember this Danelle," he said, putting his hand upon my shoulder, "Always there is choice."

Chapter 9

Aureillia

I returned to the temple of the Snake Goddess, apologized for my previous outburst and requested private council with the leader. Her being was tight with anger; nevertheless, she led me to the back of the temple where there were private rooms in which we could be alone. I followed her into a small, dark chamber that I remembered well. A room that had layers of my being left in it. She lit a lamp, dispelling some of the despair and motioned for me to sit upon one of the two pillows facing each other on the floor. She was aware that I had a relationship with this room. Here, I had received most of my visions.

The walls had been replastered and repainted, making it different in appearance, yet in sensation it remained the same. I looked at her inquisitively, wondering. She did not respond, refusing to acknowledge her choice of setting. I met silence with silence and, after settling myself upon one of the pillows said, "It has been brought to my attention that your temple has been overcome with those who would be better served by the temple of the Bird."

She observed me suspiciously, "Some say it is so," she answered. "Your prophecies have affected the community in a way unexpected."

Like most mature Snake priestesses, her face possessed the readily perceived signs—deep creases around the eyes and mouth, rivulets and empty rivers lining the contours of the cheeks. Her hair was held together in a tight knot upon the top of her head.

"I have come to tell you that you may send those people my way," I said.

"It would offer us the greatest relief," she said.

I breathed a deep breath, anchoring myself more firmly within this space, attempting to become present to what it was that remained which wished still to speak to me, but my effort was met with great resistance. I shivered and held my arms tight to my chest.

"Aureillia," she said, placing her cold, hard, hand upon my arm. "I wish to apologize for the harsh words I spoke. I am afraid my temper is sometimes fierce. I deeply respect the duty you performed here. I am simply overwhelmed by the repercussions we are now encountering. Truthfully," she said, lowering her voice and leaning toward me, "I am rather frightened by it. It is most disturbing and it seems to be growing."

"Growing? In what way?"

"Affecting more people in more ways." She readjusted her weight upon the pillow. "The thing that troubles me the most about all of this is that I know Snake would not give us information we cannot use. I have pondered this question over and over and I arrive always at the same conclusion. It seems that we have not made proper use of the information." She made a sweeping motion with her arm as though to indicate the information still present within the room, "and that is why it is showing up in the community in this manner. I continue to ask myself, 'In what way could we make better use of the information? What is it that we did not understand?' Perhaps you, in the work you do at your temple, will discover the answers to some of these questions."

Though I sat in stillness, my insides were rife with confusion. It was curiously unclear whether she was implying that we had not made proper use of the information or that I had not. I did not know what to think of these things she and Leida had been telling me. The seriousness in their tone and manner while speaking of it gave me great cause for concern. How was it possible that prophecies I had given years earlier foretelling of events in a distant future could have become a problem for the community now? Indeed, the leader herself puzzled me. Though her words were seemingly kind and repentant, why had she brought me here, to this room, where I was so obviously vulnerable? Certainly I did not feel inclined to share confidence with her now.

"There is one more thing," I said, for I was ready to leave. "I have recruited Leida as a priestess of the Bird."

"You help me twofold," she said. "It is good. You will need help."

As I exited the temple I stopped to consider a sculpture of the Snake Goddess I was unfamiliar with. She wore the tiered skirt and exposed breasts of a priestess in ritual attire. Two thick, black snakes wrapped around her, meeting in an entwined knot at her womb. Two thinner, mottled snakes spiraled down her arms, coiling around her wrists. She held her arms forward, palms open, serpent power rising from within them. Upon her body were swirling, undulating, painted snakes. There was no distinction between her and the snakes. She was serpent energy embodied. The snakes had become her, and she had become the snakes.

* * *

An egg is pure potential; a. circle of possibility. Females carry this potential within them. When Her magical spark alights upon this potential, creation happens. Out of this meeting, all things manifest.

The eagles had mated successfully. We had watched them gather sticks, grass, leaves, and soft moss, admired their talent in weaving these together, building a new layer into which the female released two speckled eggs.

The colors of the Golden eagle, molten browns blending with gold and yellows, seemed to capture the sunlight within them. The feathers stood up and out around the eagles' faces, rays of darkness and light.

Lilith and I sat at our lookout, watching as they took turns sitting upon those eggs becoming, bringing each other food. Then she said it. All at once, it came out of her. "When will my father return?" she said. And I saw it, her brave little back, how it collapsed into sadness. She blinked her eyes, forcing back the pain.

"Oh my darling," I said. "I am so sorry. Of course you miss him so."

"I think he is my favorite person, next to you," she said. "I simply have found no one I like better."

"What is it that you like best about him?"

"His eyes," she said, clicking her tongue as though I should know that and what a silly question.

"Naturally, his eyes," I said, correcting myself.

"I wish to have eyes just like his," she said, smiling a sparkling smile.

A feeling of regret passed over me because it was something that could never be. I did not tell her that, however. Lilith's eyes, though blue, were a dark blue, almost black. Into Danelle's eyes, one liked to look, found comfort. Into Lilith's eyes, one dare not. They seemed to challenge. She was an altogether disquieting child. I often felt pain for her. It seemed her gifts would separate her from others. I had seen it already in her interactions—how they tended to shy away from her. Though she was an entirely lovable child, there was something about her that kept others at arm's length.

Eagle	**Owl**
Nest builder	*Nest user*
Creating safety	*Taking risks*
Power through exposure	*Power in silence*
Capturing sunlight	*Utilizing the darkness*

"She is truth serum itself," Hypia said as she sat beside me at the central hearth of the block where Lilith and I lived. Thela and her children also lived here, as well as four other women and their young. Together we shared the tasks involved with nurturing. Tonight had been my turn to attend to the children's bedtime needs. Hypia had stopped to see me here.

I looked at her in alarm. It was true. "Do not despair, Aureillia. It is not an entirely undesirable trait. I daresay it is in her blood. Rory was one of the greatest seekers Minoa ever had. I watched her extract information from people more than a few times. They barely knew what was happening before they revealed their deepest truth to her."

Hypia was speaking of my mother's mother, Rory, who had served Minoa as a seeker. A seeker is a person who seeks out hidden information for the benefit of the community. I had only learned later in life that Rory had been a seeker. She had told everyone she was a sailor. The identity of a seeker must remain concealed.

"You knew about Rory?" I asked.

"Yes," she said. Then whispering, "I guessed."

Hypia's face had become wider with age but it still possessed the same intensity and great strength. Her hair, which she continued to wear cut very close to her head, was now almost entirely white. "It's all right," she said, patting my hand reassuringly. "I never told anyone. As for Lilith," she said, returning to our original subject, "I only wish Danelle were here for her. It is one thing to feel wary of a child but then to remember who her mother is."

This remark surprised and hurt me, causing unexpected water to arise within. I looked down to try to stifle it. The sight of the bite marks on my own arms repulsed me. I crossed them in front of my chest and looked away.

"Aureillia," Hypia said, "forgive me. The words were not meant to hurt. You have done nothing wrong. I am deeply ashamed of the way the community is treating you, confusing the prophetess with the prophecy. It is a most shameful way to behave, surely not a Minoan one." She sighed a deep sigh, "In spite of all my efforts, I am afraid it is only a matter of time until we turn into one of our neighbors. It seems to be a tide that cannot be stopped."

It saddened me to hear Hypia, the one who had always been the fighter, express statements of surrender such as these. "This is a very grim thought indeed," I said. She was right. Even on my trip to Malta, I had felt it—a difference in approach among the other people in the seas. On Malta itself, the priestesses compromised their beliefs and instincts to protect themselves. These things were not yet occurring on Crete, but were evident in more and more places around us. Hypia acquired her information from Minoans who journeyed to the Minoan settlements in the lands surrounding us. The reports brought back had become increasingly worse. Sheena, my mother, was presently on the island of Thera, to the north of us, gathering information from the elders in the settlement there.

Hypia and Sheena were deeply involved—the closest kind of friends. I knew these visits were part of her response to having both her beloveds away.

"For myself, I do not worry," she continued, "but for Lilith and Lilith's daughters and granddaughters, life will be difficult indeed."

"She feels his absence now. She awaits his return. Oh, Hypia," I said, feeling the weight of my present situation, "What ever shall I do?"

"You must get him back, Aureillia," she said sternly. "It is as simple as that. The child needs him."

"But how? I do not even know where he is."

"It has never been a problem for the two of you to find one another."

"I wish not to interfere," I said.

"You must interfere," Hypia said, grabbing my hand within hers. "Oh behalf of a child, one must always interfere."

Her face, so close to mine reminded me in an eerie way of Danelle. Something about the lines around the eyes and the cheekbones. I backed away. "It is a most difficult situation, Hypia," I said.

She pulled me toward her and said in a low, confiding voice, "I do not know what happened between the two of you. I know that there is more than what you have told me. I also know that it must be something terrifying or you would have surely told me the all of it. But, Aureillia, I also know that Lilith needs Danelle. He is the only one who can save her from becoming a stranger within her own community."

Hypia's words, though blunt and cutting, were true. I knew this. I also knew that Danelle had asked me to leave him alone. How could I make peace with these two opposites?

"There is more than one way to contact another," Hypia said. "I know that you know this, Aureillia. You are simply not applying it to your present situation. And you must. You must find a way to connect with him, no matter how far apart."

The responsibility for the well being of a child is a weight heavier than any other. I began to worry incessantly. If Danelle were here, he would have told me that worrying serves no purpose. Somehow the visions I had witnessed had brought this condition of anxiety to me, anxiety over things that have not yet occurred. This was a condition I had not previously experienced. "Only action can effect a change," he would have said to me, scolding, and he would be right. But, in which way to act?

I had not been truthful with Hypia. I did know where Danelle was. I had known all along. I knew he was in the place called Libya in the land to the south. When I left Malta, it was clear to me he was going there. I knew he was still there. Others had told me. People on boats who had sailed there, returning without him. This, I began to understand, was information enough.

Stories They Told Me

The Time of Which My Grandmother Had Foretold

We had to abandon the Center when the time came, the time of which my Grandmother had foretold. We had been preparing for years, preparing ourselves. Still there is always hope, hope that something will happen – change – to make us not have to perform this task, to allow us to stay, A new prophecy. A different future. We had to prepare ourselves for many things, for the arrival of the earthquake, the impending invasion (many had fled already). The first task to be carried out was the dismantling of the sacred labyrinth beneath the Center. It was the time of the festival of the Bees, the time where we would normally build something new for the community. A time, usually of great energy and combined effort. What was usually a joyous working together now had to be devoted to tearing something apart, disassembling a form designed and built by our beloved ancestors, a space we had used over and over, something everyone on our island had an intimate relationship with.

Her labyrinth, which had transformed us from girls into women, from boys into men. It had been there underneath the Center, supporting it. It was our foundation, the base of our community.

We knew we had to remove it. It was too powerful to leave unattended. It would have been a dangerous act to abandon it. We understood the power of the energies it contained. We had created it and were therefore responsible for it and whatever may happen to anyone entering it unaware. We also knew, for the people who were to invade and overtake us, it could most easily be turned into a weapon.

Dismantling was not easy, rather, it was very difficult work. It was very difficult work that we did not wish to do. for one full lunar cycle, we broke apart walls with large axes, carried debris out in heavy wagon loads, our fingers bloodied, our legs weak. It was work which we took no pride in, work which we only wanted done. It hurt, it hurt in our beings to break apart – to take an axe to something we held so dear – a place so very cherished. In destroying the labyrinth, we were destroying Minoa. As the dismantling progressed, this made itself more apparent. It became clear that we were relinquishing a life we had labored to acquire, a community we were all an integral part of.

The seeds of anger that had been planted in us long before, with the original prophecy, began to blossom and flower as we demolished the labyrinth. This we had not considered. We had not anticipated the anger this mutilation would evoke, disconnecting us as a people, shattering and scattering us everywhere. We did not realize the energy this act would release, setting loose in some the need to destroy again and again, creating within us a labyrinth – an internal confusion, a maze, leading us away from our center.

Upon completion, instead of pride and celebration there was only silence – not the silence of stillness but a silence of inner unrest.

The place we thought we could never leave, our beloved island home, became something other, something no longer ours. It became easy to leave, groundless, rootless, a hollowness at our core, we began to wander, carrying our anger with us.

We began to fight.

To call ourselves warriors.

The first time I saw the feathered headpiece, I knew. I understood the energy released in the dismemberment of the labyrinth had crystallized into a form – a Minoan warrior.

Chapter 10

Aureillia

Long ago, I had been told that from the highest mountain peak on Crete, southwest of Knossos, on a clear day, one could see the tall hills of Libya. I began to think about this place until I felt drawn to it, until it pulled at my insides. I took Lilith, and, together, we journeyed there.

The twin peaks of Mt. Ida, the highest mountain on Crete, were a frequent place of pilgrimage for the people of Minoa. If one found herself in an especially difficult situation or in need of a renewal of the lifeforce—it was to Ida she traveled, to Her nurturing breasts. Often it was that She called people to Her, as She had to me, filling me with a longing for her so strong and overpowering that I felt I had no choice. It was a long and strenuous journey; one not taken often. My being was burdened with the weight of how to help Lilith and the pain that my prophecy had brought to the community. I knew that my time had come.

For the beginning of the journey, we were pulled along by mules in a cart with other pilgrims. I had not often been in the middle of the island where one could neither see nor smell Mother Sea. She had always been present in my environment, her salt breeze, her rhythmic sound. Here, removed from her, there was a stillness, a calm I was unfamiliar with. The air was permeated with the spirit of relaxation and luxury. Here, where there was less to resist, to buckle against, the plants and trees stretched higher, opened themselves wider, their branches hanging heavy with the blessing of abundant growth. The absence of the ever-present wind allowed for a constant melody of insect voices and a deep, settled heat.

At the base of Ida, we were provided with mules to take us up the steep side of the mountain. Our guides led us to the temple of Ida, a building which, though nestled within thick forest, echoed the Center building in Knossos with its three stories and peaked roof design.

Little sunlight broke through the dense cover of trees, making it very cold. The priestesses who greeted us wore large woolen shawls and thick leather boots.

"Is it always this cool here?" I asked, rubbing my hands together in an effort to warm them.

"This is the warm season," they responded. "For half the year there is snow on the summit."

"Mother," Lilith said, tugging at my dress and bringing my attention to the gold labrys of remembrance she had removed from her sack and now held forward in her hand.

Before embarking on this journey, I had sent her to the Temple of the Butterfly. It was the first time she had entered a temple alone with a concern of her own. She emerged proudly, displaying the labrys to me.

She had been given a ritual to perform. The last part of it entailed presenting the gold labrys to the Goddess of Ida in honor of her father. She was eager to carry that part out now.

One of the priestesses noticed and approached her, kneeling down to her height, she said, "You have traveled so far and you are so very anxious to make this offering, but it is a long trip to the peak summit and it is best to wait until morning."

Lilith nodded her head and leaned into my legs before releasing a long, open-mouthed yawn.

"I will watch over this until then," the priestess said, relieving Lilith of the heavy weight.

"There are quite a few children here today. You will find them in the clearing there. You see," she said, directing Lilith's attention to a patch of bright sunlight within which small figures danced in play.

She stood and, addressing me, said, "We could use your help in preparing evening meal."

The preparation of a group meal is a lively affair. There is the smell of the fire, the energy of people working together, the anticipation of eating. There are the discussions that can only happen over the creation of food.

After the long journey, such satisfying, human work was enlivening to the spirit. I was put to work shaping soft, workable dough into oval forms that would be baked into bread. The priestess with whom I worked asked about the reasons for my journey. I told her gladly of my twofold dilemma.

"You must trust," she said, after considering what I had said for some time, "that the Goddess has a reason for everything that she does, including the things that are difficult and unpleasant. What we see is but a small part of Her story, which is vast and all-encompassing.

"It is my sense that these two concerns are one and the same, only you do not see it yet. Allow one to lead you to the answer of the other. Remember that She who presents us with the questions is the same as She who presents us with the answers. In time."

She took the shaped loaves, placed them onto the heated charcoals enclosed within the stone oven, and sealed the door tightly to allow the heat to better transform them. I heard Lilith's laugh, confident and distinctive, echo for a moment over the voices of the other children.

Sleep was deep, so deep and complete that when I awoke, it was as though swimming to the surface of the water from a place of great depth. I soon determined that Lilith had experienced a similar sleep, since her usual morning perkiness was replaced by requests to sleep longer.

We lay together under the warm blankets, listening to the jangling of goat bells as they foraged on the steep slope outside the temple.

The walk to the peak invigorated us. The flowers growing within the grasses along the hillsides possessed a tender beauty unexpected in such a harsh climate. The guide was a skilled climber who knew the trail intimately. Her strong legs stretched with grace over large rocks, and up the steep course, leaving her energy enough to assist us.

When we reached the peak, into the large, wide, and wanting crevice, we both lowered our offerings. I stood, astounded once again by the majesty of this island. Never before had I encountered such views in every direction. Her exquisite combinations of jutting peaks, dipping valleys full of green groves of trees, the stretching blue sea beyond. The unimaginable assortment of colors. Such a wide panorama offered a feeling of vastness. Looking around I was struck with the realization that this sort of view, eagle enjoyed always.

I remembered what the priestess had said the night before. How we are but a small part of a much larger story. I experienced those words as I stood there.

I located a place on the peak that was facing southward. There Lilith and I sat. There were some clouds, and I was unable to locate anything that looked like the tall hills of Libya, but I pointed in that direction nevertheless and said to her, "Your father is there."

She nodded her head, solemnly observing the horizon. I felt myself stretching across the water that separates Crete from the land to the south, as though I were growing, expanding, and might actually reach that far. It was an extraordinary feeling—as though I were the vastness, and the story was but a small part of me.

Lilith's face was serious and pointing with intention and effort in the direction to which I had pointed—bottom lip pulled in. I put my arms around her and pulled her up onto my knees. "Close your eyes and think of your father. Imagine you are with him. Think of him and I am sure that he will feel it."

She closed her eyes, squeezed them tight together. I heard her whisper his name.

Eagle

Eagle – vast view

Knowledge of vastness

Sees larger story

Owl

Owl – knowledge of darkness

Night time awareness

Knowledge of minute

Chapter 11

Danelle

I longed for my daughter. It was a persistent, aching pain that never left me. It was an inner tugging.

Often, walking the beaches of Libya alone, my hand would stir with the memory of her hand inside it as we walked together the beaches of Knossos; her legs bounding along, trying to keep pace with me. As she jumped, I would pull her arm and she would, for a moment, fly—eyes wide—big, open smile. In that small, warm hand gripping mine was a trust so absolute and pure that it awakened in me feelings of protection and nurturance.

In so many ways Lilith awakened in me things before unawakened. Her presence added to my life a triangular aspect I had not before experienced—a feeling of continuance, an understanding of connection. Nurturing her recalled to me the nurturing I had received. Often it was that I would pass to her things that Hypia had passed to me. When this occurred I felt myself to be participating in an extension both back and forward. This extension stretched and reached in both directions, rooting itself firmly in shared wisdom.

At these times I became filled with an overwhelming sense of gratitude for my mother and the nurturing I had received; I understood that this allowed me to nurture in turn.

In the evenings I would sit on the bench outside my quarters and look seaward toward Crete. I would think about

Knossos and wonder what was happening there. I would squint my eyes and imagine the outlines of Her peaks rising out of the water, swaying in the hazy dispersement of the sun. I would think of Aureillia and Lilith. I would hear them calling my name.

I had made the surprising discovery that I am not a solitary man. I longed for the company of others—most especially other Minoans.

I had observed the regular rhythm of boats arriving from Knossos and made sure to be at the beach when they landed so that I could meet and visit with the boat people. It was enjoyable to hear of happenings in Minoa and to speak my native tongue. Some of the men and women I knew from before, others I had only just met. There were those with whom I had become quite friendly who would come to my quarters when the boat was docking overnight. These were good nights, sitting around the fire, sharing stories.

"Word is you shall not be staying here long," Promo said to me one evening as I sat around the fire with other Minoans. The moon was bright and half-full. His comment clamored loudly through the cool, clear air. "They already have a shaman. A village cannot have two shamans."

Promo was a Minoan I had, unfortunately, known on Crete before. He was a troublesome person, possessing the undesirable habit of picking fights and antagonizing people over unimportant matters. It was said a groan could be heard over a court when Promo entered it. I had witnessed him at the center of many public disturbances. The community was always relieved to see him board a ship that was sailing far away.

Now, he sat before me, at my own quarters, here in Libya. I had felt a cringing within when I saw him arrive with the others. There was, however, nothing to be done. Minoans do not exclude. If an invitation is extended, it is extended to all. I knew, when I had presented my invitation to the boat people down at the beach that it included Promo as well.

"What is a shaman?" I asked, reminding myself not to react to provocation.

"Rodin is a shaman."

"What is the meaning of the word, 'shaman'?"

"One who flies."

"'One who flies'," I responded. "How is it possible for a person to fly?"

"It refers to flight between the realms. A shaman is able to travel or 'fly' between the realms."

"Travel between the realms? I am not familiar with such a thing, therefore I cannot be a shaman."

"The villagers tell me that you are a shaman," he insisted, looking not at me but into the fire. He crossed his arms in front of his chest, leaned back, and continued to look at the fire. He had short, curly dark hair and a pointed nose and chin. His chin pushed forward as he spoke, lifting his head in a motion of defiance. "They said," he continued, arching his eyebrows, "shamans are skilled in entering and gathering information from other realms. They say Rodin is such a person and that so are you." Now he sat up straight and raised his eyes to meet mine. "They say there is no way you could have access to the images you create without possessing this talent."

"I tell you," I said, my jaw tightening, "I know nothing of it." I looked around the fire at the others present. I was hoping one of them would say something to change the subject but none of them did. They only remained silent, watching the two of us.

I was agitated. I wished for him to leave me alone but I could feel him, still looking at me, his small slits of eyes penetrating, ready to challenge me further. I had never been quick to temper, until now. Since I had witnessed the vision on Malta, it was easy to spark my anger. I had noticed this about myself. I was aware of it, yet this did nothing to help me control it.

"Do you think," I said, my voice loud, "that I know of such accomplishments yet choose to keep the information from you?"

"I did not say that," Promo said.

"Then what is the reason for your hostility?"

"I am sorry. Do I seem hostile? I do not mean to be hostile. I simply do not understand it," he said. "Why is it that everywhere you go, everyone admires you so. These people, the way they speak of you." He was shaking his head.

"I tell you, I know not of these things that they attribute to me. They are mistaken. They like me for reasons that do not exist."

"I think it is you who are mistaken," he said.

I raised my hands in surrender. "Perhaps they know something I do not."

"You know, Danelle, you shouldn't make it look so easy. It makes it hard on the rest of us."

"Make what look easy?"

"Being noble," he said. "I know it not to be so easy." There were a few grunts of agreement around the fire.

"Noble?" I said. "In what way am I noble? I assure you I am anything but noble."

"In what way are you not noble, then? Tell us. We would be comforted to hear."

I looked at him, at the others, all looking at me, waiting for my answer. I crossed my arms in front of myself and shook my head 'no.'

* * *

I continued to observe the fishing people from my hill above the cove. As I sat outside and carved, I would look down occasionally to watch them. They began to wave as they passed beneath me, and I began to wave back.

One day, as I watched them cutting and cooking their catch on the beach, I noticed one of them calling to me, motioning for me to come down.

"Please," he said, as I reached the white sandy cove where they sat, "join us." He offered me a seat around the fire of cooking fish. The smell was sweet succulence. In his hand he held out toward me a plate of cooked fish.

I was overwhelmed. This was the first time anyone from this community had invited me to share in a gathering, had offered me food.

I looked at what was in the plate he held toward me, the curving sizzling limbs of freshly cooked octopus.

"We had a good day today," he said. "She was very gracious."

He was a small man. His black skin was stained white from the salt of the sea. His hair was cut tight to his head. He had an extremely kind face with cheeks that rose to his eyes when he smiled, eyes that sparkled.

"Come," he said, motioning for me to be seated in the space beside him.

"I am most honored," I said, smiling and bowing slightly toward him.

"Come. Come," he said, brushing away my thanks and patting the space beside him.

I sat next to him and took the plate into my own hands. I watched him eat. I wanted to be sure to eat like him and not to offend in any way.

After watching him and the others eat for a while, I began. It was so delicious. The soft octopus flesh releasing its juices into my wanting mouth, upon my receptive tongue, as my teeth pressed against it. I closed my eyes to better savor it. They laughed.

"You are enjoying it," he said.

"Indeed," I answered, "it has been some time since I have eaten anything this good."

"You must join us. Come and join us. We have plenty. We have seen you watching. You come. You join us," he said.

I looked around at the others. They were nodding their heads in agreement.

"To be truly welcomed is a great pleasure," I replied.

"Good," he said. "It is good."

After we ate they all began to clean up after themselves. I rose to help. He put his hand on my forearm to stop me. "You are my guest," he said.

I nodded and stopped.

"I am most grateful to you," I said.

"Jeftu," he said. "I am Jeftu."

"Danelle," I said.

"Danelle," he said. "Return tomorrow."

* * *

I began to join the fishing people each day upon their return for a meal of that day's catch. I would hear them leave in the early hours. When I saw them making their eventual return, I would go down to the beach to meet them. Each day I would help a little more, pulling the boats in as they arrived, unloading, building a fire. The cleaning and cutting, the cooking, I only watched. They would catch different fish every day. What they caught, they would immediately cook. The first of each fish they cleaned, they returned to the sea as an offering to the Goddess. Then they would eat. After cleaning up, they would carry what remained up to the village. Everything they caught, they shared with me. Every one of them was kind to me. They seemed an altogether gentle breed, smiling a lot, singing to themselves as they worked, enjoying each day their catch. They explained that, though they lived in the same village as Rodin, he and his people were of a different tribe.

Around the fire, they would converse in fast dialogue about the day's trip, changes in the sea, the moon's cycle. I understood very little of what they said, but Jeftu would sit next to me, sometimes translating, sometimes just talking to me. He seemed to be one of the leaders of the group. I could not understand why he was pouring so much attention onto me. I was, however, enormously fond of him and looked forward to our daily discourse. Never had I met a man who seemed so at ease with himself. He seemed to radiate sunlight from within.

Finally one day I said to him, "You have been so generous to me. Is there not something that I can give you in return?"

"There is one thing," he said, putting his plate down and looking at me. "It would be our good fortune if you would join us on our fishing trips."

"Good fortune? Me?"

"She has been good to us since you came."

"If it is your wish for me to come with you then, of course, I shall come with you," I said.

He clapped his hands once and held them together in front of his chest.

"I must tell you I have not a lot of experience at this."

"We do not need you to work," he said. "We simply require your presence."

"I would be willing to learn."

"And I would be willing to teach. Tomorrow morning, at sun's return."

Stories They Told Me

The World Within the Rocks

Once, before the dry time, this land knew water in abundance. Moist mornings, damp evenings, rainy winters. Vigorous waterfalls enlivened the wadis. The dry paths of dirt that traverse the area now were lush, flowing rivers.

Tall cypress trees grew, spreading over and bending around us, containing us in groves of shade. Within this shade we rested while walking our cattle. We knew Serpent would protect us. She was the One. The Creatrix; the energy that is present.

The cattle we kept, not only for the nourishment and power in trade they provided but also for the added gift of the wise ones which, during the rains, sprouted from their droppings. It was they, these moist, spongy plants who first sang to us of our Mother, that revealed to us the world beyond, the world hidden within the rocks. It was they who taught us the dance.

The more we visited this different world, the more we came to know it, the more it became a part of ours. Some of us were able to see it emerging from a crevice. Others followed moving shadows through the rock face into the place beyond. It is there always, ever-present in our environment. The plants only let us see it, offering form to the form-free.

To remind themselves and show each other, some of us began to paint or scratch the realm beyond onto the exalted rock surfaces that surround us. from then on, looming over and within our environment, was this other world. Herds of shadow giraffe, spirit cattle, outlines of tiger guides, and figures like ours engaged in the dance – the Serpent dance.

My mother slipped between the cracks readily. She perceived doorways no other had. She recognized new teachings. It was she who learned to preserve the wise ones for use in the dry season. It was she who led us to a previously undetected wadi full of crisp freshness when the usual ones were becoming reduced. Naturally it was she who slipped into a world unlike any other – the world of the dryness.

Until then, all the other realms we had experienced were similar to our own, with animals and plants; similar but altered. The realm of the dryness, however, sustained barrenness; utter desolation. Life did not move Herself there.

"The giraffe have led me there," she would say, shaking her head in dismay. "They who see far in front of themselves. Something there is they are trying to show me. But what? A land full of sand? A land so dry I taste it for days upon my return?"

* * *

Here the rocks are carved and sculpted into lofty, stretching planes and wind-rippled curves. Long ago water pushed persistent urgings against mountainsides until the mountains surrendered, allowing the water slowly within. This connection created corridors and tunnels between thick towering walls of rock. Along these corridors we travel with our cattle, resting at places of green that border the river, or circle seasonal wadis. There, in huts of tied-together straw, arranged beneath the shadows of cool stone, we stay. When the cattle have lowered the grasses so entirely that the sun burns it brown, we move on, once again, in search of green.

I was young, too young to eat the magic when my mother was witnessing the dryness. Often, even without it, if I sat for some time watching an image depicted on the rock face, the animals would begin to move, flow, and dance, as the chalk and pigment they were composed of dissolved, giving way to the other world.

I would enter, running with them into the land of shapes, the place of thoughts becoming. Still young and unsure of myself, I did not venture far, keeping to the periphery, remaining conscious of both worlds.

"It is true," my mother said, in the evening around the fire, "we are no strangers to dryness. We have dry seasons. But what could create such sand? Lakes of dust! Hills of heaping powder, as though all has evaporated into randomness, all has become particles of sand."

It was clear, the dryness was overwhelming her, haunting her journey through this world. It had instilled in her a sense of foreboding, not previously present. Others began to turn away from her.

Chapter 12

Aureillia

When they began to come to me, I was glad I had taken on Leida. There were more of them than I alone could help. It was only after I had worked with them for a while that I began to see how my prophecies had created a hole in the community. Trying to help them with warnings about the future had brought pain into the present. Those who came to me all seemed to be suffering from a similar affliction: a sort of anxiety—despair. They could not name it, but when pressed, many would say, "What shall become of Minoa? Our children? Our future? If these things come to pass, what is the purpose of the now?"

There had been a delay. It had taken some time for this despair to develop. Many years earlier, I had given my final prophecy, yet here it was among us, affecting many in the form of individual worry. There seemed to be a pervasive feeling of helplessness, a hopelessness, a lethargy.

There was something else, very disturbing. There were those who came to me to tell of terrifying dreams that had taken over their dreamtime, repeating themselves over and over. The telling of these dreams were frequently detailed descriptions of one or more of my visions—parts I had disclosed to no other. This frightened me. How could they know these things I had seen in my visions? How is it these things were coming to them without invitation? It was as though there was a source of information they were accessing, the same one that I had access to with the assistance of the venom. My having had the safety of a mentor and a reason for receiving such information had, though difficult, helped me process it. But these people, and they were all different kinds of people, had no means of reconciling with these dreams they were now receiving. There was no discernible reason for the information. It served no purpose except to make them always afraid.

Leida and I welcomed them, our companions, accepting them into our small, underground temple. We listened. They needed to speak. They seemed to be overfilled with words.

We taught them the dance of release.

* * *

The dance of release must be practiced outside on a tall hill with an open view of the world around it. It must be practiced often, and with intention.

We start out as a small ball upon the earth, our feathered wings wrapped around us, slowly rise, spine unfolding, feet begin to move up and down, down and up they move, up and down upon this earth until they pulse fire, becoming claws.

The power, rising up through, straightens the body, lifting breasts, chest high as wings begin to extend up and down, down and up, flapping, flapping until it begins to unhitch—detach, disperse into the air, the atmosphere around us.

"Loosen," I say, as Zula and Rory, my teachers had said to me so long ago when I was learning. "Release further," I encourage. "Make room for Her once again within you."

From my own experience I knew that the holding that happens when one is in pain or despair can block the energy of the Goddess. As had happened for me, witnessing the horrors of my visions had affected my whole being, beginning the grabbing, the fierce holding of fear within.

Leida and I took our winged companions to the hill to teach them the dance alone. We tried to afford them some privacy. We assumed they wanted and needed this. There were, however, those few times where we would, quite without meaning, arrive there at the same time. At those times, I had noticed how our companions eyes' would meet each other with interest, behind the shyness and confusion. As we danced together I perceived a ring of power forming around us. This combined effort of release seemed to intensify the effect—unifying us in our struggle.

With work to do, and a place in which to do it, Leida began to thrive. Never had I seen her so full of life, and what passion. Her energy carried me many days. Much of the toughness and anger had left her, now that she was able to put her talents to work. Though she was still an apprentice, I allowed her to do the same work I was doing. Since we were in the process of creating a temple, there were no guidelines to follow. We worked closely together, trying to understand in what way Leida could utilize her gifts in the service she was being called to perform and what it was we were being asked to do as priestesses of the Bird. Already a great ability to nurture had been awakened within her in response to our winged companions. She was committed to the purpose of the temple, eager to learn all I had to teach her about snake, birds, and the dance.

"It is strange," Leida said, "for though your prophecies were about the future, they seem to have happened on a certain level already. These people are responding to them as though they have already come to pass."

"It is this which is so disturbing," I responded. "I know not why it is so. It is as though a door became opened, as though more pushes through it all the time."

"Where do the messages of prophecy come from? How is it that we are able to see things that have not yet happened? Where are the voices from?"

Leida's questions surprised me. Then it was that I remembered that she had never been schooled as a Snake priestess. "The Serpent," I said. "It is the Serpent who speaks to us. It is She who brings us our dreams. It is She who possesses the wisdom we receive and transmit as Her priestesses."

"So it is the Serpent who speaks to these people as well, who enters their dreams in this way?"

"I suppose it must be," I said, though I had not before considered it. "Indeed it must be Her."

"But why? Why would She do this? This seems a terrible thing to do."

"The priestesses at Ida told me that She has a reason for all that She does. What we see is only a small part of a larger story. Because of this, we may never understand all the reasons. Our work seems to be about helping our companions make use of it, helping them to digest it. Did you know," I asked her, "that a snake eagle can swallow a snake whole?"

"Indeed whole?"

"Whole. Without being poisoned, without suffering the ill effects of the venom. We would be well served by finding ourselves a snake eagle."

* * *

The trip to Ida, though long and hard, had done Lilith good. She returned telling everyone she had seen her father and that he would be home soon. I determined to continue. Such a long trip, however, I could not make often. I found a hill close to Knossos that faced south. Together, Lilith and I journeyed there often. We would sit and look southward and think of Danelle. Our ritual seemed to invoke his presence.

She felt him. I felt him. Sometimes, his presence was so thick in the air surrounding us that I would reach out my hand to touch him.

Stories They Told Me

The World Within the Rocks

In the heat of midday, I swim with my mother in a deep wadi. She who thinks only of the dryness. I am now her only friend. The stone hole is filled with cool rain water. All around us, beside us, across from us, the tall towering walls are painted, engraved, covered, and recovered with images. The sun reflects off the water, making patches of shimmering light upon the forms, which begin to move.

"Too much sun," my mother is saying, her brittle body submerged within the cool water. "Too much sun."

She has begun to understand the dryness is already here; already present among us in this place. This place is the place of dryness. Her eyes are wide and puffy for lack of sleep. Her skin is hard and cracked. Her body an empty reed. She is forgetting to eat. I submerge into the clear water, swim over to her. I put my arms around her neck. She pulls me to her but the embrace is empty. My mother has left me for the dryness.

She brings back grasses for them to taste. "Taste," she says, "within these grasses you can taste it. It is here already. The dryness. Too many cattle." Her eyes are wild. It is clear. They will not listen to a ranting woman. "The spirit animals tell me there are too many cattle. This is one of the reasons for the dryness."

They look up at her, registering their disgust, then away. Around them is no dryness. They cannot see it. When they look, they see flowers, they see abundance. There is water, there is green. It is enough knowing for them. They are satisfied with this.

At Jebarren, my mother ascends the high peak of Ahournet. I wish to go with her. I beg, I plead, until she surrenders.

We walk for a long time up the steep, rocky hills. The wind is fierce. I have heard of this place; it is where important questions are asked. Girls and boys coming of age are brought here. Here they are introduced to the wise ones for the first time.

Here, the Goddess of Rain dances across a huge rock face, water streaming from her arms, sprouting from her head. She spreads it around. She shares it generously – moisture – long, flowing streams of life.

We sit in front of Her. My mother eats the magic. She passes me a small bit of it, which I chew on slowly, surprised by its straw-like texture; the way it dries out the insides of my cheeks. We sit beneath Her, watching Her dance. She is moist, cool, and nourishing, inspiring within me inner gushings. Moisture passes between my legs, life streams pour down from my eyes, sprout up off the top of my head, through my fingertips until I become moisture spreading myself around, dispersing droplets of me. from these droplets life arises – color – enhancement. I am enchanted with this profusion of moist sprouting, and I dance wildly, lost with the ecstasy until a smell arises – the smell of damp on dry; the singeing odor of water upon rock, hot sand. The sun, huge and yellow – such a clear, bright ball of yellow – fills the horizon, the sky – evaporating me, the many lifeforms I have sprouted until the dryness spreads around me – around me becomes everywhere sand.

"No! No!" I call out. I call out to Her. "Goddess of Rain, where have you gone? Why have you abandoned us?"

Return Return
Return to us

She appears, a faint image maintaining Herself within the dryness.

"What is the reason for such dryness?" I ask.

"Upside-down serpent."

"Upside-down serpent?"

"I have not gone. I am still here. I am only upside-down."

Chapter 13

Aureillia

Once, I had practiced with the Serpent of Fire. My teacher had been the high priest Tolles—Danelle's father. The Serpent of Fire is the divine energy that fills the cosmos. She is the life force, the Goddess within. She lies dormant at the base of the spine until awakened. One may awaken Her in many ways—through dancing, chanting, bringing forth. In Minoa, the most common way used to awaken Her was to engage in a practice with Her. This involved working with a high priestess or priest in a series of postures and extended silent time, all working toward conscious activation.

When I had activated my serpent, I had also been blessed with the ability to see other people's serpent lights spiraling up through them, pulsing with power. However, much pain had resulted from that effort and I had lost that ability. In my anger and desolation, I had discontinued my practice.

With all the new questions about the serpent arising within me, it seemed the time had come for me to return to my practice.

I approached Tolles again after many years. He welcomed me back graciously in spite of the fact that I had not always been pleasant toward him about my decision to terminate my practice.

"Why is it that you return to me now," he asked, taking his seat across from me in a large, spacious upstairs room of the Center.

"New questions have arisen within me about the serpent. I have an inkling a practice with the Serpent of Fire may offer some answers."

Tolles smiled. It was a defeated smile. He looked frail and drawn. He had been a dear friend of Barbara, and had not fared well with her passing. Now, the absence of Danelle appeared to be unbearable for him.

"Aureillia, why has he gone?" he asked. The change in subject was disorienting. I took several minutes to answer. I was thinking about what to say to him about why Danelle was gone. It became more difficult to not speak of it, the longer he stayed away.

"I do not feel it is right for me to speak about why Danelle has gone," I answered finally.

"A father wishes to help his son."

"You have helped him, always."

"Please, Aureillia," Tolles pleaded.

I shifted my weight upon my knees and sat up taller. "This is very uncomfortable," I said to Tolles. "Danelle is gone because of something that happened between us on Malta. Something that he feels he needs to process alone."

"And you will not tell me what that is?"

"I cannot," I said. "Though it would surely offer me comfort to speak to you of it, it would not be fair to Danelle. I must remain silent to grant him his privacy."

"I understand," he said, shaking his head. "It is not that I do not understand the reasons for your silence. It is simply that I am bothered by something. Aureillia," he asked, greatly changing his tone. "Do you know Danelle to be an oracle?"

Tolles's question caught me unawares. Though Danelle and I had spoken of this matter often, no other had ever mentioned it to me. "I know that many do," I replied, "though he wishes it not to be so."

"Why? Why is that?"

"He simply wishes not to be called that. The reasons why have always been unclear to me."

"I am afraid it is not that simple," he said. He stood up an approached one of the windows. He crossed his arms in front of himself, then turned back around toward me. "Aureillia, Danelle must assume the title he has so clearly earned."

"It makes him uncomfortable."

"Why? Why should it make him uncomfortable being who he is? Don't you see? There is something he is afraid of. He is terrified of this title, though it is a blessed one indeed."

A stone settled in my stomach. "I always considered it a sign of humility," I said, standing up and approaching him. "How foolish I have been."

"He is very good at hiding it," he said. "I am ashamed to say I did not even know he was an oracle until just before he left. You see, that is why I am so concerned. Only days after I tried to speak to him about it did he leave. I had intended to work through it with him. I had a plan, but now he is gone and I am unable to carry it out."

Tolles and I stood looking out the window. It was quiet. The island stood calm as a picture before us. Each time I had the opportunity to come up to this highest part of the Center, I was impressed by its open airiness. A place above all the noise and clamor of the lower levels. Even the rooms were larger. Tolles's dark, curly hair hugged his face, which was full of concern over Danelle, his own son unreachable and distant. "Perhaps he is gone for more reasons than I understand," I said.

Chapter 14

Danelle

In the mornings the air is cool, the water is warm. After I meet them on the beach, we set out in our small boats. The fog is lifting, the water is calm. The sun, only just returning, is hugging the edge of the sea, casting its burnished red sheen across the liquid surface, over the hills, out toward the other side of the horizon. It ascends slowly, hovering momentarily in each position as it climbs its steep rising arc.

* * *

"Is it true," I asked Rodin, when he came to see me at my quarters one evening, "that you are able to travel between the realms?"

"It is true," he said. He took a long stick into his hand. He held the stick over the fire until it became fire. He watched the burning stick. The crackling noise filled the silence. "Since you ask," he said, placing the entire stick into the fire, "I must now tell you. The spirits have requested that I teach you this craft. They say there is something you do not understand, some knowledge you require that spirit flight may help you with."

"Why do you tell me this only now?" I asked.

"The craft is taught only to those chosen at birth," he said. He spoke softly now, in a whisper almost, but still accentuating each word in that way he had, "by the elders. It is forbidden to teach any other. The spirits, with their request, are asking me to break with custom. Because they have not yet made a request of me, I must do as they ask. I may have to contend with much trouble from my community, however, if they discover that I am passing the teachings to you."

"From what I have been told, it seems that the community considers me to be knowledgeable in this matter already."

"It is so," he said. "I have, for reasons you may now understand, not discouraged this kind of thinking. However, this brings to light the other problem. The problem of not having two shamans."

"Why is that?"

He clicked his tongue impatiently. "Again, custom," he said. "They consider you a threat to my power. I have assured them that you are only here temporarily. I am correct in that statement, am I not?"

"Yes," I answered. "I do not intend to stay here."

"Well then," he said, standing and stretching his legs. "We must begin. I will come for you in a few days. We shall journey together. You will be prepared."

"Yes," I said.

He nodded and took his leave.

* * *

Rodin began to lead me in long treks through the forested hills beyond the village. Inside these hills was a world I had not imagined. Magnificent greenery with lush vegetation; tall peaks with views stretching over the dry land beyond.

"Do you know," Rodin said to me one day as we stood observing the immense sea of sand beyond us, "this land was not always like this. Once this land was full of grass, lakes, and grazing cattle. It was not so very long ago, for the elders still speak of it. Sometimes there is too much sun, Danelle.

Too much sun creates nothing but a great dryness. We must allow time for the sun to be away."

We walked at a steady, even pace, barely speaking. Rodin's silence seemed deliberate. He only spoke to give instruction or to point something out on the trail. The paths were very wide, as though well traveled by many at a time. Though we rarely saw others on the path, I was aware of the presence of others. This place had an underlying hum to it, which I understood to be sacred. Though the vegetation in these hills did not appear to be anything beyond the ordinary, there was something about these places where we walked that seemed to have a strong pulse. Everything seemed a little bit bigger, a little bit greener. The trees seemed taller; one felt their trunks breathing, smelled the moist wood beneath their hardened exterior bark. The underbrush stood tall and perky. All seemed to have a glow around it.

The largest difference, however, was the animals. Because it is an island, animal types are limited on Crete. Here, I saw animals I had not before seen, and some were extraordinarily large. I was not sure what I was seeing, as we encountered the same animals often and Rodin seemed to know them, calling them by name. I had always wanted to see a tiger. I had heard tell of these cats which possessed equal amounts of power and grace. I knew there were tigers here, in the land to the south, and looked forward to meeting one.

These treks were very tiring for me at first. My being grew enormously tired, even shaking toward the end of the day. Rodin was most difficult to keep up with. I now understood where he acquired his great strength. In the first few treks, my being was so exhausted I would fall off to sleep at once by the fire in the evenings, and even in the breaks during the day.

I would wake up to Rodin nudging me with his foot saying, "Wake up, tired man."

It seemed there was a schedule to keep. We rested for certain amounts of time in the same place. If I wanted to stay and rest longer, Rodin would not allow it, saying, "No. We must go on. It is time."

Slowly, after many trips, my body began to adapt. The terrain began to feel familiar. The pace became comfortable, and I was not as tired. This helped me relax and enjoy the treks more. A pattern began to emerge. Every ten days, we would journey for three. We would travel the same paths, stop to rest in the same places, and always overnight in a wide circular clearing where there would be a large pile of wood set up and food prepared and waiting there. I did not know who prepared the wood or the food. I never saw any other, but it was always there for us when we arrived.

The most curious part about these journeys, however, was that after we had walked all day, Rodin would set himself up for what appeared to be another journey in the evening. He would build himself a large fire, setting a lot of extra wood beside it and, after we ate our meal, arrange another plate and set it beside himself. When I awoke in the morning all the wood would be burned and the food eaten. At those times, it was I who would need to wait for him to awake.

"Tell me," I said to him one evening when he began to build his fire. "Tell me what it is you do after I fall asleep."

"Begin by telling me what it is that you have observed," he said.

"I have observed that we follow a rhythmic pattern in journeying, that you come to collect me for journey every ten days, that we travel for three. Within these three, we seem to follow certain rhythms of walking and resting. I feel a presence in these woods, a presence of something other. I have observed you setting yourself up for what would appear to be another journey at night—after we have walked all day."

"Always I have been taught," Rodin said, "that inquiry displays readiness. These paths we travel are spirit paths—well-traveled ones indeed. It is the spirits you are sensing when you say you sense the presence of other. In walking these paths in the day, we are requesting to enter them on the spirit level at night."

"You simply walk the same path at night?"

"These paths are but entryways—doorways to other places—but you must know them well, most especially for when you wish to return."

"Where do you go?"

"You go where your spirit leads you. It knows where it needs to go. The spirits do not always grant me permission to enter their world by night; often they deny my request. They have detected something within me, an energy I have carried through the paths in the daytime, which they do not wish to have cross over. Then I must clear myself of whatever it is they have rejected. This can take much time. They seem to be welcoming you, however, and have asked me many times why it is that you have not yet accompanied me in my evening journey."

I was intrigued by what he was saying. On Crete it was said there were people who had visited other worlds. Indeed, Aureillia, in her trance dances, had. I knew there to be other planes of existence, but I had not knowledge of these things. They were secret teachings reserved for those initiated in the role of priestess or priest.

"When you travel into the spirit plane," I asked, "are you aware of what it is that you are doing?"

"Most certainly. It is this precise art that is spirit travel. Conscious journeying," he said, accentuating the words. "Taking your awareness with you is essential. A shaman enters the spirit world for a certain reason—to seek out requested information. Therefore it is necessary for him to be able to bring the answers he finds back with him. For this reason one must be conscious. The shaman of the village serves as the bridge between this world," he said, pointing to the area surrounding us, "and the otherworlds. Villagers come to me with requests, questions for me to present to the spirits when they are in distress or need some healing. It is they who stack the wood and provide the food. It is what they do in exchange for their request. The heat is essential. Sometimes, answers are received, instructions offered, warnings given."

"Much like a Snake priestess," I said.

"Yes, but no venom," he said. "No venom and, you should know that here in Libya, it is only the men who journey."

"Why is that?" I asked.

"That is the custom," he said with a finality that made me understand I should leave the subject alone for now. "The paths are only open at certain times of the sun and moon cycle. Access is tenuous at best. I am not sure why, but the doors seem to be wide open for you. I suspect the spirits are satisfied to see me working again. I suppose I had settled into a placid state, which is not good. One must never stand still."

Stories They Told Me

The World Within the Rocks

Serpent Dance

It is not so much a dance as a remembering. It is not so much a union as a reconnecting. It is not so much an act as a way of being.

It is a way of engaging serpent energy, allowing it always to swirl, about moving with the energy that is present in a flowing, lucid dance.

Chapter 15

Aureillia

A raptor must kill to live. Does she think of what she did? Conversely, does a bird think about being noble? Does a bird strive toward better?

"Can we travel between the realms?" I asked Helena, who was sitting on a pillow across from me. I had been filled with this wondering since Lilith and I had been making our journeys to the south-facing hill.

Helena sat in silence pondering the question. The purpose of our meeting was to design an initiation ritual for Leida. Though she was already engaged in work at the temple, she had not gone through a formal entry.

"It must be that we can," Helena said, "otherwise how would one explain those who communicate with us after they have been returned."

"Yes," I said, "we are sure of travel after return, but what I am wondering about is whether we know how to accomplish it while we still possess a physical form. Do we know how to travel then?"

"Travel to where?"

"To other places. To where another person is, a person we need to communicate with."

"Aureillia, why do you not simply get on a boat and go to him?"

"Because this plane will not serve me now. I cannot name the reasons why, but I know within me that I must reach him on a different plane."

Helena returned to thinking. I watched her, observing her face, young for her years. Where Snake priestesses aged more quickly than normal, being a priestess of the Butterfly seemed to elicit the opposite effect. My face had the unmistakable lines of a mature Snake priestess. In many ways, I knew, I looked older than Helena.

The air coming in through the window smelled of rain. I wondered if I would emerge from the Center to find the earth damp from a morning shower.

"Ah, the elders," Helena said in a tone of satisfaction. "I do not possess information on this matter, but it is my feeling that the elders may."

"You are quite right, Helena. If anyone possesses this knowledge, it would be them," I said, recalling only then the new moon celebration I had attended as a Snake priestess. At this ceremony I had observed the elders communicating with beings from other layers of existence.

"About the girl," Helena said, referring to Leida and bringing me back to the reason for our meeting. "I have given the matter much thought. It is clear to me that she must journey the labyrinth."

"The labyrinth?" I repeated, surprised, for I had not considered it. The labyrinth was a large series of winding and unwinding corridors built into a dug-out space underneath the bottom floor of the Center. It was a space of utter darkness through which one may pass at important times of passage.

All the girls and boys of Knossos experienced it as part of their initiation into female and male being.

"It is what you did, Aureillia. What you felt you must do to ease the transition from snake into bird."

"I remember," I said, "and it did help. I, however, have never assisted anyone through the labyrinth."

"I will school you in this task and be present at all times to offer assistance. Arrangements must be made to begin the process soon, however. Leida must not remain uninitiated for much longer. Initiations must happen at beginnings when one is fresh and open to receiving."

* * *

It was with much excitement that I approached the elders a few days later requesting private counsel. Upstairs, on the third level of the Center, they sat in half-circle, observing me sitting across from them. Wind blew furiously through the windows above us.

"I have come to request information on travel between the realms," I said. "I am creating a new temple and require teachings in this craft. My mentor Helena, of the temple of the Butterfly, is unable to assist me in this matter and has sent me to you."

"What is it that you refer to when you speak of 'travel between the realms'?" The woman who sat across from me, in the middle of the half-circle, asked. She was a small woman with long, white hair pulled into a knot at the back of her neck.

"I wish to know if we have yet learned how to accomplish this while we still possess a physical form. If we have, I wish to learn how."

"Where is it that you have heard of such things?" The same woman inquired. She wore a light lavender dress and maintained a perfect upright position. Where all the others sat with their legs crossed in front of them, she sat up on her knees, making her higher. I assumed her to be the leader of the group.

"I have heard not. For reasons that are my own, I begin to question."

They whispered among themselves. It seemed to be more than a sharing of information. It was quick whispers, full of concern and even fury.

"Silence. Silence," the woman in the center said, spreading her arms wide in front of her to calm the group.

She stood and approached me. Though her face was young and supple, the skin below her chin hung slack. There were bones on either side of her neck that stood out in pronounced lines, extending to her shoulders; they moved when she spoke.

"Please, if you would wait in the hallway while we discuss this matter between ourselves," she said, leading me to the door.

I went out into the bright hallway. As she closed the door behind me, a gust of cold wind seemed to pass out of it. This closing of the door felt cruel. I was surprised to find myself feeling slightly wounded from this action. It was such a different reception than the one I had expected.

I sat on the ledge of the large window across the hall from the door. From this window was a view looking out across the valley surrounding the Center. It was the time of the cool moons. The island was full of lush bright green due to the many recent rains. I sat looking at the island, my place of origin, my home. From here, I could see so much, the dipping valley, the hills beyond the blocks of rooms, people walking below. From here, I had a view as a bird has from a perch in a tree. I thought of my little temple at the bottom of the Center: dark with no view. It occurred to me that a bird would never live there. A bird requires a view to watch for prey, protect herself from predators. Dark caves and holes in the ground were for snakes who welcomed the dark solitude. I knew my temple could never be up here, on the top floor of the Center, but it was suddenly evident that it could not remain where it was.

The elders kept me waiting a long time, until the sun arced in the sky and my stomach turned over upon itself in hunger, until I leaned against the window ledge and fell asleep.

I awoke to the leader's voice calling my name, and followed her back into the room. After we both sat back in our places, she began to speak.

"We have taken much time to discuss your request," she said, looking around at the others who were nodding their heads in agreement. A fleeting feeling of ill will passed over me. I brushed it aside and tried to focus on her. "We have decided that since only those who receive invitation are allowed access to our teachings, we must decline your request."

"Am I not invited by simply possessing the question? The desire to learn?" I asked, trying to appeal to their sense of fairness.

"You must receive invitation," another woman hissed. "Invitation from Her," she continued. Her face was full of rage.

"You act as though I have committed offense simply by making a request," I said. "This I do not understand. I ask only for the good of the community."

The other woman moved to answer but the leader stopped her, extending a hand out toward her. Then she turned to me. "Aureillia," she said, "you have not received proper invitation. Since you received it once before, in your younger years, you know what that is."

I understood her meaning. I had received invitation before, the proper way. About that, she was right, but I could not ignore the knowing that this was not the real reason they were denying me. There was something else they were not admitting to. It seemed unfair. "Have I not proven myself to you all through my deeds?" I asked looking at them, many of whom looked away, averting their eyes from mine. "Please do not send me away."

"If you truly seek this information for the correct reasons, you will most certainly receive invitation. Go and wait patiently. It will be sure to come."

* * *

One received invitation from the council of elders through an inner voice, an inner call made by one of the members or the Goddess Herself. I did as she said. I prayed. I made my request to the Goddess. I sat silent time, made pilgrimages to Her caves with offerings. I waited and I waited but nothing came.

One day, at the Cave of Medea, as I sat in the center of the main room, yellow light streaming down upon me from the small hole in the ceiling above, it became apparent that I would never receive one. None of the council members would extend one and even if I did receive a call from the Goddess, they would not believe me. Instead I asked the Goddess for guidance to find a way through this in whatever form it may take.

On my way back from the cave, Thela approached me. "Aureillia," she said, forcefully, "where have you been? I've been looking everywhere for you."

"What is it?" I asked, for I detected the alarm in her voice.

"You must not send Leida back into the labyrinth. She did not fare well the first time."

"Of what do you speak, Thela?" I said, shaking my head in confusion, trying to reorient myself from my quiet time in the cave.

"Leida," she said. "I am speaking of Leida entering the labyrinth as part of her initiation."

"She told you?" I said, surprised. Ordinarily initiations were secret from everyone, even the person being initiated. Since we were only creating this one, I had included Leida in the decisions. I did not, however, expect her to discuss it with others.

"She told me because of what happened last time."

"What happened?"

"She passed out. They had to go in after her. She was terrified."

"Was that during her initiation to female being?"

"Yes."

"She did not mention it to me," I said.

"She would never want to disappoint you, Aureillia."

"I would not have been disappointed."

"She has a very high opinion of you," Thela said, angrily. "She wishes only to please you, regardless of her own well-being."

The words were cutting, but I tried to overlook them. Since Leida and I began to work together, there had been tension between Thela and me. I kept waiting for it to dissipate, but it seemed to be getting worse.

"Thank you for telling me, Thela. I will speak to Leida."

"With me. I want you to speak to her with me. She will not speak the truth if I am not there."

"At least give her the chance, Thela."

"No. You give her the chance. You give her the chance to be honest. I know where she is. Let's go. Right now."

She led me to our block where Leida was engaged in play with Lilith and the other children. She was not surprised to see us walk in together. Thela must have told her she was going to get me. We waited as Leida disentangled herself from the young ones and approached us.

"Leida," I said, "Thela has told me about your experience in the labyrinth the first time. I am sorry. I was not aware of it when Helena and I decided to send you in again."

Leida looked at her mother and said, "I have given it a lot of thought and I have decided that I want to try it again."

Thela made a move to say something but Leida stopped her. "I wish," she continued, still looking at Thela, "that my mother had not done this. I would have liked to have had the opportunity to tell you about this in my own time."

"Leida," Thela said now, "you must not be foolish. You must not do this simply to please Aureillia. She understands that it is for your own well-being."

"I wish to try again," Leida said, now speaking to me. "Aureillia, please, do not stop me. I wish to pass through the labyrinth successfully."

I did not know what to say. Anything I said would upset one of them. I understood Thela's concern but I also understood Leida's desire to try again as well as the wish to make her own decisions, to be treated as a woman by her mother.

"Thela," I said, "I have listened to your concerns and I understand them. I do. Any mother would feel the way you do, but Leida must be able to make her own decisions."

"It is not her decision. It is your decision."

"No, mother. I want this," Leida said.

"This you must be sure of, Leida," I said, "for if you do it only to please me, it is foolish indeed. Why don't you take some time to consider the matter carefully and make sure."

"Aureillia," Thela warned, "No good will come of this. You could stop it all right now if you wished to. You are choosing not to."

"You are right, Thela. I want it to be Leida's decision, not ours."

"It is too dangerous. I tell you. You did not see her the last time when they dragged her out of there. She barely had life. You weren't around. You were off at your cave. If you had been around, you never would have considered it."

"But that is not the case, Thela," I said with force, for she had said too many hurtful things and now I was mad. "I wasn't around. I didn't know and I am sorry. But this is a matter for Leida and me to discuss at the temple."

Stories They Told Me

The Tiniest of Seeds
The Black Sea
3500 B.C.E.

It was in a slow and sneaky way that they took over our village, our way of life. It was so slow and so sly, some did not even notice until it was too late. But I did. We did. from the start, we had a plan.

We understood what we must do. To have any hope of surviving this incursion, we knew we must gain access to the one thing that they had that we did not. We knew we needed to build our own relationship with the horse.

At first it was odd, seeing this graceful, powerful animal, once our food, once running wild in packs, being used as transport. This wild and precious beast tied up – caged. We had goats and sheep, even cattle – but the horses, the horses we had left alone to run -wild with the antelope and the deer – their sisters.

In the beginning we fought back by releasing their horses when they stayed in our village overnight. Sneaking out in the dark when all others were asleep and opening the gate of the fence where they were keeping them. I would watch them leaving, running into the star-flecked night air, still so freshly caught they had not yet forgotten life before, life in the open plains. Often, I could feel a part of myself running away with them, the part that had become caged since these strangers had landed upon us; a part I did not even realize was free until it shrunk itself in response to these people.

For so long had we stayed still, wanderers welcome to join us in the community we had created, growing larger and larger, expanding wide and large upon this fertile valley within which our village lies. What need had we for horses? There was nowhere we needed to go. All we had want for was here. Here she sprouted Herself happily within the rich, black soil into which we placed Her; offered Herself to us in the budding berries of wheat. The rivers were fitted with fish; their banks oozed with thick clay. In the nearby mountains She flowed forth in rich mineral streams. There was no place She did not give of Herself. And we took, receiving gladly while always remembering to give thanks, to offer something in return.

In the Northeast Steppes, however, She is not so kind. There the summers are short, too short to offer floods of abundance. There where the wind blows hard and fierce – breaking the calm within – the winters are long and merciless. The huntable animals come to us. So it was that they became wanderers.

At first they came only now and then, a few men, using our village as a stopping point on their journeys, but I saw it even then, the lust in their eyes as they looked upon it. At first they did not stay long. We were hospitable. It was our way. We were also aware of what it was people like these had done to other villages, villages less fortunate than us, the ones they set up camp in immediately. The ones who may have been a little less hospitable than us. Word had spread, from far beyond the steep mountains that separate us from one another we had heard: what did not get offered, they took. Any resistance was met with devastation and destruction. By the time they came to us we knew, with these people there were no choices, only the illusion of them.

Slowly, they built themselves a stable and a coral on the outskirts of our village. They began to bring more of themselves. They began to leave themselves there. They began to stay longer and longer until they finally stayed for good, kicking villagers out of their own shelters, claiming them as their own. Too impatient to work the land and wait for results; too greedy to share what they had, they simply took from us our food, our housing. This, I knew, was only the beginning. It was clear, inside their beings the harsh winters had made their home. They were always wanting, never offering. They had forgotten the necessity of exchange. Because of this, there was no intermingling of a friendly nature between us villagers and them. If they had offered to give back now and then, all would have been different. They did not, therefore, the energy between us did not move.

Though their relationship with the horse disgusted me, I also envied it. The way in which they combed it, patted it, fed it. They way they sat upon it, their legs spread wide about it. I recognized the power in riding that high, in moving so swiftly. It was a power I wished to possess.

Slowly, I came to know the horse. After repeated and persistent requests, they allowed me to feed them, to clean their stalls, to comb them, until I became accustomed to the presence of this strong, graceful animal. I began to enter the pen without fear, approaching them, talking to them. I began to rub down their warm, pulsing bodies. To relish the feel of sleek muscles under coarse, short hair. I came to recognize a body that sweat like mine, a body that smelled like mine. When she finally allowed me to look into her eyes, big, black and wanting; when she finally looked back at me – it was then that I saw Her. When I recognized Her within the horse, everything changed. My legs ached for Her. She allowed me to mount Her.

"Together we shall ride to freedom," She said.

Chapter 16

Danelle

The octopi they catch, they must immediately kill. If left alive, upright, they will surely find their way back to the water. They are tremendously talented at escaping and have been known to lift lids off clay amphorae with their tentacled arms and crawl away. Storing them upside down is a sure way to prevent escape but they are able to live a long time like this and it is a long time of unnecessary suffering.

The octopi are caught using a system similar to the one used on Crete. A row of small amphorae are strung along a tree limb, which is lowered into the water and left. Octopi love to crawl into small spaces such as these. Every few days the amphorae are checked. If any octopi have decided to rest there, they fall out when the amphorae are emptied, water and all into the boat. Any that are collected are gathered by hand and, to assure instant death are swiftly bitten on the back of the head.

On Crete I was removed from any of the methods needed to acquire food. I had simply been fed. I had forgotten what is re-quired in the harvesting of the meals I had become accustomed to. I eat octopus. Octopus I love to eat. I had forgotten this custom.

* * *

"What you see when you journey into the otherworld is only that which you have already imagined on the conscious level," Rodin said to me one evening. "The other realms will appear to you as you perceive them.

"Aureillia saw you murdering her only because she had first been witness to the horrors of her visions. She could never have seen such a thing without having first been exposed to the material of her prophecies. This is not to say that what she saw was wrong, or that she should not have foretold of it. She was tapping into an energy from which only Minoans have succeeded in insulating themselves.

"When you travel, you will indeed see things that scare you. You must understand that they are only there because you have already imagined them. They are a part of the material that is your very being. They exist within you. This is one of the purposes of journeying; to examine the contents of your entire being, even that which may be hidden or dormant, in a detached yet interested way so as to effect a change."

He had begun the teachings, teaching me how to release myself to flight. The fire burned high. The wood was prepared and stacked beside us. We sat before it. The first few times, he would travel with me.

"Study the flames," he had told me. "Feel the heat. Become the fire. Think of nothing, only study the flames and become the heat."

The concentrated focus I knew from my work with the Ser-pent of Fire. This my father had taught me. It was a similar teaching.

It was a long time that I sat there feeling the fire, so hot against the front of my body—a heat that ordinarily would have made me back away. I felt the heat until it was so hot it hurt and the hurt gave way to a heat that entered me from below, rising up through. There was a sensation of the front of my body melting away, my forehead, my face, my forearms, my legs and knees, of my hair rising, an all-over expansion.

"What are you most aware of?" Rodin asked. "A bird," I said, "the trilling of a bird." In the stillness the sound of one particular bird had become penetratingly insistent within me.

"Follow that," Rodin said. "Let that be your guide."

I focused on the trilling. I became aware of its curved movement, how it lifted and fell. I began to follow that line of movement with my awareness until I felt my self lift to follow it into the space in front of me.

It was strange and, at first, shocking, this feeling of lifting, this sensation of moving without moving. I became frightened and gasped.

"Yes," Rodin's voice came, calm and reassuring. "This is what it feels like. Indeed, it is strange at first. But that is the feeling you want. Stay with it. Allow yourself to lift. Allow yourself to go with the bird. I am here watching over you. Try it once again."

I breathed deeply, again focusing on the trilling. Again I felt the lifting sensations and, instead of resisting them, I allowed them to take me up high, to swoop and twirl. Once above, I moved backward a bit before lunging forward awkwardly to a space out onto the path to which I had become accustomed, knowing I was somewhere else, though I was still here. I was someone else, though I was still me.

I noticed immediately how it helped, the familiarity I had with my surroundings and the path itself. It offered me a confidence with which to move forward. I followed the path I knew, all the time aware of another layer, a different path also there. In the same place as the path I knew was this other layer, as thin as a piece of silk—the shadow of another world—a different forest existing at the same time as the one I knew, only visible to me now.

Then I seemed to leave the path I knew and enter the other forest entirely. It was still a forest but a forest as none I had ever seen. It was bigger, larger. The flowers were as tall as me. Their leaves I could examine in detail. Into their large open eyes could I peer, examining more closely than ever the detail of their petals—the interior workings of their bubbling fluid.

Color! Until I entered this world, I had never experienced color. There were fewer colors than I was accustomed to. One green, one red, one blue, one yellow, yet they were brighter, more powerful than any color I had ever seen. The green in this world made me aware that I had never before seen green.

I stand within the green surrounding me, encompassed in green until I become green. Porous yet strong, moisture travels in streams through me. I grow, reaching toward the sun with the intention of becoming more green. I become aware that the sun is making me more green—the more I eat the sun, the more green I become. I am wet, droplets of dew. I am fresh. I am new. I am green.

* * *

The boat glides silently over bright blue waters. Here, in this rocky area, is where the octopi live. The rocks rise up beneath the surface of the water, close to the bottom of the boat. Here is where we lower the amphorae. Jeftu raises the long tree limb. As he does this, an octopus slides out and drops back into the water from the movement of the lifting. I watch her swim at once round, at once flat in front of me, floating, gliding, stretching her wide-legged body. I put my hand into the water as if to catch her. She dashes away swiftly, leaving behind only a purple blur.

The tree limb hangs across either side of the boat; Jeftu empties, one by one, the remaining amphorae. I look away as he opens his mouth wide, exposing his teeth, which he sinks into the softness of her head. Though I am performing most of the other tasks, he does not ask me to help him in this. He also does not mention my not offering. Here is an area of silence between us.

The days the amphorae bring us octopus are good days. Our return is filled with excited anticipation for our forthcoming meal.

On these days Jeftu always makes sure to serve me first saying, “Look at the good things you have brought to us.”

Stories They Told Me

The Tiniest of Seeds

I began to ride everyday. The journeys became longer and longer, the ride more and more comfortable. My being enjoyed more and more the rhythm of her walking, her four legs moving, shoulders and spine swaying, moving my body upon her back, myself spread wide upon her, the heat of her body entering mine, strong neck – thick and erect – before me, together becoming one. I allowed her to go faster. She took me far.

We began to search for a place, together exploring the far reaches of the forests – up into the tall hills – where the trees grew so thick there was sometimes no room for us to travel between them, to the banks of the river, to the place where She spreads herself in vast meadows and fields full of grazing deer and antelope. I saw her look at the wild ones with momentary longing, but I felt it, how she remained loyal to me.

Once we found the place, we went each day asking the Goddess to receive us, to welcome us. It was an uninhabited part of the forest that reached itself to the river's gentle bend that we had decided upon. Here, in this mild curve of the river, fish were plenty. The adjoining forest was full of edible plants and animals. There was a small, natural clearing in which to cultivate a crop. Here She would provide for us well.

I made a circle of stones around a tall, wide tree in which She lived and I waited. Thinking of leaving my village sent strong tuggings through my being. Often I thought perhaps it would not come to pass. But there were other moments-moments of realization – that the place where I lived was no longer my village. My village was already gone. In the villagers' eyes, fear had already made its home.

In those times I would remember my place by the river's bend, how the air there was fresh, crisp, and clean. There – where there was a newness – all things were possible. This feeling I clung to – the feeling of possibility. I understood I must adapt myself to the world that was now forming. In this new and different world, I could no longer remain the same. I must turn myself into a new woman, a woman of my own choosing.

I returned each day to the place by the river. Beneath the tree where I waited for Her to welcome me, I spoke soft prayer.

Beneath this tree
I ask of thee
Release me
Set me free

Welcome me to this new home
Grant me the strength to become
The new one that shall give pause
A woman with teeth and claws

The day a tall purple flower bloomed proudly within my stone circle, I knew we had been welcomed.

Chapter 17

Aureillia

Things were not good. Leida had made the decision to enter again the labyrinth. Together with Helena, we were preparing the initiation ceremony. Thela, however, was furious. She refused to speak to me.

Since I had not received invitation from the elders, I decided to again approach them to try to persuade them to change their minds. The leader would not even allow me into the room. She came to the hallway and, in a scolding voice, said, "I know that you have not received invitation. You show the greatest disrespect to the Goddess with your actions. Do not dare to approach us here again or we will consider removing you from your role as priestess."

"Of what nonsense do you speak?" I said. I had never known such treatment. "These rules are not the rules of the Goddess. They are your rules. If I have shown disrespect, it is to you, not to the Goddess, whom I know myself to hold in the highest regard." My anger was high. My words were ahead of me. "I have cooperated with you always. You would call yourself teachers who turn away a person who aches with the desire to learn?"

"Aureillia, it is best for you to leave now," she said, opening her eyes into wide, large circles and pointing toward the stairs.

I held my tongue, but threw the large, clay bowl that I had brought as an offering against the wall. It made a large sound before shattering into many pieces upon the hall floor. "That is what has become of any respect I may have had for you," I said.

The rage that was surging within me was so powerful it terrified, but it was not as powerful as the sense of injustice I felt from their treatment and the behavior of the community in general. I could neither ignore it nor pretend it away any longer. All the pain and hurt I had been ignoring came rushing full view into my awareness.

* * *

The eggs had hatched and there were now eaglets to feed and care for. Mother and Father bird shared in this task, bringing food to the wide, wanting mouths of their young. Lilith and I sat at our lookout, watching them. With everything else around me having become so difficult, I cherished these walks, these talks with Lilith. The ease of simply being with her; her open, receiving nature; her innocence.

"It's a miracle, isn't it, Mother," Lilith said, "that birds can fly?"

"It certainly is," I said.

"How is it that they fly?"

"Their wings," I said.

"You have wings, yet you fly not."

"I am far too heavy to fly," I said. "The birds are so light weight. Do you know that they have hollow bones?"

"Hollow bones?" Lilith said, scrunching her nose up and looking at me. "Nothing at all within them? Nothing?" Her hair was pulled back into a braid, displaying her not-often-seen, smooth, broad forehead.

"Not entirely nothing," I said. "Lots and lots of air. It is this, this weightlessness, that enables the flapping of their wings to lift them to flight."

"Hmmmmmm," she said, looking down into the gully below us, "perhaps if I could find a way to hollow out my bones, I too could fly."

"I am afraid that is not possible. We humans are bound to the earth, except for our souls, of course."

"Our souls do not possess weight?"

"I used to think not, Lilith, but now I am no longer sure," I said. I thought of those who came to me at the temple, how I perceived it, a weight, a heaviness within them. In their bodies I had been able to detect areas of hardness, actual physical density left by the experience of pain, the witnessing of horror. Was it possible that this was happening on a soul level as well? Had it happened to me? I had taught them the dance, together we had danced it, yet they suffered still. The endurance of pain. What indeed was the cause for the endurance of pain?

Was there a way, I wondered, to lighten the physical being—make it weightless, so it could journey? I thought about the new moon vigil with the leaders so long ago, the centrality of the fire, second only to the chanting. Heat, I wondered, can heat be used to lighten?

"How much they eat," Lilith said. "Isn't it astounding? Why those parent birds have not stopped working the whole time we've been sitting here."

"Amazing," I said.

She watched them, shaking her head in disbelief then she turned to me with a look of fright on her face. "Oh my, mother. Was I that much work?"

On the wall we wrote:

> Birds: weightless
> light
> free
> the gift of flight

hollow bones
lots of air
lightweight even though they eat a lot (Lilith)
heat = release (Aureillia)

The next day, during practice with Tolles, I was distracted.

"Aureillia, what bothers you?" he asked.

"The elders," I said. "They have denied my request, yet my yearning for knowledge grows stronger each day."

"Which knowledge?"

"Travel between the realms; that is the knowledge I seek."

He lifted his eyebrows, "You wish to accomplish this?"

"Yes," I said.

"On what grounds did the elders deny you?"

"I did not receive proper invitation," I answered.

"Invitation?" he repeated. "That is what they told you?"

"Yes, and I daresay I did not handle it well."

"I do not expect you would have. What will you do now?"

"I am going to attempt it on my own. I am going to create my own new moon ceremony. If I can recreate the ceremony, perhaps I can encourage my being to travel."

Though no other was present, Tolles looked around the room before patting the floor beside himself to indicate that I should come closer. I moved over and sat next to him. He leaned in toward me. "These are very secret teachings," he whispered.

"You know of these teachings?"

"This is but another way of working with the Serpent of Fire," he continued. "These are the teachings Barbara transmuted in her time as a priestess of the Snake. The Serpent of Fire," he said. "There is much you do not know."

"Barbara?" I said, my body sparking with excitement.

"Though I am not permitted to pass these teaching to you, I plan to do just that. Barbara would have wanted it. Not one can know that I am doing this, Aureillia."

I nodded my head. He took my hand into his.

"Have you accomplished this kind of travel?" I asked.

"No. I have never experienced it. My will was not strong enough. But you, your will is a mighty force, and you so wish to accomplish it that I am sure that you will." He whispered, "You are right about the fire, and the hill that you have chosen is good. There are doorways. That hill is one of them. These doorways become open at certain times. The time of the new moon is one of them. You went through one of them when you went to the healing temples of Malta."

"Malta?"

"Aureillia, there have been no temple priestesses on Malta for over one thousand years. The Tarxien is a crematorium now for people of that sort, those who burn their dead."

"Tolles, I was just there."

"Yes. Yes. You were, weren't you," he said, smiling.

"But how?"

"Shhh. These are secrets."

"Does Helena know?"

"Very few know. These are teachings of the high priests and priestesses, and the elders of course."

"Yes, the elders. Tolles," I said shaking my head for I could make no sense of what he was saying, "they tell us there are active temples there. They sent me. Why would they tell us we were going there when.. .why not tell us we were on a journey, why hide that sort of information?"

"I can say no more now." Tolles repeated. "You must be very discreet. I tell you, if they find out...," he looked around and whispered yet again, "You will come here. I will teach you all that I know. What you will do, the things that I shall tell you, they are not so different from that which you already know from your work with the Serpent of Fire. Start by imagining, imagining it so."

* * *

On the morning that Leida was to enter the labyrinth, Thela approached me, breaking her long term of silence.

"Aureillia," she said. "I had a dream. A horrible dream. A dream about Leida in the labyrinth. She was calling for me. She was in danger. I could do nothing about it. You must call it off. You must not make her go through with it."

"Your dream concerns me," I said. "But I cannot cancel now. I will, however, allow you to be present at all times during the ceremony and I will be sure to have all the rescue equipment available in case anything goes wrong."

Thela stood looking at me, confused about what to do.

"Hurry. Go and arrange yourself," I said, "We start soon."

I had become very thankful for Helena this past moon in preparing for this event. Thela's insistence of danger and anger toward me had almost caused me a few times to abandon the whole idea, but Helena insisted that I follow through.

"Your sister does not understand the trials of a priestess," she had said. "The Goddess sometimes asks the most difficult things of us. The trust of a priestess, she always challenges. It has all been most difficult for her, I know, but you must not let that stop you. You must trust yourself. You must trust in the process."

"But within me too there is a nagging fear."

"Then take every precaution and be most prepared, but do not stop."

I prepared all the emergency equipment, put it into proper place, and left Thela at the exit of the labyrinth. Then I went to get Leida from the pillar crypt where she had spent the night.

Carrying out this process reminded me of the two times I had been through the labyrinth. Those two times, the danger had never loomed this large in my mind. The first time because I was not even aware that I was entering the labyrinth, the second time I knew what I was about to do but I was not overly concerned because I'd had no trouble the first time. However, always, circulating throughout Knossos were stories of people getting into distress on their journey through the labyrinth. Though Helena assured me she had pulled many people out and would know exactly what to do, I had made her tell me step by step what would need to be done in the event of a problem. I was taking full responsibility for Leida's welfare and if something were to happen, I wanted to know how to respond.

The feelings of fear I felt for Leida forced me to recognize the enormous task it is to mentor someone—to send them through something you are aware may be dangerous is the greatest act of faith. It gave me cause to stop and nod my head in appreciation to all the women who had mentored me and their strength to not interfere but see me through even the most difficult of passages.

The pillar crypt was a dark room in the bottom of the Center dug deep into the earth. It was a small, square room with a pillar extending up through its center—a symbol of serpent energy rising from the center of the earth.

I entered, carrying a lamp, and found Leida sitting in front of the pillar. I handed her the cup of mint tea I had brought for her. She had been fasting for three days and drank it down thankfully.

"Are you sure you want to go through with this?" I asked her.

"More sure than ever," she said. I could tell she was ready. The transformation that had happened to Leida in her time of apprenticeship was remarkable. From a wavering, angry girl she had changed into a woman committing her entire being to the role of priestess. A confidence exuded from her now. A sense of purpose had smoothed out her sharp edges.

I helped her into the white robe of initiation. "Leida," I said, when she was fully dressed and ready, "I am so very proud of you, not only as your Aunt and your mentor but as one priestess to another."

"I am proud of myself Aunt Aureillia. Right now I would rather be no one else. There is nothing else I would rather be doing."

I presented her with one of the snake eagle feathers from my own set of wings. "After today," I said, "we will no longer be aunt and niece, mentor and apprentice, after today we will be sisters, sister birds."

I placed the blindfold upon her, around her long, thick, red hair and led her to the opening of the labyrinth. "May She lead you safely through darkness into the light," I said. I took a long look at her, knowing a different person would emerge from the labyrinth than the one I was sending in. I kissed her on the forehead, removed the blindfold and the white robe and watched her enter the darkness, naked and vulnerable. I stood by the opening through which I had sent her a long while until I was sure she was not coming back. Then I went and joined Helena and Thela.

Though there were many ways to enter the labyrinth, there was only one exit at the west end of the Center. Upon its low stone rooftop, around a wide circular opening, were spread a few benches and sculptures. The opening looked down into the shrine room at the very end of the labyrinth, which was the exit. In the daytime, the light from the sky above it filtered in through the opening. This light acted as a guide to the traveler within, directing her to the exit. From above, one could see the altar on which were the many ivory labryses placed by all the many who had recently passed through. One was not required to complete the labyrinth, only to experience it.

I wove the eagle feather into Leida's wings, which we had made together and which were hanging on a beam above the exit of the labyrinth. When Leida emerged from the labyrinth, I would place them upon her, making her full priestess of the Bird.

Helena and I invited Thela to join us in our prayer circle for Leida's journey, but she declined. She had returned to not speaking to me. A long time passed and Leida did not emerge. Helena had warned me to be prepared to give her plenty of time. It took some people as long as three days.

The light faded away, exposing the stars, still no sign of Leida. I lit the lamps above the circular exit to allow her to find the shrine even at night.

Helena brought food which we all shared, but Thela continued to remain silent. I had never been this separated from Thela. Her actions cut through me with a stinging bite. It should have been a happy time, a time in which her daughter, my apprentice, was about to become full priestess, but it was not to be that way.

We must have fallen asleep, for when I awoke it was to daylight and Thela shaking me vehemently.

"Do something," she yelled. "Do not wait any longer. I had a dream again, only this time she was not breathing."

I looked into the open space below me seeing the lamps burnt out but still no sign of Leida. Panic filled me.

"Get the rope," I said to Helena.

"Aureillia, it is too soon. Give her more time."

"No," Thela yelled. "You must go get her or I shall go myself."

"We must go, Helena," I said.

She gathered the rope. We went to the entrance where I had left Leida. Helena was to stand there with one end of the rope while I traveled inside with the other end. When I had found Leida, I would follow the rope back to Helena.

I entered the dark tunnel with a lamp and a large pile of rope around my shoulders. Thela followed behind me frantically pushing into me. "Thela you must not push. I shall drop the lamp and we shall never find her."

"I am furious with you about this, Aureillia," she said.

"Thela, please, not now," I said, moving forward, trying to imagine which turn Leida would have taken. There were so many different paths and ways one could try. We could be looking a long time. But I was guided that day. I felt it so entirely, almost a pulling at the rope, something leading me in the right direction.

Being in the labyrinth with a lamp and another person changed the feeling of it enormously. Actually seeing the tunnel stretching before me, turning abruptly or ending, changed a place of perilous pilgrimage into a hard, cold, tool. It gave me a strange feeling of foreboding. I was able to see the work, the brick laid upon brick, the sharp corners and deliberate misleadings. Still we had to crawl, into tunnels with smooth surfaces for floors, squeeze ourselves into tight spaces, but the difference was that all the time we could see what we were doing, we knew what was coming next.

Thela put aside her anger momentarily and accepted my help as well as offering me help in turn. This cooperation between us made me feel how desperately I missed her. I wondered how I would feel if it were Lilith trapped inside here for the second time.

"I'm sorry, Thela," I said, turning toward her. She stood, hands on hips, in the stone hallway where we had both once been alone and scared. Her body softened for a moment. "We must continue," she said.

We found her, in a narrow tunnel, lying on the floor barely breathing. There was blood on her head. "Oh, my darling," Thela said, throwing herself upon her. "Aureillia, you must go for help."

I looked around at the surrounding area. "What could have happened to make her fall this way? There is nothing here to trip over or bump your head on."

I looked around some more and realized I could detect light. I put my hands over our lamp to block it. Light was passing into the tunnel from the opening of the nearby shrine room.

"Thela, she was so close. Look," I said, pointing to the light. "So close. Only a few more steps and she would have been there."

"None of that matters now," Thela said. "We must simply get her out of here."

"Yes, but we shall pull her out that way. Come, let's carry her to the exit shrine that she may breathe some air."

Thela and I lifted Leida to the circular shrine room. "You wait here," I said. "I'll return to Helena and we shall pull her up this way."

I went to Helena, who went to find a Center healer. Together we lifted Leida up and carried her to a room inside the Center.

After we'd settled her in she roused. "Aunt Aureillia," she said, grabbing my hand, "Did I make it. Did I earn my wings?"

"Yes," I said. "You made it. You are full priestess now."

She smiled at what I had said and relaxed back into slumber.

"The wound on her head is only a bruise," the healer said. "It should be gone in a few days but she is greatly weakened and will need time to recover."

"Aureillia," Thela said, when the healer had left the room. "I wish to be alone with Leida. Come and see her when I am not here."

"Thela, you cannot still be angry?"

She said nothing only stared at me with a look that told me she still was.

"I wish to be alone with my daughter," she said, holding Leida's hand and pulling a chair up close to the bed.

"As you wish," I said, and took my leave.

Stories They Told Me

The Tiniest of Seeds

At the village, I began to teach other women to ride – those of us who had been planning our exit together. We worked in secret and gradually, so as not to be noticed. The young ones were the easiest – forming a relationship with the horse quickly. I led them on visits to our new home. We journeyed there two at a time to begin the task of setting up shelter, planting seeds to sow at our first harvest there. The plan was to leave in the next warm season. We became impatient. It seemed too long. We knew, however, there was still much to be done.

We learned to steal horses. Slowly, and one at a time. If they thought only some of the women left, especially the difficult women, they would not care. If they knew we had taken horses, they would come after us for sure. We took them at night so that it seemed they were escaping.

Before I left the village completely, there was one thing I still had need to learn-something I myself had never been schooled in – metallurgy. This was a sacred art which I had not been called to perform. I knew we would need weapons, that we would not be complete upon the horse until we were armed.

Long ago I had been schooled in the art of clay baking. My mother was a potter, as had been her mother before her, and she had passed that sacred teaching to me. It was the mothers before them who first discovered metals hidden within the clay; shiny flecks cooked to smoothness in their fiery pottery ovens. It was those mothers who refined the craft of softening hardened rock into thick liquid which could then be pounded into shape, into strong, sharp tools, sharper than anything we had known.

Before they came, before I came to know the horse, I spent my time working soft warm clay into rounded, open wombs in which to contain Her. I sat, satisfied, humming songs to myself as I painted swirling whirls and spirals – eggs electric with Her presence – onto rounded female forms. Before they came, I worked beside my mother, our fingers sinking into deep clay, in the workshop below the temple where I would go often to offer Her my best work.

When they came, the within me grew wild and restless. The workshop could no longer hold me. I began to create only horses, clay horses running, sleeping, standing-painted horses on vessels – women riding horses, until I stopped going to the workshop altogether.

"Why do you not come and do the work you were chosen for, the work the village needs you to perform," my mother said to me one day upon meeting me on the path to the stable.

"I have a different job now, Mother," I said, avoiding her eyes, for I knew that I had abandoned her. "I am busy with other things."

"It is an insult to Her to turn your back on the gift She has given to you. An insult to me," she said, lowering her tone.

"Mother," I said, whispering at the utterance of words such as these, "I no longer find Her in the work with the clay. Not as I once did. I now find Her in the wind that rushes through my hair as I ride the wildest of horses, in the heat between my legs as we gallop, by the river's gentle bend and the tall tree encircled with stones. I must go to the place where She leads me, Mother, I must follow Her call."

She eyed me suspiciously. "I know," she said, "that you are planning to leave."

"You must know that it is no longer safe here. Please, Mother, you must come with us."

Her lips were pursed but there was water staining her eyes, which looked toward the village. "I wish to see this tree," she said, "this place by the river's bend."

I took her hands into mine. "First," I said, "I must teach you to ride."

* * *

I approached the village smith at his workshop. I asked him to teach me his craft.

"Only men may learn it," he said.

"It is women who discovered it," I said.

"Do you think I do not know that?" He said, pounding hot metal thin with a hammer and shaking his head. It was enormously hot inside this smelting hut. He was sweating. Dirt clung to his bare chest. He put down his hammer, took a piece of cloth from the bench and wiped his face. "I only wish to protect myself from danger," he said, throwing the cloth back down onto the bench. "They will not tolerate me teaching you."

"Then don't tell them."

He snicked a laugh and smiled at me. The smile contained tenderness. "Why is it that you wish to learn?"

"I and some others, we are leaving. This is a skill we shall need, yet none of us possess."

"Where are you going?"

"I cannot say."

He looked down at his work, then out the window. "Leaving," he said, "leaving is a good idea."

"Leaving is the only option," I said.

He looked at me. Sadness covered his face. I began to perspire. He returned his gaze to the window. "Not here," he said. "You must not be here."

"Then where?"

"I know a place," he said, approaching me, the metals he worked, mixed with the juices of his body, gave him a strange metallic smell. "There is a cave," he whispered, "a cave behind yonder hill. It is a small cave with a hole in the side of one of the walls."

"I know the one."

"There. Meet me there." I looked into his eyes. The fire reflected within them. "Tomorrow."

"I must go now," I said, backing away. "It is too hot in here."

He walked me to the door and stood in it, filling it with himself, as he watched me walk away.

* * *

"The first thing you must learn," he said to me the next day when I met him at the cave, "is how to remove the metals from the places in which they are found." He had cleaned himself. His hair was tied back into a long mane of deep browns and auburns. In the morning light, I noticed specks of green in the browns of his eyes. The heat, the fire was still there upon him, pulsing in waves from his body; revealing itself in the deep creases that lined his dark face. He was dressed in clean trousers and a soft, wool blouse. He carried with him a large, leather bag. "We shall walk together to the places where She gives forth."

"We need not walk," I said, "I ride."

"I have seen you ride," he said. "I, however, do not ride."

"You shall ride behind me."

I helped him onto the back of my horse. He held me tight around the waist. I turned to face him. He hid not his fear. "It is all right," I said. "She is a good horse."

I put my hand upon his that held me around my center. I rode slowly. His hand, warm within mine began to relax, my center melting to molten liquid beneath the heat.

We arrived at the place between two hills where She offers herself in rich streams of minerals. He set his bag down and extracted a long pick. I watched as he inserted his tool into Her, as She gave Herself to him in rich dark copper. In other places, he showed me how to determine which rocks contained Her, to chip away at the hard wall of stone, forming workable clumps which we would smelt, freeing the copper hidden within them.

"Now you," he said, handing me his tools, heavy and foreign. What he had made look easy, for me was extremely difficult. I struggled, became frustrated.

"It is difficult at first," he said, "but you shall become accustomed to it. Your hands are strong. They match your will. That is all you really need."

He took me to a stream bed. He taught me how to pan and dredge for tin. "The tin is hard to come by," he said, stooping and bringing up a pile of black dirt into a clay bowl which had small holes in the bottom of it to allow the water to spill back through it. He sifted through the remaining dirt, extracting large clumps of hardened black rock and showing them to me. "Sometimes," he said, "I use arsenic to harden the bronze. I am not going to show you that way. I want you to use tin to harden your bronze."

Back at the cave, he taught me how to build my own smelting oven deep into the earth. "The hole, "he said, making a small opening in the back of the bottom of the oven, "there must be an opening. Through the opening will be released the slag. The copper will be left within."

He stacked within the small oven layers of charcoal and the pieces of ore we had mined. Then he lit the fire and covered the oven. With his foot pushing on a small leather pump inserted into the side of the oven, he fanned and fanned the flames, stoking up the fire until it became so hot, he removed his shirt and the stone released the copper in a gush of steaming hot liquid.

This, he then took and reheated, purifying it more. Some he took in a warm, semihardened state and hammered into shape. Others he cast, pouring a steaming, white, liquid mixture of copper and tin together to form bronze.

"I used to work only with copper," he said, "but these new people, they have a taste for bronze."

I watched him moving quickly from fire to floor with a heated heap of copper to pound with his hammer. I watched his face, serious and focused, his lips, pouting as he worked. I watched his hand, skilled and quick with the hot metal, his arms quivering from the stress of the work. I enjoyed this, this watching him work. There was something profoundly comforting in observing this act of creation.

In the extreme heat, combined with the intense effort it was taking me to learn this skill – something I was not naturally inclined toward – I began to lose my will.

He could have let me. He could have let me sit there watching him, allowed me to melt into another piece of workable material for him to form into any shape he wished. He could have let it happen. I was not aware until it was too late. But, he didn't. He saw what was happening. He would not allow it.

He began to force me to work. "It is only certain people," he said, "who can tolerate such heat without melting. You must stand tall, strong to the heat, Sadie. You must not allow it to reduce you."

He pushed me, every time I was exposed to the heat, presenting me with chore after chore. "You must learn this," he said; leading me out of the cave when I was overwhelmed, to take in a breath of coolness, to harden me back into shape. "You cannot go out into that world without this skill."

He ceased to work, began only to watch me pound clumsily against softened metal, pour liquid rock into a cast I had made, my arms moving involuntarily in staggered, jerking movements under the weight.

"It is the heat," he said, "the heat which transforms, fire which alters. Only with fire may we change things." He took a cloth from the belt around his waist and wiped my damp face with it. "You possess this element within you," he said. "It is good. You will need it. You must be careful, however, because you are made of fire, so you are especially vulnerable to it."

I looked at him, he who had pulled me out of the flames, yet left me intact. "Why do you do this for me?"

"I do not do it for you. I do it for us, our people, our village. Do you think I like these barbarians?"

"What will you do?"

"I have not yet decided."

* * *

My skills improved. Alone, I mined for minerals, built the fire, transformed stone into liquid heat, pounded soft metal into a hardened, sharp-edged sword.

"You no longer need me," he said to me one day and smiled. It was a crooked smile, its right side higher, a smile I had come to look forward to.

"How can I ever thank you?" I asked, touching the sharp edge of

the blade I had only just formed.

He came and stood himself before me so that his chest touched the cloth of my dress. "Take me with you," he said into my face, in a voice so innocent, so full of need and longing that it took my breath away.

"I cannot," I said, there was a galloping in my chest. "It has been agreed. Only women. I thought you understood that."

"I thought by now you would see that I am not one of them."

"Of course, I know that," I said, touching his chest with my hands. "I am so grateful to you. There is so much that you have done for us, more than I ever could have expected. I have also grown very fond of you." I sighed, collapsing a little. Then I remembered the burning in the women's eyes when they talked about the men. These strange and different men, at whose hands so many of them had already suffered, still bearing the bruises they had acquired when they were forced to share themselves against their will. How could I explain to him the torment this was having on us as women? The distrust that now permeated every encounter with men?

"I cannot allow it," I said, looking at him. "In spite of my feelings for you."

"You cannot leave me here, Sadie," he said. He held my face within his hands. I allowed him to kiss me. His warm mouth encompassed mine; a furnace deep with leaping flames. I felt myself surrendering within, the 'yes' beginning to form within me. I felt the opening that wanted to happen, to let him in, to merge together into something other, something new. But the 'no.' I needed the 'no.' The 'no' was what sparked the fire, what fanned the flames. "I cannot," I said, breaking away from him, from his strong, confident embrace.

"Sadie," he said, "even if you do not allow me to join you, let us at least have this."

"I cannot," I said, backing away from him. "Don't you see," I repeated. "I cannot."

"No, I don't see," he said.

"I cannot feel this way about you. This opening, this spreading of my being that wants to happen. I cannot allow it. It will ruin everything."

"Nothing has to change," he said.

"But everything will," I said, pounding my fists against my chest. "Inside, inside. I need, more than anything, this cool, hard shell I have grown."

Chapter 18

Aureillia

Lilith and I began to create our own new moon ceremony on the peak of the hill facing Libya. Like the elders, for the period of no moon and the three consecutive days until She appears again in the night sky as a gentle sliver, we slept during the days and kept vigil at night. We worked very hard together, gathering wood enough for a fire to burn the whole night through and preparing plenty of food.

I could ask no one for help. I knew that no one must know. Even Tolles could not be with me here. If the elders were to discover what it was I was doing, they would be furious. I was stunned still by the revelation about the healing temples of Malta. A journey, going on a journey together, to another time? I was desperate to know how they had accomplished it. Tolles had assured me I must learn first to journey alone. "You are learning it all in the appropriate order," he had said, "just as Barbara taught it. First the Serpent of Fire, then to journey alone, then the other: a group journey."

Lilith told no one. She was a supreme secret keeper. Without any instruction or explanation as to why, she instinctively understood the necessity of silence.

And she helped. She assisted me with her entire being in this task. I was not sure if it was her longing for Danelle or her intense loyalty to me, but she was motivated to help.

"What next?" she would say, hiking swiftly ahead of me, her firm legs bending as she stooped to gather sticks.

"More sticks," I would say.

"More?"

"More and more and more. We must keep the fire burning the whole time that the sun is away from us."

"The whole time?"

"The whole time."

"Mother, that is a lot of sticks."

Increasingly, I was enjoying her company, the person she was becoming. Our relationship was now much less about me taking care of her needs and more about guiding her in becoming herself.

I had made the decision not to use the assistance of the poppy. There were already enough toxins in my body. Tolles and I had decided that though it would take longer and be more challenging, it was essential that I remain aware of what it was I was doing that I may do it again.

"Conscious journeying is the secret," Tolles had said, "We travel often. Indeed you have journeyed far. The challenge is to take our awareness with us."

The first few times, nothing happened. There was the darkness of a moonless night, the crackling of the red-yellow fire. There was Lilith's face outlined by her hair glowing against the background of the fire. There was the comfort of each other, a relationship that never ends, our shared desire for Danelle. There were all these warm and wonderful things. And there was me, becoming comfortable with the darkness. There were animal sounds, an owl hooting. We saw deer, fox, and rabbits. But there was no journey or even the indication that there was anywhere to go. After hours of silent time, I would lie down next to Lilith who had fallen asleep beside me. I would pull her warm, slumbering body into mine and surrender to the luxury of sleep.

When I returned to Tolles and told him of my unsuccessful attempts, he took my hands into his, which shook lightly as with illness. "Aureillia, if you continue to listen, the darkness will eventually speak to you. Now, as with anything, it is a matter of practice and patience. You are no stranger to these qualities. I have the greatest confidence that if you persist, you will succeed. You must go forward without my help, however, for I have decided that I must go find Danelle. I must bring my son back."

"Tolles," I said, holding his hands firmly within mine against the shaking, "Are you sure it is wise to set out on such a journey in your present condition?"

"What could be more unwise than not being present to the very person who means the most to you in your life?"

"You should not be so hard on yourself."

"Alas, Aureillia, I am ashamed to be esteemed by my colleagues as a high priest yet not be able to see the person of my own son standing right before me. I must go find him. I must earn the honor of being father to such a man."

Danelle

For a while, it was the most wonderful thing I had ever done, entering the other-world, seeing things only before imagined, until I fell into the realm of horrors and I could not get myself out. I could not find beauty, though I searched for it everywhere. I longed to return to my world of color and fascination but I could not find the way back.

"I do not wish to continue," I said to Rodin when he came for me.

"You must," he said, tugging at my elbow brusquely. "You cannot stop now. You must continue. This is where your work lies. Though you wish to deny it, this horror lies within you. It is a part of you."

I follow after him begrudgingly. Again the path leads me to the same place.

There is an enormous circular stone court. There are stairs and benches to sit upon, built into the edges of this stone circle ascending gradually in four tiers. There is a cloth covering, held up by ropes, sheltering the court from the sun. People sit upon the benches within the stone court and look down into the center.

Beneath the stone circle, in a dug-out, cavelike space, I sit. I am a dark-haired man, wider, thick with muscle. My arms are tied tight at my elbows behind my back and then forced up high onto a bar above my shoulders. There are other men around me forced into a similar position.

I am frightened. Within me is a small shaking thing. The men around me are frightened as well. They are not showing their fear as I am, but I can smell it. I can smell their fear. The pain in my shoulders is overwhelming. I begin to moan.

"Keep quiet," the man to my right says. "If you show your suffering, they will make it harder on you."

"Why?"

"Show no emotion," he warns, clenching his teeth and grimacing. "Don't do it, I tell you. That is what got us here in the first place."

There is another smell. A damp, ripe smell. "What is that smell?" I ask.

"The animals," he says.

"Animals?"

My awareness alternates between being within this person, this different body which is also me, and that of an outside observer of events. Once, I am within this other me, looking out, seeing things from within him, through his eyes, then suddenly it changes and I become a movable awareness. As now, I am witnessing rows of cages made out of some form of dark metal and lined up underneath this circular court, within which are animals. Boar, deer, lions, and—to my astonishment—a tiger.

Several men come in and release our arms from the upper hold, wrists remaining fastened together. My shoulders ache at first upon release, then begin to ease and relax a little. But there is no time to enjoy this freeing, for we are prodded up thick stone steps, pushed and shoved and, if we're not moving fast enough, sometimes whipped, as we make our way up to the floor of the circular court. When we arrive to the archway that leads into the court, our wrists are released and we are each handed a long spear.

As we enter, the crowd begins to cheer and make raucous noise. The court is filled with trees and greenery as though to imitate a forest. Many men work together to push a large, heavy stone onto a wooden plank, which lowers once the weight of the stone is upon it. Simultaneously, a large iron cage rises into the court. The cage is opened and the deer within it set free within the court. They continue to lift more cages up until there are many animals loose within the court. One can tell from the hollows in their bellies that these animals are starving. I stand considering the other men, myself one of them—holding a weapon in a circular court with hungry animals. I look up at the crowd watching us. The men who set the animals free flee the court quickly. I am reminded of the Minoan bull leaping. This can only be some sort of sport.

Then the festivities begin. Some of the animals charge the men. Some of the men charge the animals, loosing their spears into a running deer who stumbles, falling under the assault. A boar corners one of the men and begins to tear his flesh apart. He releases screams of agony. To this, the crowd cheers. What kind of people are these? I make a move to go and assist him. A guard interrupts my intention and points me instead into the direction of the tiger who is approaching me with deliberate confidence, her shoulders rising and falling with graceful, defined movements. Her proud white chest extends before her. She is the most elegant creature I have ever encountered. Just as I had imagined her. What grand paws she has! They are supreme. Everything about her is ferociously large. Her tail swings down, curving up at the end. Strong black stripes traverse her orange coat. Her green, knowing eyes meet mine.

"You are most elegant indeed," I say, bowing in sacred gesture toward her. She stops and sits before me. I put my weapon down and extend my hand toward her. She smells it, sniffing at it for a long time before returning her gaze to me. I reach my hand out to touch her, run my hand down her large head over her sleek fur. She allows me to caress her. My fingers descend deeper into the thickness that is her coat. It is irrepressibly warm and enticing. The crowd is a wild cheer. We turn and face them, neither quite sure of what is happening.

Aureillia

On the third try, the darkness changed. It seemed to separate from the stars that had twinkled within it. It seemed to turn into a something, a presence, full of being rather than empty space. The space between me and the stars that before had seemed so removed by emptiness now seemed full, almost puffy with life. Within this puffiness of life there was movement, and, within this movement, I began to perceive shapes—shapes of things other than what I knew to be present. At first there were so many shapes, it was confusing, shadows of shapes that appeared to be passing in and around, between and through one another. I became fearful. The fear made them disappear, sent the stars back to their distant location, and returned me to the fire, to being Aureillia sitting by Lilith. I understood that I had broken through to something. I also understood that fear had ended it.

In the days that followed, I made myself think about what I had seen over and over so that I would not be afraid the next time. I made myself feel again the darkness, the seeming empty space that is thick with presence, the warm blanket of movement. Clearly fear added weight to the soul.

On the morning that Tolles was to depart, Lilith and I went to the marina to bid him farewell. He was surrounded by a crowd of well-wishers, yet he removed himself and approached us.

"Return in good health," I said, embracing him. In his being I detected a hardiness, a determination. The intent to go and find Danelle, that alone, seemed to have already made a difference.

"Aureillia," he said, "Sometimes mere spaces are more than what they seem. Barbara always said we must learn to walk into the place between the trees. Look into the space between the trees, Aureillia. Try to see the unseen."

I knew what he meant. At the vigil, a pair of trees kept attracting my attention. There seemed to be something between them. At the next new moon, when the space around me began to bubble with thickness, I stood and walked to those two trees. As I walked between them, the space hollowed out into an opening. I gasped as I entered it, a hidden pocket of otherness which stretched as I walked through it; bending into forward depth. This space was like none that I had ever before experienced. The air had a qualitatively different feel to it. There was a vortex-like spinning my being responded to, vibrating more quickly its rhythmic sustaining.

It was clear that I was only in the opening, that I needed to go further within. I hesitated and asked for assistance. That is when they appeared: Rory and Zula. Their shapes flickered in and out as a lamp light reacting to the presence of wind. I knew this flickering was caused by me; my uncertainty in this space, my newness to this world was making what I was seeing uncertain. It did not mean that which I was seeing was uncertain. So comforting was the presence of Rory and Zula, however, that I relaxed immediately into the trust I had always felt for them. They were not only my Grandmother and her friend but my teachers. It was they who taught me the dance of release. They were motioning for me to come farther within. As I walked toward them the space around me opened wider, and what seemed to be only a pocket spilled open into an entirely different realm. It was as though I had been standing on some sort of threshold. Still, within this newfound realm were areas of complete darkness and shadow. I understood these to be my own.

"Again you come to me when I most need you," I said. "I am ever so grateful."

"We have come to assist you on your journeys," Zula said. She reached her hand out toward mine. I reached my hand toward hers, but there was a pulling from behind and I found myself sitting again by the fire. I looked to the space between the trees, the opening was gone.

Lilith was asleep by the fire, lying on her mat before it. I studied her face, always so peaceful as she slept, her soft little body seeming always younger, more tender in slumber, revealing her for the child that she was. I pulled her blanket up over her and caressed her soft, black curls.

The sun was beginning to return, spreading pinks and orange across the sky. Light came, slowly brightening the land. I sat and breathed in the particular smell of the sun's light as it first touches the moist earth in the morning, dusty red and freshly hot.

Danelle

The work and design of this court are exceptional indeed. There are tall columns with intricate designs carved into the tops of them. Stone sculptures of men whose forms are graceful and defined. More animals are brought here—so many—only to be killed, slaughtered.

The tiger tells me how they came into her land and stole her young when they were still too young to be alone. How they captured her and brought her here. She tells me they are wicked people who love the smell of blood. She tells me she wants to die. She asks me to kill her.

There are those that are called gladiators who seem to have more importance. I have heard that they fight one another, that the people come to see these fights, that the fight is unto death. They have given me a shield, a helmet and a sword. They have made a gladiator out of me.

Again and again we are brought into the court together. Again and again we walk toward each other in the same way. I bow toward her. She sits before me. She allows me to caress her.

But the tiger is so very hungry. They have decided to feed me and starve her. "You will need to kill me or I will have no choice but to take your life," she says. "Though I wish not to, I cannot fight the need to feed myself as you can. They know this. Because of this they have chosen not to feed me."

I understood it then. It was this which they wanted, which they waited for, the benches becoming fuller and fuller each day until it seemed no more could fit upon them. They wanted not only the death of one of us, they wished to watch one of us die, watch one of us kill the other. They know the time is drawing near.

Aureillia

I began to determine that there was a path I must take—a path that they were on—it seemed to be a straight line. If I followed this line, the black pocket slowly opened itself to me as though creating itself as I walked along it. Scenes began to appear, layers of scenes, one over another. If I would focus on one, it would become clearer. Still, I could only go so far before I felt it, this behind me tugging. Something there was that would not release me. The next time I approached them

Rory said, "The girl. It is she whom you do not allow yourself to leave. I shall stay with her. I will sit by the fire with her while you travel with Zula. You know she will be safe with me."

A surprising amount of relief filled me when Rory said this. She came toward me and touched me, turning herself into the likeness of me. Then she sat down next to Lilith. Lilith of course was unaware of Rory's presence. She was watching me, sitting by the fire. I had not considered that my concern about Lilith might be keeping me from venturing deeper into the other realms. Only now did I see this to be true. Attachment, I thought, attachment also adds weight to the soul.

I turned back toward Zula. She held her arm out toward me. I locked my arm within it so that our elbows interlocked. I followed her lead to a beautiful blue green coastline. It was daytime. As the waves came toward us, we leaned our bodies forward, our legs lifted, and we began to fly.

Danelle

Of course I give myself to the tiger. I ask her to be gentle as I lie down on the hard, hot earth of the floor of this court, offering myself to her as food.

Take this body I offer you, I say, *and eat of it. Eat that I may become part of you.*

I was ready for the pain. I was ready for the fear, for the sharp and cutting teeth, the grotesque cheering of the crowd. But what I was not prepared for, what I could not get over was the sorrow—the regret in the tiger as she killed me. "Forgive me," she had said, before gently flipping me over and snapping the back of my neck with her large, engulfing jaw.

I had not said that to Aureillia. I had wanted her dead.

The Tiniest of Seeds

Finally the warm season came. We began to leave, one by one, early in the morning, before the sun returned, each carrying as many supplies as we could upon our backs. I was the last to leave. After all had gone safely, after all were there, I too took my leave. As the morning light began to filter in and mix with the darkness, creating shadows where there were not normally shadows, bringing noise into the stillness, I walked away from our village and, except for one long, lingering gaze toward the smith house, I never looked back.

All through the warm season we worked, using every bit of light to make ourselves suitable shelters and clothing enough to pass the coming winter. We tended our crops with an almost over-attentive eye. Hoeing, weeding, watering. We built winter shelter for our horses. We traveled deep into the forest together, exploring the area, staking out escape routes and hiding places to use when the protective leaves left us.

At harvest, we rejoiced in our first crop of grain by gathering together to roll it and form into sacred bread. We celebrated in the main room, where there were two large ovens. The room became hot with all of us in it and two ovens burning with the heat that transforms grain into bread.

I looked around the room, hot with power, with excitement over what we had accomplished, the women we were becoming – and I was filled with a longing tall and long-reaching, for only then did I realize that She is not only in the wheat we pound into grain, in the grain we mix into dough, She is in the process – in the fiery act that turns goopy dough into warm, velvet bread. She is transformation. The One Who Changes Things.

I exited the shrine, released puffs of hot slag from within myself into the cool night air. I looked up at the stars, burning fires transforming them even as I looked at them, at the cool dampness of rotting earth around me and I fell to my knees to ask forgiveness for all I had said 'no' to.

* * *

The first winter was long and hard, but we survived. Never had we been so happy to see the snows recede, the birds begin to return. Outside, during the day, I began to notice it, a small pillar of billowing smoke at the place beyond the hollow in the river. I knew of no settlement there. The entire village was agitated over this. As soon as the mud dried, I went to explore.

There, inside a small hut he had built for himself, did I find him alone, smelting.

"What is it that you are doing?" I asked. The heat within was, once again, shocking, but this time I welcomed it. I welcomed him, his presence. I think I may have even smiled when I said, "They shall find us for sure, simply by following your smokestack."

"They know where you are," he said, calmly pouring liquid metal into the mold of a long sword. "They do not care," he said, when he had finished pouring it. He stood and faced me. "They have the village. Many of our people have left, most retreating to caves in high hills. All is calm there now. The ones who remain are there because that is the choice they made."

"Do they know about the horses?"

"I suspect so."

"What about you? How is it that you came to leave?"

"They cast me out," he said, looking at the door through which I had come. "I am ill."

"Ill?" I said, panic overtaking me.

"Something in the work," he said, "something in the metals has made me ill. They say I have smith's disease."

"Smith's disease?" I repeated. I had not heard of such a thing. "You require healing," I offered. "There is a healer in the new village."

"It is too late."

"Too late," I said. "How do you know? You do not appear ill."

"I am greatly weakened. Some days...," he stopped his words and walked over to me. "I am glad you came, Sadie," he said.

I could not look at him. I looked down upon the sword he had only just poured. "It is magnificent," I said.

"Do you like it? It is for you," he whispered into my ear.

"For me?"I said, surprised.

He put his arms around me. "You will soon need it," he said. "There are more coming, ones who make these look meek." His hand moved up my back, touching gently the base of my neck. My body shook within his embrace. I leaned into his shoulder. "I am sorry," I whispered. "I should have let you come when you asked. I should never have said 'no' to you."

"Oh, no," he said, lifting my face up to look at him. "Only women. I understand. You had a commitment to the others. I knew. It was unfair of me to ask. Why, if I were a woman...."

I put my hand up to his mouth to silence him. "No," I said, "it was unfair. I was unfair to your kindness. Now, I must suffer losing you."

"I am not yet gone," he said.

Chapter 19

Aureillia

Leida was regaining her strength slowly. She remained, for the time, with the Center healers. I went to see her there often. The bruise on her head was healing, and she had been taking daily walks to strengthen herself.

"Leida," I asked her finally one day. "What happened in there? In the labyrinth? You were so close to making it through. What caused you to fall in such a way?"

"Yes," she responded, sitting down upon the bed, "something did happen."

I sat beside her on the many-colored blanket.

"The journey was going well. Much better than the first time. Naturally, I was terribly lost for a time but then, all at once, I began to feel led.

"Something, someone was in there with me. I perceived Her presence and I trusted Her completely until," she stopped and sighed, "until She showed Herself to me. I think I must have passed out from the sight of Her. I daresay I found Her rather frightening."

"Who was it?"

"A woman. A woman with the face and feet of a bird. A woman with wings."

"Lilith," I whispered in surprise.

"Lilith?" she responded. "Are you speaking of your daughter?"

"No. Lilith of the Cave. The one after whom I named my daughter. Lilith was in the labyrinth with you? Yes, it makes perfect sense."

"How is it that you know of Her?"

"It is She who nurtured me at the cove in the time of my retreat. It is She who helped me reenter the world of the living. It is because of Her that I wished to become a priestess of the Bird."

"She was there with me, Aureillia. I recall now how She turned Herself toward me in an opening inside the labyrinth. She revealed herself to me, spreading Her wide, expansive wings. I remember thinking she was magnificent. Then, the next thing that happened was that I awoke, inside the Center with this bruise on my head."

"She comes to all who have discovered the murder of the Goddess," I continued. "She comes to help transform this knowing. She presents them with human work. Only human work can transform this pain. Lilith is the Bird Goddess. She is an essential teaching. And yes, her form is, at first, disquieting."

Leida's almond eyes opened wide as she thought about whom she had seen—Lilith of the Cave, a power larger than any other. Until now, Danelle was the only other I was aware of who had witnessed Her. Now Leida too had an experience with Her.

"I knew, when she appeared, that I was in the presence of something awesome. If I had been prepared to see Her, had I known who she was, had I a name to give Her, I may not have felt so afraid."

"In this way it was a true initiation," I mused. "She must have come to welcome you as one of Her priestesses."

"Do you suppose," Leida asked, "that this is what is happening to our companions in the temple of the Bird, the ones we are teaching the dance of release, that they have discovered the murder of the Goddess and they need help transforming this knowing? Is our task to assist them in finding human work around this pain?"

Gather Her many pieces
Make her whole

I chanted, remembering the song Lilith had sung to me at the cove.

"I had not understood that the experience of our companions would so closely resemble my own but now, I see that it does. Perhaps this is the way to approach our work."

Leida sat, swinging her legs beneath her, then she turned toward me, "Tell me about your time at the cove, Aureillia."

* * *

Zula knew where Danelle was and she knew how to find him. She told me she would teach me. I knew from the start that her motivations were for reasons other than only to help me. There was something she wanted. I could sense it, but it did not bother me. I was thankful to be benefiting from her needs.

Tall, with a face that had strong, angular features and hair that was thick and hung in long curls from the clasp at the back of her head, eyes that were deep brown and penetrating, she swung her long elegant brown arms in front of her as she spoke. Her power was palpable.

My Grandmother had met Zula in her time as a seeker in foreign lands during one of her trips to the land to the south. Their connection had been immediate and lasting.

"A message received in Malta is not to be taken lightly," she said. "It is wise to know there are other ways to approach certain matters. It is true that concerns of this kind require work in many realms. This is about much more than that which you have been made to witness."

"Zula, do you know about the healing temples of Malta, about the elders telling us we are going to the temples there when they are no longer truly there?"

"I am aware that they do this, yes."

"Why would they tell us they exist now when they don't?"

"To get you to participate without knowing you are participating. Your beliefs are what you will experience."

"But why don't they tell us we are going on a journey?"

"Power. There is great power in keeping secrets. Aureillia, the art I am about to teach you, women have always known. Since the beginning of time, women have found entryways to the otherworld and journeyed into the beyond. I am doing this so that you may pass this teaching to the priestesses you initiate into your temple. This is an essential craft for women, especially women helping others to process the difficult. Difficulty is a sign that work is needed on many levels. Through journeying, one may obtain a deeper knowing. A deeper knowing helps bring about much-needed changes."

"Are you telling me that this, too, is a teaching of the birds?"

"Most certainly. Birds are those creatures we see passing between the realms everyday. We see them disappearing into the blueness often. By following them, we have learned many secrets. I too was once a priestess of the Bird. You are not creating, Aureillia. You are remembering—remembering things as old as the moon."

Hearing Zula say this made me feel ever so much better. It removed my feelings of isolation and connected me once again to the women before me and the women yet to come. This made all the difference, this connection.

"The first step," Zula continued, "is to imagine. Imagine yourself a bird, the mighty eagle—taking to flight."

There began to be left every morning offerings of sword tips, axes, daggers, bits, and harness links. There began to be left every day offerings from him. first, he left one of each by the tree of the Goddess, then piles and bucketfuls by the entrance to the village.

"Promise me you will not smelt," he said. We were at the place in the tall hills where She gives forth, collecting copper. We had stopped working and were sitting on the crest of the hill, looking down at the river below. "Do not poison yourself in the way I have poisoned myself. I will make you more, all that you will need before I go."

"It is the arsenic," I said. "The healer told me. The arsenic you are using to harden the bronze. It is this which makes you ill."

At first there was no movement, just a still silence that echoed everywhere, sending pangs of sharp ache through me. Then he shook his head, slammed his fist against the ground. "I should have known," he said. "I suspected. I coughed every time that I warmed it. But they needed more and the tin is so hard to find. Does she know," he asked, looking at me, hope in his face, "is there anything?"

I shook my head. "You were right," I said, "There is no recovery."

His eyes filled with pain. He stood and twirled slightly, looked down at me in dazed confusion. I stood to help him. "No," he said, shaking my hand off his. He fled, running down the steep incline furiously, dangerously fast. I stumbled behind him but could not keep up. When I reached the bottom, I saw him, slamming his pickaxe against the wall of hidden copper in furious repetition. I did not approach him, stayed out of sight, allowing him privacy, until he collapsed down on to the ground and leaned his back against the wall of stone in exhaustion. Then it was that I came to sit next to him.

"I had a mother," he said, his breath hard and heavy, "they killed her. I had a daughter," he continued, squinting his eyes to the bright sun, "they raped her. There was a woman," he said, looking

at me, "who made me feel things I had never before felt..."

He touched his fingers gently to my cheek which was flushed red with heat. He leaned forward slightly over himself. "I suppose," he said, looking away from me, "I kept using the arsenic, though I suspected. I suppose," he struggled. "I suppose I didn't care."

* * *

At the stream I pan for tin. I hold my colander down in the shallow section where she often leaves deposits, and I bring up smooth sand, pebbles. The water falls back upon itself in soft music. I sit back against the mossy bank behind me, my fingers panning through the gravel.

"That which kills me shall kill you as well," he had said to me. "for it is not really the arsenic which makes me ill but the hate. The hate festering in my very being for these people. Once, I knew not what hate was," he said, laughing an eerie laugh.

"Now, I have come to welcome it. Where before I drew my power from other things within me, now hate is all I have."

"Hate?" I said. "Have you hate for me?"

"No, I have not hate for you, but it is our hate, our common hate, which binds us together."

A wave of hurt passed over me as he said this. He saw it but he did not alter what he had said. Instead, he took my hand into his. "Don't worry," he said, "they're not so far apart, hate and love."

The water runs clean and constant in front of me. I listen as She winds her winding way down the hill, passing over rocks and steep embankments. She continues. In spite of what She passes through, She flows.

Aureillia

The first time I found him, I was so pleased, I ran toward him. He disappeared instantly. I looked all over for him. It was only then, in searching for him, that I began to notice where I was. This was a place like no other, a place of unimaginable beauty.

"I never imagined Libya to look like this," I said.

"Foolish woman," Zula said. "We are not in Libya."

"Where are we?"

"We are in Danelle's journey."

"In Danelle's journey? How is that possible?"

"It is the only way. He will not allow you on the conscious level now. There is too much in his way. It is lucky that he too is learning to journey between the realms."

"He too?" I said. "That seems more than lucky."

She smiled a sly smile.

"Of course this is his journey," I said, looking around myself. This place spoke his name. It was the natural world enlarged. Flowers taller than I whose long, fuzzy stalks I walked through, as a forest of trees. The colors were glowing in bright distinctiveness from one another. But what impressed me most about this different world was the abundance of sound. The sounds of the small things around us. The sounds that are inaudible to us normally, I could hear. I could hear the sounds the flowers were making—a high-pitched humming. The plants were whispering, the grass was breathing. The trees large above us croaked and whistled. I listened to each sound separately, and then all of them together. Everything on this earth is gloriously alive. My being joined in pulsing strong aliveness, gaining more strength from union with them. At that moment I was sure, without a doubt, that there are Serpents of Fire in each and every tree, flower, and blade of grass—and that our serpents communicate. Whether or not we notice, in a voice inaudible, in a language unknown, they speak and speak and speak.

Stories They Told Me

"Put it on for me. Let me see," he said. He was sitting on his bed. He had been sweating and shaking with fever. It was happening like this now. I wrapped him within his blankets, fixed him a cup of hot tea. He sat smiling and sipping at it.

I put it on, the armor he had made me, the shield, the helmet. He had decorated it with an intricate design of small sword tips. He had made it out of gold. "It is exquisite" I said, gently stroking the design with my fingertips.

He smiled, but then his face filled with concern. "It is very dangerous," he said, "to become one of them."

"I am not one of them. I shall never be one of them," I said, but I crumpled down onto the bed beside him. He was right. I knew it. Already we felt it, the need to move again. Our village was no longer safe.

"Remember when," he said, looking beyond me, "remember when we were young. The smell of Mother, the taste of field berries in the warm season? Remember not knowing all this?" He asked.

I looked at him, at his face. The memory had covered it with the innocence of a boy.

I removed my armor, my helmet. I set my weapon aside. "I remember,"I said, taking him into my arms, "men who walked proud. women who felt safe. I remember," I said. "I remember."

I buried him in the earth beside the smelting hut. I buried him, with the tall sword he had made me, horses galloping across it, women riders astride. I removed all the arsenic and smelted without it, the way he had taught me. All that I made I took to the earth where he lay buried to show him how well I had learned.

On good days I would hear him whisper again what he had said to me right before he had left. He had said to me, "She is so large; She can hold within Her the entire earth. She is so small; She is a tiny seed. She is watching us now, though it feels as though She's left us. She has not. It is just that now She has become the tiniest of seeds."

Aureillia

Zula and I returned to the same place often, to try to find Danelle. We often succeeded in finding him, but always when he saw me, he would disappear. It was very disappointing after so much work to get to him, only to have him disappear.

I tried to be more discreet, to approach him less abruptly, to sit casually off to the side of the path he walked upon, to allow him time to slowly process my presence. It did no good. He continued to disappear even when he understood that it was me he was seeing.

Another person, a man, had been with Danelle. He seemed interested in me. As I would search for Danelle, he would appear and disappear behind me. I would feel a presence, and turn to see him fading. It was clear he wished to observe without being observed. I, however, did not wish to be observed. I began to play a game. When I felt his presence I would turn around swiftly, forcing him to blink out before he was quite ready. It surprised me how I enjoyed watching him struggle in this way.

The next time I met Danelle, when he disappeared, I tried to follow him back to wherever it was that he went. This man who had been following me stepped into the path before me, stopping me instantly by interrupting my intention.

"You must not follow him," he said.

"Who are you?"

"A friend of Danelle's."

"A friend or a teacher?"

"Do you perceive a difference?"

"If you are a teacher, you might be able to help me."

"I am teaching him how to journey," he said. He was small, much smaller than I. "He is quite surprised to see you," he said, his lips moving over white teeth that seemed too large for his mouth. "As am I. Surprise can send one back to ordinary consciousness quickly."

"Take me to him, please," I pleaded. "Show me where he is. I must speak to him, even if in ordinary consciousness."

"No. No," he said, "it is much better this way." It was clear that it was difficult for him to look up at me but, being that I was taller, he had not choice. I did not feel inclined to lower myself for him. I did not like this man.

"Tell me," he said, "how did you accomplish it? It is a very sophisticated teaching, getting into someone else's journey." He stepped very close to me. Too close. I backed away from him and as I did, became aware of another person behind me. It was Zula. She stood directly behind me with her hands on my shoulders.

"You?" he said, a look of fear covering his face upon seeing her.

"Yes, me. You shall never be blessed with the ability to forget me. This traveler has my protection."

He was backing away, his face alternating between expressions of fear and rage. We watched him until he was gone. I turned to Zula. "Am I to assume," I asked, in great anxiety, "that Danelle is in danger?"

"From Rodin?" She said, laughing. "Goodness, no. Danelle is indeed in danger, but not from Rodin. The only one who threatens Danelle is Danelle."

"But how can he have such a teacher?"

She looked at me in surprise. "You do not believe that teaching is a one-sided endeavor? No. Students and teachers choose one another for very particular reasons. Rodin is about to receive the lesson of his life," she said, laughing a rather sinister laugh.

"But Rodin can journey. Is this not a high level of the teachings?"

"Anyone can learn to journey."

"I do not understand. Is not journeying an indication of an educated sort?"

"Educated in the art of journeying, yes. But, dear Aureillia, there are many other lessons that have nothing at all to do with journeying that are equally as challenging. I can assure you that Rodin has chosen to turn his back on many of the most important teachings."

"How is it that you know him, Zula?"

"It does not concern you."

"I wish to know."

"No," she said and the no was final, so final that for a moment I feared her. She recovered herself quickly, however, adding, "Perhaps later I will tell you more on this subject, but for now, I can only tell you this. Do not assume simply because someone appears to you in a journey that they know more than you do. Also, stop assuming that everyone's intentions are good. Walk in fear of this man, of all men, Aureillia. Do not close your eyes to the truth."

Stories They Told Me

The Winged Goddess of Creation

God formed Lilith, the first woman, just as He had formed Adam, except that he used filth and impure sediment instead of dust or earth. Adam and Lilith never found peace together. She disagreed with him in many matters, and refused to lie beneath him in sexual intercourse, basing her claim for equality on the fact that each had been created from the earth. When Lilith saw that Adam would overpower her, she uttered the ineffable name of God and flew up into the air of the world. Eventually, she dwelt in a cave in the desert, on the shores of the Red Sea. There she engaged in unbridled promiscuity, consorted with lascivious demons, and gave birth to hundreds of lilim, or demonic babies, daily.

Chapter 20

Danelle

I was sculpting a small tiger when Rodin came. The piece of wood I had chosen was, like a tiger, naturally striped. Deep brown and black circles ran through it. My fingers caressed the smoothness the knife left behind.

I did not stop working when he approached me. I continued to shave away at the piece of wood within my hand. He settled himself on the seat next to me outside my hut and watched me work.

I had told him about my time in the circular court. He had only looked at me with confusion present in his eyes. "I am afraid I have no words that might help you," he said. "I find this most peculiar indeed."

He took some seeds out of his pouch and began to chew them, one at a time spitting the shells onto the ground beside him. "You must continue until you understand," he said.

"Why the fire?" I asked.

"What?"

"Why the fire? Why the necessity of the fire?"

"The heat," he said. "Heat is necessary, essential for the transformation that spirit flight requires."

I knew he had come to take me on another journey. "You come for me too soon," I said.

"I come when it is is time."

"What if I say 'no.' What if I do not come?"

"You cannot escape it. If you say, 'no,' if you do not come, you choose to proceed without help, and that seems to me an unwise choice."

He was right. I did not want to do this alone. I was grateful to have Rodin. He had even brought food to me the first few days after my return from the circular court as I had been left again without the capacity to care for myself. With someone else I may have felt ashamed, childish, to be brought food. But, with Rodin, I did not feel that way. He treated me with respect and compassion, making his presence, his efforts inconspicuous. Simply setting the food beside me, keeping my water jug full of fresh cool water. Quietly taking my clothes to wash in the stream. He even swept my floor and shook out my mats. All the while saying, "You'll get through this. You shall come to an understanding. A shaman passes through difficulties an ordinary man could not tolerate. Don't forget to eat now."

"Tell me," Rodin said, beside me now, "Why is it that you do not sign your work?"

"'Sign it?'" I said, observing the tiger within my two hands, "In what way 'sign it'?"

"Why do you not indicate somewhere upon it that it is you who have created it?"

"Most know that I have done it. I hand it to them."

"These here," he said, pointing to the carved objects around us. "These here you will trade at market. You will release them for further trading and none will know it is you who have created them."

"Why should they know that?"

"Why else do you do it?"

"Certainly not so that others shall know that I have done it."

"Then why?"

"Because it is what I do. It is my gift. It is what I have to offer—the way in which I serve. It is also one of my greatest joys," I said, looking at Rodin. "When I carve wood, for instance," I said, holding up my not yet completed tiger, "the way it smells, releasing more of its smell with each cut that I make—releasing the colors—darkness and light. Wood I adore because it is always surprising me with its circles and spirals. No one piece is like any other."

He smiled and looked out in front of himself. "This is very beautiful, what you have said, but I am afraid I do not understand it."

I shrugged my shoulders and returned to my work. "When do we leave?" I asked.

"I'll give you until tomorrow morning."

"Thank you," I said.

"Danelle," he said, "perhaps you should stop for a time. Your eyes are quite red. Do they not hurt you?"

My hands instinctively reached to cover them. "I forget to notice," I said.

"This could become a problem. You must make an effort to notice."

I nodded my head in agreement. "Aureillia scolds me about this as well," I said, recalling the many times she had found me working when my eyes could no longer tolerate it.

"She is right," he said. "Only a foolish man ignores pain."

This remark embarrassed me. I looked away from him.

"I shall return with something for the soreness," he said.

Aureillia told me often of her worry over the red lines in my eyes after hours of intense work. I pretended not to know what she was talking about. Yet there was the dizziness, the stinging, the evenings spent covering them with cool cloths only to stop the burning enough that I may close them.

On Malta, when I had first arrived, the priestesses who had bathed me in the cool, clean stream had given me an ointment. "You see without seeing," they had said, "but you do not accept it. You force your eyes to work when they need not to, when you would be better served by closing them and seeing within. What is it you do not trust?"

They observed me patiently, waiting for a response. But there was not one, only a long, profound silence within, an echoing quiet. A deep well of nothing.

"Your eyes are at risk," they said when I did not respond. "You must try to correct this behavior."

"I wish not to be a foolish man," I said to the empty air in front of me. I set the tiger aside, stood and stretched my body, stiff from sitting for so long, before entering my quarters to try to locate the ointment the priestesses had given me.

Stories They Told Me

The Winged Goddess of Creation

Lilith roams at night, and goes all about the world and makes sport with men and causes them to emit seed. In every place where a man sleeps alone in a house, she visits him and grabs him and attaches herself to him and has her desire from him, and bears from him. And she also afflicts him with sickness, and he knows it not, and all this takes place when the moon is on the wane.

Chapter 21

Aureillia

I returned and returned, but to my dismay, I no longer found Danelle. I rather wished to stop the whole process. It was difficult and trying to my being. I would have given it up completely but for Lilith. Lilith sitting there so hopeful each time that I returned, asking me eagerly, "Have you seen him? Did you tell him?"

Only then would I remember that my intention had been to do this for her, though it no longer felt that way. Questions began to bother me. What was this about? Why had Danelle gone from Minoa? From me? For it was, in fact, me he was avoiding. And why couldn't I find him? I knew if I really wanted to, I could. I knew I needed not any of these rituals. I knew I needed only to close my eyes. Why wouldn't I then?

Leida was fully recovered and back to work at the temple, but I had not been able to find a way to make things any better between Thela and me. Though I had approached her with apologies and pleas to end this situation many times, she refused to listen.

One day, as she walked by me hurriedly out of our block, I followed behind her into the grove of trees below.

"Please, Thela," I said, grasping her arm. "We cannot go on this way."

"I asked you. I begged you not to do it," she scolded. "And yet, you did it. That shows me how little you care for me."

"Thela, this was not about you. It was about Leida. She is a woman. She must be allowed to make her own choices. It would have made her feel like a child to have been forbidden."

"What if I were to do something you specifically asked me not to do while taking care of Lilith?"

"It is not the same thing, Thela. Can't you see? She is a priestess. I am her mentor."

"You and your temples," she said, disdainfully, almost spitting the words. "What good is being a priestess if you have to almost die to become one?"

"Thela, why do you insist on being so hurtful?"

"Because I am worried."

"Leida is fine, Thela. She's never been so well."

"I am not worried about Leida," she said, exasperated. "I am worried about you, Aureillia."

"Me? Why me?"

"Yes, you. You and Danelle. Aureillia, where is he? What happened between the two of you. Why haven't you told me?" She said, collapsing down onto the bench behind us. "You see," she said, "I know that if you haven't told me, it must be something terrible."

"Forgive me, Thela," I said, sitting beside her. "I see now that I should have tried to explain it to you. It's only that giving voice to the whole thing terrifies me."

"Everyone knows Danelle would never leave Minoa willingly. For this reason we worry so."

"And blame me?"

"Though I am not one of them, there are those who do. There must be someone to blame, Aureillia. It is not easy for a community to lose their oracle."

"Their oracle?"

"Our oracle," she corrected.

"Do you see him as an oracle, Thela?"

"Certainly, though I would never tell him that."

"Why not?"

"Because he would be furious with me."

"Why?"

"You know why, Aureillia."

"No, I don't. After thinking upon it for some time now, I realize that I actually do not. I know that I must not call him one because it upsets him but I don't know why that is so. Do you?"

"He prefers to see himself as an artist."

"But why, Thela?"

"Because...," she said, pausing, "I suppose I don't know why either. Aureillia, do you think that is the reason he is gone?"

"No," I said. "It has only just occurred to me that this may be part of the reason, but it is not the main reason."

Thela and Danelle had a kinship like a brother and sister. She, like I, grew up with Danelle, and they were even closer in age. For some time, it was their mutual feelings for me that had connected them. More recently, however, they had developed a friendship independent of me. Danelle spent much time with Thela's young sons, who were close in age to Lilith. He had known their father, Keynou, well. They had met him in the time that I was away at the cove. He was a traveler from the land to the south who had been drawn to Crete by the work of Her artisans. He had spent time apprenticing with Danelle. Through Danelle he and Thela had met.

I looked at Thela; her eyebrows arched slightly and her jaw clenched. I wished not to tell her what it was I was about to tell her. I wished not to add more weight to that face. But she was waiting, bracing herself to listen. The time for the truth had arrived.

"I will tell you what I know," I said, "but none other can know it. It is a sister secret."

"Sister secret," she said, sitting up tall and spitting onto her first finger.

I spit upon mine. We held them together. "This secret I shall share with none other than my sister," we both said, giggling at ourselves. It had been a long time since we had shared a sister secret.

"Thela," I said, when my seriousness returned. "Danelle is gone because he needs some time to try to understand something he saw in a vision in the healing temples of Malta."

"What did he see?"

I drew in a breath. I had never spoken these words out loud. "He saw himself killing me," I said.

A look of horror passed over her face. "When?"

"In the future," I said. "In my last vision I saw someone killing me. When we went to Malta...."

"Is that why you went?" she interrupted. "To find that out?"

"Yes.

"Why, Aureillia? Why couldn't you just leave it alone?"

"I needed to know."

"Why? Why know things like that?" she asked, her eyes were not focused on me but rather on a point in the distance.

"I couldn't bear to be around him, Thela. I didn't want to feel that way."

"And now? Now that you know?"

"I am not sure. He is not here."

"You see? You should have left it alone. You and Keynou," she said, "always needing to pluck the feather, always needing to pry underneath the floorboards. For what? Why? It serves no purpose. Only to make things more difficult." She stood up. "Poor Danelle, how will he ever recover from this? All this time, I have defended you, when in truth, you really did send him away. You are the reason why he is gone."

"Thela," I said, "Keynou and I, it is our task to ask questions. It is part of what we have been sent here to do."

"Don't you dare speak his name," she said, turning and walking swiftly down the path before me.

I sat back and blinked my eyes hard to the tears that wished to push forward through them. I would not cry. Not now. Not here.

The trees waved their leaves above me, making a play of light and shadows around me. I sat and watched the contrast.

Some people can live more easily in the world of contradiction than others. Thela needed everything to be either one way or another. She had trouble dealing with things that were at once one thing as well as another. This was the world I inhabited.

"My mother does not handle well information that does not fit easily with her idea of the world," Leida said, emerging from the bushes behind me.

"Leida," I said, "What are you doing here?"

"I heard you two fighting."

"You must stop following me around," I said. "I must be afforded some privacy."

Her cheeks flushed. "You are right," she said. "I apologize. When I heard the two of your voices, I was so hoping...," she stopped herself from making further excuses and sat down next to me.

"How much did you hear?" I asked, looking at her.

She said nothing, kept her head bowed.

"I see," I said.

"I keep secrets well." She made a closing motion over her mouth. "Aureillia, please forgive me. I will try to end my habit of always following you around."

"Please do," I said, taking her hand into mine and squeezing it to let her know all was fine between us. She took my hand into her two and kissed it. "I went to him once," she whispered. "He made me this." She reached into the space between her large breasts and pulled out the amulet that hung from a cord around her neck. I couldn't believe that, after all the time we had spent together, I had never seen this. The way she wore it, hidden in her dress, I had not even known it was there. She held it out toward me. I examined it. It was an image of a body with a double body drawn around it, lines of energy emanating between the two bodies.

"What is this?" I asked.

"For the longest time I did not understand it," she said. "Everyone else, upon receiving their stone, had felt so enlightened, had been given a sense of illumination, yet I felt only confusion. I thought perhaps the magic didn't work for me. Perhaps some mistake had been made, until now. Only now, when I returned to my work at the temple, was it revealed to me."

"What was revealed?"

"I can see them, Aureillia." On her face was an expression of disbelief. "I am able to see where it is they are holding their pain."

"See it?"

"Yes. Our companions. I see a sort of cloud around their bodies and in these clouds are places of density and darkness I have determined to be the area, the place in which they hold their pain."

"You did not see these things before?"

"No. I am sure it has something to do with my time in the labyrinth."

"How terribly fascinating."

"Yes," Leida said. "Now I need to try to understand why we hold to it and how we can release it."

"So it seems that this is the question we find ourselves left with. The insistent clutching, the persistent pain. Leida," I asked. "What about me? What is it that you see in me?"

Her face turned solemn. "Dear Aureillia, I thought you knew," she said. "Your heart. Your heart is broken."

Stories They Told Me

The Winged Goddess of Creation

She forsakes the husband of her youth and descends to earth and fornicates with men who sleep here below, in the uncleanliness of emission. And from them are born demons, spirits, and Lilin, and they are called 'the plagues of mankind.'

Danelle

Inside me, this hollowness seems never to end. There is nothing, only this work, this ceaseless, hard labor that makes one day resemble the next in a way I have not before experienced.

I cannot understand why it is I am doing what it is I am doing. Each morning I meet a group of men in front of a cave-like enclosure. There is some talking among us. We are each handed a single-sided axe and a head piece with a candle on it. We are then led into a box that moves down low into the earth, where we are directed toward a certain area we are to work on that day. With our axes we chip away at the walls of the earth inside this opening they have blasted into Her.

We load it onto a cart, heavy black chunks of rock. There is little air here. It is difficult to breathe. The chamber is thick with a heavy black dust that I swallow. In hard gulps it moves through my throat. Each day as we work there are loud noises, as they force more openings into Her. While we are working, large rocks fall around us—we shield ourselves with our arms—as they tear her open, to remove more from her—to strip Her of Her insides. She gives so much. She gives so freely. What amounts we take! Cartload after cartload are led away by the horses who live down here in this lightless chamber, this airless tomb.

Sometimes, I talk with the men working along side me but, after a while I tire of the talk. It takes all my energy to keep working. I have not enough strength for both. I cannot leave until I am told to! My being aches. Such pain there is in my arms and shoulders. They burn hot. Sometimes they cramp into tight knots. I wish to stop, but I do not. I cannot. The persistent pain causes anger. This anger, I can feel how it sits within me, turning into something tough and impenetrable.

Stories They Told Me

The Winged Goddess of Creation

Lilith, God preserve us, has dominion over children who issue from he who couples with his wife in candlelight, or with his wife naked, or at a time when he is forbidden to have intercourse with her. All the children who issue from such unions, Lilith can kill them anytime she wishes, because they are delivered into her hands. And this is the secret of the children's smiling when they are small—because of Lilith who plays with them.

Aureillia

Before my visions, I had never feared a man simply because he was a man. But I understood it then. I heard it in her voice. I recognized how she feared him simply because he was a man. A man whom she had provoked to anger. In this new and different world—the world of my visions—the world that now claimed an inner part of me—provoking a man to anger is a dangerous thing. In Minoa, in my world before, often I would, I could make a man angry. It was not a dangerous thing. The man's anger was the man's anger. Once provoked, he would become angry. Nothing more. He would understand that the anger belonged to him. It was a feeling coursing through him, a feeling he would handle. In Minoa, men had not yet begun to use anger as a weapon.

There is great power in being feared. A person who is fearful has surrendered their power to that which they fear. This is the only way one attains more power than another—by stealing it.

I could not see in that journey. As in my earliest trance dances, I could only hear. I was trying to open to information I resisted. Always in these situations, I allowed myself only to hear.

In their voices, I heard it. I heard her responding in fear. I heard him leaving her powerless. I knew he was Danelle. His is a voice I know.

Stories They Told Me

The Winged Goddess of Creation

Lilith roams all over the world, then approaches the gates of the Garden of Eden and observes the cherubim watching over the gates. She sits down there, next to the flame of the sword, since it was from that flame that she originated. When the flame turns around (indicating that the world has entered into a phase of punishment), she rushes off and again goes roaming all over the world to seek out the children who deserve to be punished. And she smiles at them and kills them.

Danelle

I am dirty. I cough a mean hack from the soot and dirt I have inhaled as I walk home to my quarters. Often I go first with some of the men I work with to an indoor place where I drink a bitter drink that helps. For a little while I feel better, warmer —the pain leaves me, for a time. It is because of this that I go there.

There is a woman that I live with. We share the same quarters. She is angry with me on these nights. I cannot understand why I am sharing quarters with this woman. There is nothing at all within me that feels anything at all for her. She rages at me about my meal being cold, about her waiting for me. Why does she sit there waiting for me? I do not understand. There is nothing to wait for. Why does she look at me that way? Cook me these awful, cold meals I do not even want?

Sometimes, there are days, moments, when, quite unexpectedly, a candle flares up, sputtering light around the tunnel while we are working. In one swift movement, the flame extends a long arm of light, causing the entire wall of this dug-out cavern to shimmer. This glistening awakens something deep within me. At my core, a small, sleeping thing quivers. I am filled with a feeling of recognition laced with a deep, unquenchable longing.

When the light dispels, I am standing there wanting. I know not for what, but I understand that something is lacking.

On these nights, there is a different kind of pain to erase. On these nights, the bitter liquid does not help. It deepens the ache. It increases the anger. Returning to my quarters on these nights, the woman gets hurt.

Stories They Told Me

The Winged Goddess of Creation

Lilith goes out into the world and seeks out the children; she sees the children of mankind and attaches herself to them to kill them, and to draw herself into their souls. And as she is about to go into such a soul, three holy spirits appear there, and they soar toward her and take that soul from her and place it in front of the Holy one, blessed be he and there (the children) study in front of him.

Aureillia

It is one thing to hear anger and fear, but to see it is quite another. Because I had experienced the fear of men in my visions, I understood her. I too had known the clenching inside, the terror, the small and vulnerable thing that is left of you after they have robbed you of your power.

He was a horrible man. Such an angry and ugly man. She was terrified of him. The place they were in was utterly dark and unappealing. I could not believe Danelle, lover of beauty, would allow himself to live in such an ugly place. Here there was no color—only everywhere stunning gray. He looked ill. His face was drawn and colorless. His clothing was covered in a blackness. In his hand, he held a bottle from which, when he was not swinging it around, he took, long, deep swallows. He ambled around the room clumsily. He did not seem to be in control of himself. Then it happened.

He began to hit her.

Hard and with intention.

Though she cried out in pain, and blood flowed out of her, he continued. I stood watching but, of course, I could not tolerate it.

"Stop that," I said, loudly, my words echoing into the room. They both looked at me.

I stood still, surprised to actually be in the room, to have been heard. I looked at Danelle. "You stop that, now," I said.

The woman looked at me in fright.

"Aureillia, what are you doing here?" he asked.

"This is entirely unacceptable," I said. I was furious.

He looked down at his hand, poised and ready to strike again, then back at me. Recognition flashed through his eyes. At that moment, he became Danelle. He began to approach me, but not all of him. It was the strangest thing I had ever seen. Danelle walked out of this man, this other Danelle.

"Aureillia," he pleaded, approaching me. "Aureillia, help me," he said.

But there was a rock at my center. "How could you?" I said. I began to shake with rage. "How could you?"

And though he stood there before me, helpless and vulnerable, I hated him.

Chapter 22

Danelle

"Welcome, we have missed you," Jeftu said, when I returned to the cove one morning. "Did you have a safe journey?" he asked, his small slits of eyes smiling above high pressing cheeks.

"No," I replied, averting his eyes, moving my foot against the sand. "There was no safety in that journey."

"My poor man," he said. "You are not yourself this morning. Come, the water will help. Water always helps." He extended his arm toward the boat.

I followed behind him, watching his light, lifting steps, his slight brown back—shoulder blades protruding—welcoming work that was familiar and his presence, his blessed, comforting presence.

He stepped into the boat. I pushed us off, settling into the front seat as he paddled. Silent paddling. The boat rocked upon smooth rolls of water. The light shimmered into and back out of the water's reflective surface. I relished the dark smell of the sea, the taste of salt spray upon my lips, the feel of its dried whiteness tugging against my skin. We pulled in nets, lifted baskets, set them back out again. The music of the morning turned into the noise of the day.

On the beach I joined the others, doing what they do everyday. Together we ate as we always eat. Again and again we eat. We sit on the beach and we eat together. Yet it returns. The thirst. The never-ending hunger.

"Tonight," Jeftu said, pointing toward the sky. "The moon is round. We shall hunt octopus for a celebration in the village. You are welcome to join us."

I knew this to be a sacred ceremony performed in the seasons when the octopi are present. I had observed it from my cliff dwelling above. A silent, torchlit dance on the beach followed by boats with torches entering the water of the cove. The occasional splash of a spear.

"Yes," I said. "I will be there."

* * *

The moon was round, white and hovering low within the darkness surrounding us. Her light created a path upon the water it seemed one could walk out onto.

Jeftu greeted me on the beach from within the circle of men. "Follow the dance as best you can," he said. "It is not a difficult one."

I was no stranger to dance, only they moved differently here—faster—and where on Crete we held hands and spun together, here we stood in a circle spinning separately. The energy, the Serpent rising, however, soon connected us and it seemed as though we were spinning together as one. My head grew hot, then light, and for the first time in so very long, there was a lifting, a lightening of spirit in dance and celebration; a rising up and out of the darkness—the density of the weight we carry.

In this state of weightlessness, I danced in the presence of men who had taken me in for no other reason than their own generosity, and I was thankful.

"You will start by holding the torch for me," Jeftu said. We approached our boats. I, the dance still filling me, pushed us off gleefully and assumed my seat in front of Jeftu. After he had paddled out a short distance, he stopped. I turned to face him. He motioned for me to lower the torch. The light attracted the octopus, who we would then spear. We glided along for a time, watching and waiting until we saw her.

She spread herself, fanning her being as she observed the light with interest, flashing the perfect white circles of her tentacles toward it.

Jeftu's spear crashed down into the water awakening me from the dream of her. He lifted the spear out of the water with her on it. She wriggled with movement. He removed her from the spear, efficiently bit the back of her head, spit into the water and placed her into the catch basket between us. Smiling big, he took the torch from my hand into his and presented me with the spear.

I held fast, possessing it too firmly within my hands, watching the place in the water below the light. At last she appeared, small and timid, looking at the light. Jeftu let out a small "ah" noise and glanced at me. I held the spear high, knees gripped, as though to plunge it into the water, to penetrate her being with it, yet I could already feel it within me, the place where fear had overtaken me; the impotence of my actions. I had not the will within me to do this.

"Take her, Danelle," Jeftu said. "She is offering herself to you."

I sat beholding her, how she made herself once small, once big, her large wondering eyes. Around me I could hear the plunging of other spears, the low murmurings of the men in other boats. I dropped the spear to my side. "I cannot," I said.

The concern that penetrated Jeftu's face he tried to conceal. "I see that you cannot," he said. "Would you be willing to hold the torch again for me?"

"Yes," I said, taking the torch. It moved within my shaking hand.

Jeftu took the spear from me. "It is all right, Danelle," he said, steadying my jittering arm with a firm hand. "You will get it back. I will help you."

I nodded my head, thankful for the darkness that hid my sense of utter shame to have failed in this way before such a man.

* * *

I began to sit by the fire every night by myself. I began to sit there and stare at the fire and ask myself the same question over and over, the thing that puzzled me the most, the thing that I could not make sense of. The hate. The hateful man I would become. Why? How? What would happen to me to make me become that man in that world I last visited? There was a sickening in my stomach each time that I considered it.

Though I seemed to irritate him, Promo continued to come and sit with me. He seemed to be staying in Libya for some indeterminable reason, and so he came alone when the others were away. I was not equipped to handle such a person in my present state of mind. I should have sent him away. But I did not. I allowed him to come. Time after time he sat across the fire from me spewing his bitterness. One night, still sore from my journey, he sat across the flames, speaking of the people of Libya in a way that I resented.

"Simple people," he said, laughing. "Such silly, simple people."

"They are not simple at all," I said. "It's only the language that makes them appear to you in this way. They speak to you in your language. That right there shows a level of sophistication you lack."

"What do you know of them, living in this isolated hut? You know not of them."

"I know them intimately," I said, the spark of anger lighting within me. "They come to me often."

"Ah," he said, waving me away with an inconsiderate swinging of his hand. "You were always odd. You always had crazy ideas."

"You knew me not in Minoa. You have no right to say such a thing."

"I knew you. I heard tell of you. I saw you, your workshop. Why are you here anyway?" he asked, slyly studying me. "It makes no sense."

I did not respond, only watched the fire. No other Minoan had asked me this. They had the consideration not to.

"What happened to you?" he continued, moving around the fire, closer to me. "Something happened to you," he said, his words prodding me as a stick.

I watched him yet remained silent.

He, however, was motivated. "It makes no sense at all," he said. He was becoming excited, excited to have found the place in me that was vulnerable. I was now his prey. "You have recreated exactly the life you had in Knossos. Why come all this way for that?"

"Promo, I wish not to speak to you of this," I said, hoping to appeal to some sense of decency within him.

But there was none.

"It's that woman," he continued, "that prophetess that you were always with. The Prophetess of Darkness. It is she. Yes, she has done something to you."

"It is not because of Aureillia that I am here," I said.

"Aureillia! Yes. Her," he said, almost screamed. "It is her," his heels were lifting off the ground in delight. "I can see from your reaction that it is her. Look. Just look at what she has done to you."

I stood up. The blood pulsed under my skin. "You must leave this place now," I said to him, for it was there within me. I wanted to hurt him. "Get out and do not come back."

"It is she that should be sent away, not you," he said. "It is not right."

There was a blackening, a darkness descended over my inner vision, next came the red heat. Then, I hit him. My hand reached out and slapped him with such force that he flew, landing on his back a short distance from me. I went and stood above him, raising my hand to strike again.

He shuddered and covered his face with his hands. "Please, no," he pleaded. "Danelle, do not hurt me again."

"I have much anger left within me if you wish to provoke me further," I said, holding him close to the ground with my foot.

"No, no. I wish not to. I wish not to. Please, only to leave me. I shall not return," he said. I lifted my foot and backed away from him. He crawled away, releasing slow moaning noises as he moved. I had caused him great pain.

I allowed myself to spin with the fire that raced through my being, punching at nothing until I fully exhausted it. I went into my quarters and poured myself a cup of water, which I drank down at once. Then, I stood in the doorway, looking out into the cool night air. I raised my arms to the top of the doorframe and let out a deep descending sigh. Only now could I fully appreciate what Aureillia had come through in her time as a Snake priestess. How had she managed it?

"Not without help," came a voice from long ago.

"We must be strong for her," Barbara would always tell me when she found me succumbing to desperation over watching Aureillia in her struggle with the snakes. "We must always be strong for her," she would say, her hand grasping mine, her green eyes blazing me with the same intensity as the purple in her cheeks.

She never revealed to me any fragility about Aureillia's struggle, though I knew she worried over her constantly. She knew that I was Aureillia's pillar and she needed to be mine. She knew I needed her to stand tall and promise me it would all come out right. But I did not expect to lose her. I did not know my father would go to pieces.

I had nurtured Aureillia, leaned on Barbara, and taken refuge in Tolles but She took Barbara back, Aureillia left, and Tolles fell apart.

Aureillia!

What a spirit. Pure Fire! As a boy, I wrestled with her. She was fierce fighter, but she did not use her strength until I provoked her. To engage her, I would tease and taunt until I had sparked the fire that lives within her. When this had occurred, my grip had no hold on her. She would fling me to the ground in an instant, leaving me joyously weakened. Then and always, it gave me the greatest pleasure, lying beneath her in surrender.

Throughout her entire struggle as a Snake priestess, her spirit remained strong. I was able to detect this power still alive within her. It is this which allowed me to encourage her to persevere.

But with Tolles, it was different. With Tolles, the spirit itself had become weakened. A weakened spirit I did not know how to help. There had been a delay. With Tolles, the mourning began years after Barbara's passing. I sat with him. I listened to him. I watched my father cry.

The sadness—it permeated everything. Sometimes I felt within me the desire to avoid him. Of course, I did not. There was so much he had given me.

Crete is a place of great beauty. We walked together to tall peaks where we could better observe Her beauty stretching before us in deep cutting valleys ripe with food, groves of trees whose branches leaned heavy with dripping, moist fruit. We would stand together looking at it. We would breathe it in.

We journeyed together often to the peak sanctuary, each presenting Her with a labrys of remembrance.

"The separation," Tolles said to me one day. He had stumbled and fallen on the way back down the steep hill that is the sanctuary. I stooped to help him up. In his time of weakness, he had grown frail. He pounded his fist upon his chest. "The separation," he repeated. "It is the separation that hurts. I cannot bear the feeling of her absence. She is gone for always and it hurts," he said. He said it as a child says it, shocked at the physical sting of emotional pain.

"She is not gone for always father," I said. "You do not really believe that?"

"Yes," he said, his head bobbing in a repeating up and down motion. "I do. I really do."

"Father, you have lost your way. You must seek help. You must go to the Temple of the Butterfly."

* * *

In my last journey, the woman's spirit too, seemed weakened. It was this which allowed me to inflict pain upon her; to give her things that did not belong to her. Things that were mine. It was this, this weakening of the spirit, that allowed her to accept it.

"You rotten old louse," she had said to me. She was right. I was rotten. As rotten as could be. I thought of Aureillia seeing me hitting her. How what I was doing had not mattered to me until Aureillia saw me. I knew that it was wrong, but, before she had appeared there, it had made no difference.

* * *

"They told me to see the oracle," Tolles said when he found me in my workshop a few days after he had been to the temple of the Butterfly.

"The oracle?" I said. "Who might that be?"

"They said to me, 'Surely you know him. A man of great height, fair hair. An artist. His talents have helped many,' they said. Then, they began to laugh."

My stomach tightened and dropped within me. The skin on my head became hot. Tolles was bowing to me in sacred gesture.

"My dear, Danelle," he said, taking my hands into his own. "I ask for your forgiveness. I have been involved with my pain. I have clung to it like a child. With it, I have blinded myself to you. My own son, my friend, my brother, an oracle." Pride was flowing from his face. "You have always been the greatest gift to me," he said. "Pure joy."

"No," I said, pulling myself back. "Surely a mistake has been made."

"No mistake," he said. He was shaking his head. "Danelle, you must assume the title you have so clearly earned."

I said nothing, but the shaking, the shaking had begun within me.

Tolles regarded me, a question on his face. Then he turned toward the windows at the back of my workshop. Lifting the tone of his voice up and out of the serious, he said, "I have come to request a stone. I have been told to see the oracle. I have been instructed to request a stone and that is what I am doing."

I looked instinctively toward the boxes on my shelves, then away from them quickly.

"What is it?" he asked.

"Yes. I shall," I said. "I shall carve you a stone." I was leading him toward the door. "It is good. You must leave now that I may begin my work."

He paused for a moment as if to say something, but then he nodded his head and took his leave. I watched him walk down the long corridor of the Center, away from my workshop. I knew that he wished to turn and look at me; he wished to say something. He did not, however. He held himself quiet.

I knew I was being unfair to his fairness—dishonest to his honesty. Distaste for my own actions settled at the back of my throat.

I returned to my workshop and sat at my table. I watched out the window as Tolles walked along the path outside the Center. He walked slowly, his head down, thinking. The wind blew the fabric of his purple robe against his legs.

In a couple of days, I would give it to him—the stone I had already carved for him.

Stories They Told Me

Snake Goddess

Now the serpent was more cunning than any other beast of the field the Lord God had made. And he said to the woman, "Has God indeed said, 'You shall not eat of every tree in the garden?'"

And the woman said to the serpent, "We may eat the fruit of the trees of the garden; but of the fruit of the tree in the midst of the garden, God has said, 'You shall not eat it, nor shall you touch it, lest you die.'"

And the serpent said to the woman, "You will surely not die. for God knows that on the day you eat of it, your eyes will be opened, and you will be like God, knowing good and evil."

So when the woman saw that the tree was good for food, that it was pleasant to the eyes, and a tree desirable to make one wise, she took of its fruit and ate. She also gave to her husband with her and he ate.

Chapter 23

Aureillia

I had wanted to believe I was above it. I had wanted to believe that it did not matter. I had thought that I could forgive him. I had tried to separate what happened in that vision, in those deep, dug-out chambers, from the rest of my feelings for him. But, I could not. I could not because it was not possible. It was absolutely impossible. I had not been able to admit that to myself until now, now that I was falling apart.

Once the anger came, I could no longer allow myself to work with men. Leida took all the male companions. The ones she could not help were sent away. I disliked having to send companions away, but I knew I must honor my responsibility as a priestess, the first responsibility an initiate learns: That she must be willing to face the contents of her own soul before she can be of assistance to any other.

I now allowed myself to become aware of my anger toward Danelle. It was this anger that formed itself into a hardened spot at my center. I also opened to the knowledge that this anger was not isolated to Danelle and the men of my visions. No. I now allowed myself to realize that I was angry at all men. It did not matter why, if it was fair or unfair, my being had decided to fear all men. Something had been lost, stolen, and there existed the possibility of it happening again.

"Of course, you are angry," Helena said. "Anger arises from the soul feeling that it has been violated. He violated you."

"Not him. Not the Danelle I know. The other one. Danelle, my Danelle would never hurt me."

"How can you say that? He does hurt you. You saw him. He murders you and in the most vile way. People do not do such things to others without meaning to."

"You are mistaken, Helena. It is not him."

"It is him, Aureillia. There you are again, stuck on the labrys."

"The labrys?" I said.

"The labrys," Helena repeated. "Thinking things are separate. Thinking one is two." She pointed to an etching of the labrys on the wall behind her. "Here is one Danelle," she said, pointing to one end, "and here is another." Her hand tapped against the other end. "Here are the two Danelles," she said, pointing to the labrys. "I see no two. I see only two parts of one whole."

I said nothing, but my hands were rubbing against each other upon my knees.

"Aureillia," Helena said, silencing them by placing her hands on top of mine. "I am not saying this information is easy to assimilate. It is ever so difficult, but your will to force it to be something other than what it is makes it all the more difficult."

She withdrew her hands from mine and wrapped her arms around me. I sank into her warm embrace.

"Why?" she asked. "Why do you wish it not to be the same Danelle?"

"Don't you see?" I said. "That means he really does do it and I do not wish to believe that."

"Why not?"

"Because it makes me furious. And it is an anger like none I have ever known. It is an anger so ferocious it frightens me."

"Nevertheless, you are angry."

"It is true."

"So the denial does not actually help."

"It does help. It does," I said. "It takes the pain away."

"Maybe it seems that way, Aureillia. But it is not really gone."

"No," I said. "No. It is not gone."

"It is clear to me," she said, "If you wish not be angry, simply do not allow the man to hurt you."

"But it has already happened, Helena. There is nothing to do."

She clicked her tongue impatiently, stood and pointed to another engraving on the wall so vehemently that her butterfly pendant swung back and forth upon her chest. It was the engraving of the spiral, a swirling and circling line that seemed never to begin, never to end. "Nothing ever finished," she said, "nothing ever complete," she whispered. "Aureillia, it is because of you that we know this. You have seen yourself living again. It is this part of your visions that concerns this temple."

"But how is it possible?" I asked. "And what is it? What is it that remains?"

"Yes," she said, becoming excited. "Yes, these are the questions we find ourselves asking now. What is it?" She knelt before me and made the sign of the spiral in the air. Then she held her hand in front of my chest and made a spiral there.

"This," she said, "this is what remains."

I felt the circling whirling of the energy she had moved within me and in the air in front of me combining, spinning. We sat in silence, both taking it in.

"There is something that has always bothered me about this vision," Helena said, breaking the silence.

"What is it?"

"From the way you have described it to me, it would seem that you do not even try to defend yourself."

I sat for a moment thinking about what she had said.

"Yes," I answered her. "It is true."

"Why not? What would make you not defend yourself against such a brutal attack?"

"I do not know," I said. "It seemed inevitable. In the vision there is within me a feeling of giving up. An almost offering of myself to him."

"But why?" she asked. "Why accept such a fate?"

"I did not feel that I had a choice."

"Would you allow Danelle to kill you now, here on Crete, if he tried to?"

"Of course not."

"What would you do?"

"I would stop him. I would not allow it. What nonsense, Danelle killing me."

"But why? What is so different? It seems to me this is the problem."

"Here I feel I have a choice, a chance to defend myself—the will. Here I have my will. I believe I can stop him. By the time I got to that vision, I had witnessed so much brutality, so much pain being inflicted upon people for no apparent reason, that I think I rather came to expect it."

"So because you experienced horror, you came to accept it?"

"It seems I had become rather numb to it."

"Numbness," Helena said, shaking her head. "This is a very dangerous thing."

Danelle

When she came to me, that woman, I stood there in my quarters and I looked at her. I knew her completely, though I knew her not. My body began to tremble. It was the same feeling as the one I had when the light entered the tunnel, only one hundred-fold stronger. As I stood looking at her, everything stopped. Everything that I was, everything that I had been doing, the man that I was—it all ended in that moment. I knew, standing there looking at her, that nothing after that moment would ever be the same. In her presence, I felt in all of my being the man I could be. It was a tingling sensation reaching into my bones—an awareness, so bold, it turned me inside out—offering possibility. Without a doubt, I knew that the man I wanted to be would not behave in such a way.

So it was that I abandoned the life I had known and followed it—that longing, that wanting, that surged in giant waves within me. That desire I had first experienced when the light entered the tunnel now had a form: a better me.

The woman she was, her mere presence had made that possible. The woman she was *required* a better me. I had only a name to go on: "Aureillia." The one I had said automatically—the one she had responded to. Aureillia—of the light.

It was some holy men, monks, who found me sleeping in the forest, hungry and cold, and took me in. I had been wandering for some time before they found me. My being was greatly weakened. They fed me, shared their warmth with me. I told them about the vision of the woman. I told them about the light. They understood. They nodded their heads. They said, "Now you shall stay with us. If you choose to, you may become one of us, but you will stay with us until you are stronger."

They treated me with the greatest tenderness.

"What kind of men are you?" I asked.

"We are men of God."

"God, like the Goddess," I said, but I did not know why I had said it.

They were at first alarmed but then said, "Yes. Yes, like the Goddess. Priests of the Virgin Mother."

They taught me their prayers. I said them. They helped to still my mind. But when I prayed, I prayed to a woman, though I told them not.

Aureillia

Lilith began to show signs of distress. I was not sure of the cause. At first I suspected my unsuccessful attempts to reach Danelle. It seemed, however, to be more connected to the dolphins. She required more and more time with them. It had become a sheer annoyance. She would say nothing, only begin walking toward the cove. I could not get her to speak to me. I had no choice but to follow after her. If I would say, "No, Lilith, now is not a good time," she would go to an inconsolable place.

She was often restless, cranky, unable to get into that space that children get into—that place of pure play. Within her had developed a heaviness, her mind often occupied with things unexpressed.

It tore at my insides to see her suffering so, while at the same time, I was enormously frustrated. Desperate, I would lead her down to the water and sit on the shore waiting as she swam. Of late, however, it seemed only to antagonize. She would emerge from the water looking even more shocked and upset.

"Lilith, what is it?" I would ask. "Speak to me of that which upsets you." But she would not. She would barely look at me as she walked past me up the hill back toward Knossos.

I needed to go to the red grotto. I welcomed the need. At the red grotto, the place to which women retreated at the time of their bleeding, days were long and languid—full of rest, quiet, plenty of sleep, and long talks with other women. I was in need of all of these.

I walked the dirt trail from Knossos alone, thinking, looking forward to the liquid release. The way was long but not bothersome. I meandered evenly, listening to the birds, the hot sun upon my back.

I knew Thela to be there already. We had not yet recovered from our argument. Within me was a place exhausted and empty from the loss of my sister. To my surprise as I entered the grotto, she approached me with arms spread wide, which I fell into.

"Sister," Thela said, "We must not allow ourselves to become separated."

"It offers me the greatest joy to hear you say that," I said, holding her warm bulk tight against myself. Her dense black hair smelled of earth and grass.

"I have had a lot of time to think here," she said. "I need to apologize for how poorly I reacted to the things you told me. It has become clear to me that, since you've returned from the cove, I've been expecting things to return to the way they had been. I think I rather wanted it to be like when we were girls. I had lost all those years with you," she paused and shook her head.

"Oh, Aureillia, there have been so many shifts. Mother gone, Danelle gone, Keynou and you and Leida, and me, I'm not so great at shifting." She took a deep breath and smiled. "With my resistance, I almost allowed myself to lose my sister, the most precious gift."

"Only to have you back, Thela," I said. "I have missed you so." She wore a red robe with a white sash indicating she would be returning to Knossos soon.

"Come," she said, taking me by the hand and leading me toward the wooden bench that sits beside the ravine. "Stay here," she said. "I shall soon return."

I leaned against the back of the bench. In front of me the water flowed rhythmically on its course toward the grotto. White and pink flowers climbed in creeping vines around it.

To my right was a clearing with several tables and benches. Many women sat among them, some alone, some together conversing.

Thela returned with a cup of bleeding tea, which she handed to me. I accepted the warm tea, gratefully sipping at its sweetness.

"Thela," I asked. "Do you think places have serpents? Serpents of Fire like we have?"

"They must. For we know Her to live within certain rocks and trees, indeed, even within plants."

"And do you suppose our serpents intermingle with these other serpents?"

"Most certainly. I think that is what is happening when we come here, as our serpents are more pronounced at this time in our cycle."

"But how? What is it?"

"It is the Goddess. She lives in all things. She called us forth into being and she continues to do that, to call us forth into the experience of being alive in each moment."

She put her fingers through my hair, tugging gently at the long strands. "Aureillia, how are you managing with all of this?"

"Barely," I said. "I am barely managing. But the hardest thing of all is that now it seems that Lilith is falling apart."

"Yes, I've noticed."

"Perhaps if we fall apart together, we shall heal together."

"Perhaps," she said. "Of course, it quite unnatural for a child to fall apart."

I heard the warning in her voice. "What do you have to say, Thela?"

"Forgive me, Aureillia, but I only wonder. Do you not wish to know what it is they are telling her?"

"Who?"

"The dolphins."

"They are telling her stories."

"What stories?"

"I do not know. She will not tell me. She is very private about it."

"It is not natural for a child to be private," she said.

"But what shall I do, Thela? She refuses to tell me and yet, you are right. It does seem to be upsetting her."

"What about stopping her?"

"I am not sure that I could. She is so desperate for it. I am afraid she would sneak there anyway without me and that would be even more dangerous."

"Calm yourself, Aureillia. You can do nothing from here. I will think upon it and when I return, I will keep extra watch over her."

I nodded and relaxed back into the bench.

"Thank you," she said.

"For what?"

"For being so good to Leida. You rescued her from an uncertain fate. I am grateful to you for that."

"Oh, Thela," I said, wrapping my arms around her and hugging her so fiercely that we almost fell off the bench. "You're welcome."

* * *

Later, within the grotto itself, I went to lie down. The front of the room had a fair amount of light. Offerings stood visible within the glimmering water and on the ledges that surrounded it. Taking great caution not to slip on the damp, glistening rock, I moved toward the darker portion of the cave at the back, unrolled my mat, and lay down to listen to the pulsing within that is more pronounced right before bleeding.

I met with slumber and, as so often in the red grotto, I received a dream. The ground was covered with serpents. They crawled about on top of each other, among each other.

They writhed and clumped as snakes will when, suddenly, a large, one-sided axe was thrust upon them, cutting them apart, separating them into pieces.

I awoke, disoriented, within the coolness of the cave. The small trickling sound of water moving beneath stone reminded me where I was. "The serpent among us," I said. "The serpent between us, is cut, disconnected."

Then I felt it, the liquid movement descending within, a warm release between my legs.

Chapter 24

Danelle

The wind was high and the waves were stronger than usual. It seemed there would be a storm. It was not a good day for fishing. Jeftu and I paddled around nevertheless. He guided me to places I had not before seen—places to fish when it was not a good fishing day—still, protected pools where fish would hide from the strong currents that storms create.

When it was time to pull up the basket, I turned myself around upon the small seat within the boat to sit facing Jeftu and we lifted it together. We loaded the small catch of fish into the basket within our boat and lowered again the basket into the water.

"If you eat her, you must be willing to kill her," Jeftu said.

I said nothing, only sat observing the difference in the size of our feet that faced each other at the bottom of the boat. My knees bumped against his. I was entirely too large for this boat.

"It seems," he continued, though I had not responded, "that you have forgotten when it is proper to take. This is very serious. We must take when Mother Sea offers. We must remain open to receive. Taking when she is not giving, taking when it is not proper, it is this that is wrong. It is this that is dangerous."

He kicked his foot against mine. I glanced up at him. "I do not know the reasons that brought you to this state of forgetting, but I do know that you must get it back," he said.

"It is this that weakens you, that sucks the blood down through your feet and into the ground, leaving you pale and empty, without the life force. What is it that could shatter a man such as you?" he questioned. "A man the Goddess has so clearly blessed?"

I moved to speak.

"Don't tell me," he said, extending his arm toward me to stop the flow of words. "I do not wish to know. I am a happy man," he said. "Do you see? I wish to keep it that way."

He took his paddle into his hand. It was time to move on. I turned myself around, trying not to create too much movement. I lifted my paddle and inserted it into the rough water.

"No," Jeftu's voice came from behind me, "I am sure those stories are much better suited to Rodin."

* * *

In my dreams of Minoa, together with my daughter, I swim with the dolphins. She who can speak to them, understand them. She and her gifted mother, understanding a language I cannot. The dolphins are not always kind and gentle, but they are always fair.

In my dreams of Minoa, there is sand and the blue green sea and succulent fresh fruit, which I bite into, filling my mouth with sweetness. In my dreams of Minoa there is Aureillia and the sharing of beings in touch. There is skin against skin, the feel of her weight upon me. There is the memory of being consumed by her as I enter into her depths.

* * *

"Yes, my friend," Rodin said when I told him I thought I had seen Aureillia in my journey. "It is true. You are not imagining it. You are indeed seeing her."

"How has she managed it?" I asked. We were still in the hills, at the end of a trek. It was morning of the day we would return. We sat eating our morning meal together.

"She has a very good teacher," he said.

"Who? Who is it that teaches her?"

"Someone I know to be very skilled in these matters."

"How do you know this?"

"I have seen her in the presence of this woman."

"Where have you seen her? Why did you not tell me?"

"It seemed you were not ready for such information. You, yourself, saw her in your earliest journeys yet, rather than acknowledge it, you returned to ordinary consciousness."

"I did?"

"It is a natural occurrence. She surprised you. She surprised me."

I sat thinking about what he had told me and as I did, a large smile filled my being. I began to shake my head and laugh to myself.

"What is it?" Rodin asked, smiling a wide smile back at me.

"She has done it again," I said. "Aureillia has outdone me once again. I am learning to journey but she, she is learning how to journey into my journey."

"Yes," Rodin said, shaking his head, "This is most difficult indeed."

I did not understand his meaning. I looked at him to try to determine in what manner he had said it. "What is most difficult?" I asked.

"For a woman to outdo a man. This is a most difficult thing."

"What nonsense," I said. "Why should that be?"

"It weakens a man," he said, in a low voice, "when a woman is stronger than he. I have seen this woman. I know her to be very strong."

"See here," I said, sitting myself up higher, "my strength is my strength. It has nothing at all to do with the strength of Aureillia."

"I believe you are mistaken," Rodin said.

"I know that I am not," I said.

"Perhaps it is better to not speak of this," Rodin said.

"Yes," I said, "you are right." For I had noticed how the anger had arisen fiercely within me as it had with Promo, and that concerned me. I relaxed back into a cross-legged position and opened a fig. I bit into its juicy red center full of seeds. The flesh was sweet and wet. "The thing I cannot make sense of," I said to Rodin, "is that it appears I am becoming like those people; those other men that I see. It seems to be affecting who I am now. How can that be, if these things are happening in the future?"

"As there are different levels of existence," Rodin said, "so you too exist on different levels. You, Danelle, are alive and well in many different places. Most certainly your actions in one time and place affect your actions in another. What you perceive of as past and future are actually happening right now."

"Right now?" I said. "Are you telling me that right now I am the man in the tunnel, the man in the circular court, that horrible man that murders Aureillia?"

"Don't forget Danelle," he said. "Danelle the conscious one."

"Danelle the conscious one?"

"Yes, Danelle. The one who is becoming aware of all the others. This is very good because only in this way may we consciously effect a change."

I shook my head. I could not understand what it was he was trying to tell me. I was utterly confused.

"This is a very difficult teaching, Danelle. I know," he said, sensing my confusion. "I tell you only because it is this the spirits wish you to learn. It is this very teaching they require me to give you. Traveling around in the spirit world seemed to me a good way to introduce you to the idea of layered existence."

"Layered?"

"Yes, layers. Try to stop thinking of past and future. Instead, think of layers. As the layers of an onion, if you cut it at one end, all the layers will feel it, only in a different place and in a different way."

"Rodin, this teaching does not make me feel better. It makes me feel ever so much worse. To think that right now I am that horrible man."

"What is so horrible?"

"I murder her, Rodin."

"You kill. People are capable of such acts. Yes, Danelle, even you are capable of such an act. The question is why? What led you to choose to act in such a way? Tell me," he said, eyeing me from the side in that strange way he had, "Is it possible that you detest Aureillia on some level and you are afraid to admit it?"

"What a wicked thing to say."

"Danelle, you must tell the truth. Telling the truth means asking difficult questions."

The fig had stained my hands red and I struggled with a wet cloth to clean it. Rodin stilled my hands and cleaned them for me. Then he held my hands within his and said, "Allow me to ask you again only in a different way. Could it be possible that within you there is some anger toward Aureillia of which you are unaware?"

He let go of my hands and sat in front of me. I nodded my head. I said, "I will tell you that her prophecies instilled in me a fear I had not been familiar with previously."

"A fear of her?"

"No," I said. I felt my cheeks redden. "A fear of myself. A fear of my own male being." I lifted my face to look at him, brushing the hair from my eyes, "I shudder to speak the words, Rodin, for I only now realize that it is true, but Aureillia's prophecies instilled in me a fear of myself."

As I said this, my being was flooded with a memory that filled the moment with clarity. It was a memory from my time spent with Aureillia in Malta.

We had wandered the island together, exploring temple after temple, those meticulous etchings, those colossal sculptures, those large looming slabs that were what was left of most of the temples. On Malta there had been a feeling of safety, a period of forgetting until that day we discovered the temple beneath a temple. We had explored the larger temples above, then followed the grassy path down to the secluded cove below. We were surprised to find another temple there on the shore. It appeared to have once been a natural cave that had been reconstructed into a larger one.

Aureillia entered it immediately. "Danelle, you must come," she called from within, her voice echoing upon the walls of the chamber. "You must see this."

She was far inside. I could not see her. The light from outside was so bright I was, upon entering, momentarily blinded. I stood inside the entry waiting for my sight to return. That is when I saw them. I was only a small distance within, but there they stood, in front of me. Large stones carved in the image of the male sacred limb. This was a temple dedicated to male being. I lost my air. I wished to flee.

"Danelle, come," Aureillia called again.

"I wish not to," I managed. "I am going out now. I am waiting for you outside." I left the cave and sat on the beach allowing the air to enter again my lungs. Looking at the water, I saw it as I had never before seen it; dark and dangerous— engulfing.

I looked back at Rodin and became aware of the sun, which was becoming hot upon us. "Would that she had never seen those cursed visions," I said.

"Yes, it must feel that way to you," Rodin responded.

"Feel that way? It is that way. Nothing has been the same since."

"Nothing ever stays the same, Danelle. Though we wish to clutch that which we cherish tight within our hands, it is not possible. Everything is always changing, transforming, evolving. Now, you too must change. You must learn the lessons and move on."

"I wish to have it back the way it was, Rodin. Before. I want it to be once again the way it was before."

"It can never be the way it was."

I was shaking my head. I did not want to believe it. I had somehow always imagined myself returning one day to things the way they had once been.

"You must strive for something new, Danelle. Something new but equally as good."

Chapter 25

Aureillia

I had decided to stop journeying. I needed to take time to work through the discomfort. I also needed to find a way to help Lilith. I wanted to be sure my unsuccessful attempts to reach Danelle were not the cause of her turmoil.

It was my night to prepare the evening meal for the children of the block. I was working in the food area. Lilith was playing beside me, filling a pot with peas, then emptying it and refilling it. As she played, she hummed to herself. After a while, she began to sing.

The Snake is evil
The Snake must be killed
Lilith is the Snake
Lilith is evil

I was so stunned by what she had said, I let go of the wooden paddle with which I had been stirring. It toppled to the floor.

"What did you say, Lilith?"

She stopped playing and remained still, as an animal that senses a predator lurking.

"Where did you ever hear such a thing?"

Still not moving, looking at the floor, she said, "The dolphins," so softly, I almost could not hear her.

"The dolphins?" I said. "Why would they ever tell you something like that?"

"Because I asked them. I asked them to tell me about Lilith. Mother, maybe there are two Liliths—one nice and one mean—otherwise, I think I must be very wicked to have such a name."

"Wicked? You wicked? How could you possibly be wicked? And Lilith? Lilith of the Cave? Goddess of the Bird who gave me back my life?"

I had spoken too harshly, too loudly, for all at once Lilith's bottom lip began to quiver and then she opened her mouth wide to release a loud wail.

"I didn't mean to scare you, Lilith," I said, sitting beside her and pulling her in close. "It is simply that I am so surprised," I said, trying to calm myself.

There was nothing to do. I had to stay and prepare dinner for the children. The whole time my head was working. How could they? I tried to get Lilith to tell me more of what they had told her, but she would not. She was being loyal to the dolphins. She knew I was furious at them and she was worried about that.

I had to sit with the children and wait for them to eat. I had to clean up after them. I had never seen them eat so slowly. How could anyone eat so slowly? It took everything within me not to rush them. A couple of times I could not control myself. "Finish up now! Quickly!" I urged the younger ones, the slowest ones.

"Please Mother," Lilith said, after evening meal, "Please don't tell the dolphins I told you." But I would hear none of it, and when I had finally cleaned the last dish and put it away, swept up the floors and removed the remaining food scraps from the confines of the block, I took her by the hand and we walked to dolphin cove.

They were not there. They rarely were at night, but I sat there and waited even so, my insides jumping with anger, my head full of hot words to say to them. In the morning, I awoke to their calling. I had returned to the cove after having settled Lilith into sleep and then fallen asleep in the sand.

I removed my clothing and went into the water at once, swimming toward them. They gathered gleefully around me. "What have you been telling my daughter?" I asked, wasting no time.

"She wanted to know about Lilith. We told her about Lilith."

"You told her wicked stories, stories that are not even true! How could you tell her such things about Lilith?"

They looked at each other, seeming confused, then said, "We only repeat what we have heard. We do not understand the stories."

"You do not understand the stories? How is it that you tell them if you do not understand them?"

"The language is yours, not ours. They are human stories. They have no meaning to us."

"Human stories?" I repeated. "Where are you getting such human stories?"

"We collect them as we hear them. We like to collect them, we like to tell them, however, we do not understand them."

"You must stop it. Stop it now. Not one more story. Do you understand?"

"Could we not tell her different stories?"

"I will see to that."

I began to take Lilith to the cove every night. I began to take her to the cove each night and under the light of the stars, the ever-changing moon, holding her upon my lap with my arms wrapped around her, I would tell her a story.

The earth was born of the egg of the serpent, I began, *After the egg had formed within Her, She released it into the sky. The egg split open, releasing many more eggs, among them, earth, moon, and sun. Snake roamed upon the earth, shedding her skin.*

From Her skin, people were formed. Since we are of snakeskin, Snake has much wisdom to offer us, one bite at a time. Snake is all-knowing. She planted trees. She filled the seas. She gave the earth beauty. She is our Mother, always beckoning us back into Her egg, into the dark mysteries that are life.

My mother's return was just the medicine I needed. We had been notified that she was to return. So it was that Hypia, Lilith, Thela, Thela's children, and I awaited her ship at the marina.

She descended the boat with a broad smile and was tossed into a flurry of embraces. Together we walked to her block and sat around the central court sharing stories of her journey and events that had transpired in Minoa during her time away. Upon hearing of Danelle's absence, she looked at me and made as if to ask a question, but could no sooner form the words in her mind before someone interrupted with another tale to tell.

The concern in her face revealed to me a place within myself that was vulnerable and in desperate need of mothering. It was clear I would not be able to pretend to her. The brave face I had been putting on for everyone else would surely collapse before my mother. I felt a crumbling within already as I backed out of the conversation and became silent.

Lilith cuddled into her lap and touched her long black and white curls, which had acquired much more white in her absence. Her skin, however, remained dark and supple, reflecting vibrantly the deep purple hue of her dress. Observing her, I saw Thela and Leida in her face—but not myself. After Lilith had been asleep in her arms for some time, Sheena stood and carried her into her room.

I followed behind her. After nestling Lilith into a space in her own bed, she turned to me. In the darkness I allowed her to hold me.

"My darling, Aureillia. How do you endure?" was all that she said, but it was enough—enough to open the space through which the hot tears could emerge, wetting the cloth of the front of the dress, enough for the deep sobs of the infant to arise from within me, enough for my mother to wrap her embracing arms around me and tell me, once again, that everything would be all right.

"Aureillia," she asked. "Do you know anything about an upside-down serpent?"

"Upside-down serpent?" I repeated. "No."

"I only just remembered. Before I left Thera, I visited the oracle. She sent with me two messages for you. The first, the one I cannot make sense of and hope that you can, is that she said to tell you that it concerns upside-down serpent." Sheena shook her head and shrugged her shoulders. "The second part I do understand. You must return to the cove of your retreat. Someone awaits you there."

"I shall go at once."

Early the next morning, together with Lilith, I set out. We walked for three days and three nights. The whole time we walked, I told her stories. I did not tell her we were going to see Lilith of the Cave. I told her we were returning to the place where she had been born.

The Winged Goddess of Creation

Once, there was a dark, winged Goddess who came when people needed Her. She could take all their pain into Her being. She could absorb difficulty and trouble and transform it into something other —something useful. When one called out in hurt, it was the winged Goddess who hearkened, wrapping the sufferer in Her warm, sheltering feathers, embracing the anger, containing the rage.

If one howled with the agony of despair, others knew Lilith was with her. They awaited patiently the return of their friend from the time of suffering.

The moment we arrived, I knew, as I stood in the entry way to the cove looking down on the secluded beach below. I knew, with this view, this safe lookout in which I could make my nest. I knew my temple of the Bird must be here. I did not know how I would do it or when, but I did know that birds do not live inside. I now understood that matters of the Bird Goddess require an understanding of the vastness.

Lilith and I set about to the task of collecting firewood and food before the light left us. That night, as we sat within the cave watching the moon raise her white presence into the night sky, she came, her immense wings fluttering as a ship's sail against the wind.

"Mother, what is that?" Lilith asked.

"It is Lilith of the Cave," I said. "Bird Goddess. She comes, once again, to help me. I brought you here so that you could meet her."

Lilith of the Cave flew to the entry way and stood, wings spread before us.

Long, thick, black hair. Strong, dark eyebrows. Bright green eyes. Beaked nose above a small pink mouth. Skin of copper-red.

Though I had experienced her before, her power was no less—there was no diminishment with familiarity. Her presence permeated the entire cave, filling my being with awe. I stood humbled by my own humanness before her.

My daughter clung to my leg, her nails biting in. I lifted her in my arms.

"Goddess of the Bird," I said, bowing to Her in sacred gesture. "I am deeply honored to be, once again, in your presence."

"Aureillia, though the path is difficult, you walk it with grace."

We sat together within the cave, around the fire, as before. As we spoke, Lilith the younger circled around Lilith of the Cave, examining her, touching her feathered wings, her hardened beak and clawed feet. Lilith of the Cave withstood it with great patience, speaking no words, only allowing.

"Is it true," Lilith the younger asked her, "that you kill babies and suck the blood of men?"

Lilith of the Cave closed and opened her green eyes with intention. "I would never harm a child," she replied. "It is my job to protect them. This I do often and I do it well. I have never tasted the blood of men, and I do not wish to, nor do I harbor any ill feelings toward men. They are but more of my children whom I work to protect. These things that you have heard are only stories."

"Why do they tell stories that are not true? I have heard them. The dolphins have told me many things."

"The dolphins only repeat what they have heard. The people who told them— it is they who understand the power of stories. These are strong stories indeed. Of course you believed them. You are a child, and you have great faith in the world and all the creatures in it. This is as it should be."

She took Lilith the younger onto her lap. "Do you think your mother would name you after someone who did such things?"

Lilith looked up into her beaked face and shook her head, no.

"You are right. She would not. You are too young to understand discrimination, but as you know your mother would not give you a name unless she thought it was a blessed gift, then you must know that something is not right with these stories."

"I thought my mother did not know," Lilith said, cupping her hands in front of her mouth and whispering. "I thought it was a secret."

"You must not have secrets from your mother. Your mother is the one who cares for you and protects you. Secrets between a mother and a daughter leave the door open to harm. You must not leave that door open, Lilith. You must shut it tight behind you.

"There are so many stories. It is difficult to know what to believe. That is why you must take care about what you allow yourself to hear. And you must learn, when you become a woman, to know what it is that you believe to be true and trust in that, no matter what others tell you."

Lilith's eyes were wide with wonder as she listened to Lilith of the Cave's words with intensity and focus. I imagined she had listened to the stories the dolphins told her in a similar way, taking them into her core, letting them become her in a way only a child can. But here, instead of being made worried by them, I saw her body relax back into itself in relief. Lilith of the Cave began to hum a melody, repeating it over and over. Soon Lilith was asleep within her arms.

She carried her to the nest of leaves I had made on one side of the fire and wrapped a blanket around her. Then she assumed her place again across the fire from me.

"Lilith," I said, "In trying to fulfill my duty I have caused great pain to my community. What shall I do to mend this rift that seems to be growing?"

"It is the story," she replied, her green eyes upon me. "The way you told the story. The prophecy offered no other way. They cannot let go of an absolute."

"But there is no other way," I said. "That is the prophecy."

"Aureillia, there is always another way. You must tell them a different story. Remember," she chanted, "you can change Her name, Her form, you can reject, ignore, and even deny Her—but you can never truly kill Her. The Goddess is life itself."

She rose and approached Lilith the younger. She raised her wings above her, whispering soft prayers over her. Then she plucked feathers from herself to form a circle around the sleeping child. "This is a circle of protection," she said. "Place it around her each night you are here to close the door upon that which has been allowed to enter her. Watch over her, Aureillia. She is your daughter. Women like you need protection."

She stood to leave. "Aureillia, don't ever forget that you can change a story. When you know this—truly know this inside of you—you will find your way."

Chapter 26

Danelle

"Today you will clean and cut the fish," Jeftu says. I nod my head. We have just returned from our morning trip. He has led me to the place on the shore where the cleaning and cutting is carried out. I am half a man, and Jeftu knows it, yet he refuses to fill in my other half. His tone has become harder because he has decided to help me, and he knows to help me he must fight against what it is I have become.

He hands me an octopus from our catch basket, still warm with life. "Do as I do," he says. He takes a knife and slices along the back of the head, tears around the brain, opening the supple skull, loosening the large piece of flesh. He hands the knife to me. I cut into her soft skin. "Good," Jeftu encourages, "Continue around." I continue, my fingers clumsily pulling the vibrant elastic flesh. "I'm sorry. I'm sorry," I whisper to myself. "Forgive me. Forgive me."

"Pull the insides out and throw them there," Jeftu says, pointing to the left. "They are tomorrow's bait."

I do as he says, throwing the warm black and red innards onto the pile, which will grow larger and larger.

"Take the ink sac, put it there," he says, pointing to another pile. "It is dye for our clothing. It is ink for our scribes."

I nod my head and do as he says.

"Give me the head piece," he says. I hand him the piece of flesh I have extracted from the head. "It is flesh," he says, spreading it within his hands. "Food. We shall eat this flesh as food and it will become our flesh, Danelle. Danelle," he repeats, seeing my distraction, "it shall become alive inside of us. It will become our bodies."

"Become our bodies," I repeat to show that I am indeed listening, though it is most difficult for me to remain focused. He and I both know part of me has already stood up and walked away. Together, at the same time, we cut the tentacles apart into eight separate pieces.

"Take what you have cut to the water and rinse it there," he says. "As you rinse it, you give one piece back to Her. You give Her thanks for the gift of food She has made of Herself."

I stand and walk to the water. My legs shake beneath me. I wash the pieces I have cut. My fingers, which are stained with her blood, her life, I rinse, releasing it back into the sea. I tremble, fighting back the pain that wishes to overwhelm me. I throw a piece to the sea. The longest piece of tentacle I offer to Her. "Thank you," I whisper, "for the gift of food."

Jeftu is behind me. He helps me up, allows me to lean on him as he leads me back toward the beach, the warm, embracing sand.

"Now, place it upon the fire," he says.

I walk over to the fire, through others working, others preparing, taking proper care of what they have acquired. I put my offering on the flames. The water pops and sizzles against the heat.

"That is enough for today," Jeftu says, still holding my arm, holding me up. He leads me to a secluded place at the edge of the cove, a place where I can be silent.

"Sit here," he says. "When it is ready, I will bring it to you. You may eat that which you have prepared."

Alone I try not to look at my hands, try to forget the feel, the smell of the knife blade. The sun is good, warming my insides, which slowly relax to its caress, stop shaking. I watch the waves; the wind that follows them blows against me. I am hungry. I shall eat.

Jeftu returns with the cooked flesh. He sits down beside me as I eat. I recognize her in it. I see the live octopus that she was. I consume her, taking her into my mouth one bite at a time.

"She is good, Danelle," Jeftu comments, watching me eat. "She is giving, and what's more, Danelle," he whispers, leaning into me, "She so clearly likes you. Would you turn your back on She who has given life to all?"

* * *

When the Bull came to me, standing there in the path before me one morning as I walked toward the water, I was not afraid. It had not physical density—no smell. I knew from the place where it stood in the path that it was a spirit friend and that it had come to help me.

It puffed long, deep breaths. From its nose, trails of smoke appeared. I followed those trails down to the water. At the water, I washed my face as I had intended to when I first set out. When I finished, I turned around and saw before me the outlines of a village I did not recognize. The longer I looked at it, the more it took shape. It went from first being an empty, uninhabited village to having cultivated fields around it and then, ever so slowly, it became peopled.

Though I am only now aware of them, these people go about their chores as though they have always been here doing what they are doing.

I stand at the edge of the water looking up at them, watching them slowly become the reality surrounding me.

The trail that leads toward the group of clustered buildings that is the village, I follow. People speak to me, call me by name. I respond. I am a member of the community, my consciousness once again blinks back and forth between observing and experiencing.

This village, set on a vast fertile plain edged in by hills, is concerned primarily with the cultivation of crops. I walk by many labored-over fields in which many people work. On my back, over my shoulders, I carry a tree limb from which, on either side, hang two full buckets of fresh water. I am a water bearer. I do not mind the work. I do it willingly and with pleasure.

Through an opening in the back of the clustered buildings, I enter a courtyard where stand a row of large clay urns. That is where I see her. A woman toward whom my insides rush screaming.

She stops speaking to the group of women she is standing with and observes me. I become conscious of my every movement. She approaches me, helps me lift the heavy bucket up to the height of the tall urn, helps me pour the water into it.

"Your shrine awaits you," she says. "It is prepared and ready. It requires only your presence. When will you return?"

I glance up at her, questioning her use of the word, 'return'. I have not yet entered this shrine.

"I need more time," I respond.

Together we reposition the tree limb onto my back.

"You may continue to do this work, keep this chore, if you are afraid to lose what you have."

"That is not it," I say.

"What then?"

"There are no words for that which keeps me from Her."

* * *

Dreamtime and waking were confused. Though I searched, I could not find Danelle, the man that I was. I was no longer sure of anything. So it was that I began to search for beauty. I knew that recognizing beauty would save me. My mother had taught me this.

Each morning for the entire moon preceding my initiation, she woke me and took me to the place where land meets water. In this place of elements meeting, she asked me to notice five things of beauty. Each day those five things had to be different.

"The only thing required of you to fulfill your purpose as a human being," Hypia said, "is to notice the beauty. Only to drink in the beauty. This is the purpose of human life."

"Mother," I said, "I see the light upon that leaf. I see a clump of red berries hanging ready. I hear the fluttering wings of a small, swift bird. I feel the warm sand beneath my feet. The sun has warmed the sand and the sand warms me. The sky is blue and cloudless. These things that I see are things of beauty."

She looked at me and nodded her head. The look contained concern. She knew the men were coming for me. She wanted me to be ready.

"The world is not out there, Danelle," she said, pointing to the horizon and moving her extended arm in a long, sweeping arc. "It is in here." She placed her hands open upon my chest; large and warm and safe. "When you are in distress, when things are difficult, search for beauty and retreat to the world within."

Being a boy in Minoa was wonderful, but when the priests of Male Being came to take me, I was ready. I had begun to perceive a difference, a difference that could only be explored and expressed apart, apart from the women and girls of my block.

When the men came to take me, though I wanted them to come, though I felt the need for air, I was scared. They took me deep into the forest. "Son of Hypia," they called me, "Your mother can no longer feed you," they chanted. "Son of Hypia. You must learn to feed yourself."

They left me alone. For days, In the forest, I foraged. I wandered, coming to know the trees and the earth. Days passed and I found myself in need of meat. I began to hunt. The hunting led me straight to their traps. Chasing a rabbit, I fell into a hole they had made and covered with many long grasses. I could not lift myself out. I was tired and hungry, cold and scared. I moaned as my stomach curled over itself. I called out. I called out for mother.

And She came. She said nothing, wrapped Her dense, green arms around me, lifted me out of the enclosure and led me by the hand to a stream of water moving with many fish.

I drank the water. I caught and cooked the fish. I fed myself and felt it growing—mother in me.

Sometimes, I only need to look at a person to find myself later carving them a stone. Something there is that overtakes me, guides my hand over the stone in smooth, gliding movements. It is not often that I know what it is I am carving before it is completed. Lengths of time go by unnoticed. Often my workshop becomes enveloped in darkness when it seems morning has only just begun.

Until I handed the first few people stones designed with them in mind, I did not understand. Until I saw within them recognition, I could not make sense of it. Still I did not know how I had accomplished it.

When I was asked to carve Her in tree spirit form, a large image of Her to be placed in a court, I ambled around searching, trying. Always working with others and in the form of miniature, I had nothing to grasp onto. The usual methods would not work.

I began to pray for guidance. I prayed to Her. Again She came to me and helped me. It was then I understood that it had always been Her: Her hand guiding mine. Her hand within me—deep and dark and mossy. It was Her working through me, me expressing Her.

When I heard Aureillia's prophecies, when I heard what would be done to Her, what man was capable of, when I understood what I would become – that is when it started; a blushing within, a shame so deep it reached into my feet.

Of course I had carved the stone for Tolles before his request. Indeed it had begun to happen that way more than the other way around. Naturally it was amethyst. There was no better way to describe Barbara than with purple. But I had not given him the stone. I had taken it with me when I sailed away from Minoa. Here, in Libya, I carried it around with me. I looked down at it now, sitting within my hand and noticed, as if for the first time, that it was the image of a bird, a bird in flight.

I knew that I must return to Minoa. I must hand my father this stone.

I stood up, my feet deep within the sand, the front of my body receiving the heat from the sun. I looked into the waves coming toward me from Crete.

"Mother," I said. I said it out loud, "I see it now. Even in pain is there beauty."

Stories They Told Me

Rachel's Song

I

The Earth was molten, hot liquid
Upon it, no solid ground
Only thick, fluid fire

II

Slowly
It began to cool
On this congealing, sappy surface
A great sun tide began to move
Rolling swaying
The flux grew, gaining momentum
Stretching longer and wider
larger and further
Faster and higher until
An immense chunk of steaming lava
Went spinning away

The moon rose out of the earth

Shaping Herself into consummate roundness
Caught whirling in the *orbit of Her origin*
Passionately engaged

III

It began to rain
Down pouring for days
Drizzling for decades
Showering for centuries
In cool, everpresent darkness
Did it rain
Creating the sea

Into deep craters of stone
Did She collect Herself
Reaching minerals from continental rock
Phosphorous, potassium, magnesium
Carrying Herself into Herself
Brewing briny fluid
Growing potentiality
Primal watery womb:

The first Mother.

Chapter 27

Aureillia

Some animals are gentle. Until I saw her, I had forgotten this. The mere vision of her, her simple presence reminded me. I had been back from the cove for a few days and was wandering the familiar trails again when suddenly, she stood there in the path before me eating, deliberately chewing at the dense richness of unfurling leaves. Upon becoming aware of me, she looked up. Imploring deer eyes, brown and moist, lashed with kindness, she looked at me as though she could not, at first, see all of me, as though the picture of me were taking form, being created through the act of observation itself.

When the image was complete, when I saw her see me, she fled, her swift, soundless legs making of her a fleeting memory.

I moved to follow her trail. A presence appeared before me. A shadow figure emerging. It was Zula. I had not encountered her since I decided to stop journeying.

"You must come back to the journeys, Aureillia," she said.

"I intend not to," I answered. "Not until I come to understand certain things."

"You must continue," she urged. "I need you to. Now is the time for you to teach me." Her eyes were wide, stunned. They had an uncanny resemblance to those of the deer that had only just vanished. "I too have a hardened spot at my center," she continued, "whose origin lies in hate and rage. It is this, this very hate, that binds me forever to Rodin."

"Rodin? Are you speaking of Danelle's teacher?"

"Aureillia, as our love binds us together, so too does our hate. My hate for Rodin is so strong, I fear I shall never free myself of him."

"For what reason do you hate him?"

"Once, I trusted," Zula said. "Once I believed in others. Around us the world was falling apart. Outsiders were taking over villages. I would have done anything to keep our community together. So, when he came to me, Rodin's father's father, when he told me he wished to learn the craft for the survival of the community to make us stronger in our beliefs and therefore, more difficult to take over, I believed him. I trusted him. I taught him all that I knew.

"Aureillia, I was the shaman of my community. After my mother, and her mother before her. The shamans were always women.

"After I had taught him all my knowing, after I had shared with him the nurtured wisdom, he took what I had taught him and he used it against me. 'Now only men shall know the craft,' he said. 'It is the way now. It shall be the way.' They stole my power, Aureillia. They sent me alone to live in the forest. There the hate grew within me. Rodin fears me because I haunt his dreams. I will never allow him to forget the truth."

"Zula," I said. "How is it possible? It is you who taught Rory the dance of release. Together you both taught me."

"I did. It is true. And it helped. But for this, Aureillia, for this, the dance is not enough."

"What then? What if not the dance?"

"It is this which is the teaching of the birds. This you must discover, and then teach me. Please, Aureillia, I cannot stand the pain any longer."

Danelle

The dwellings in this village are a group of interconnected rooms with shared walls. Entry is through openings in the rooftops. Some of the rooms have doorways between them, joining them to each other internally—many of the rooms are shrines.

I am in the shrine of the Leopard. The woman who approached me in my previous visit is a priestess of the Leopard. Her name is Afet. She and the other priestesses of the Leopard are dancing the dance of the Leopard.

It had been determined that there is the need for a new shrine. Today one of the men in this room shall be chosen to priest it. It is this question the priestesses present to the Goddess. It is this response they await, dancing around with the mask of the Bull until She reveals to them to whom it belongs.

Great tongues of flames flicker from the tall torches alight upon the front wall. A drum beats. The shrine is very crowded, warm with the movement of many dancing men. Afet circles and spins, holding the mask out before her, moving between and among us, until she stops in front of me. The horns on the mask are erect urgings, matching the forceful and pushing drum.

She moves to set the mask upon me. I place my hands firmly upon hers, stopping her.

"No," I say. Though I have heard Her calling, I tell her, "It cannot be me."

"It is you," she insists.

I shake my head. "Choose another."

"There is no other."

The crowd is an agitated rumbling. I push through them, squeezing past them, all the other men who wanted the role, to the ladder, which I climb, swiftly leaping over four rooftops before descending the ladder, which returns me to the ground. Safe upon the earth; I run through the cultivated fields, into the tall grasses beyond, toward the small and distant hills.

Aureillia

"I found one," Leida said, bounding into the temple. "Aureillia, I found a snake eagle nest."

I followed her out of the Center into the forest. She walked quickly, displaying her youth, with which I struggled to keep up.

Stopping before the stump of a hollow tree, she whispered, while pointing her hand up toward the top, "Up there. The nest is up there."

We waited a long while in silence before I saw her soaring down from the sky. An eagle, with a crested head, a wriggling snake hanging from her fierce yellow feet.

She landed on a branch near the nest and swallowed the snake whole, head first. Then she flew to the nest, brought what she had eaten back up into her mouth, and fed that to her young, waiting chick.

I watched this scene with a feeling of familiarity. It possessed the quality of a memory. I had seen this somewhere before, but I could not recall its source.

"It seems important to me," Leida said, as we watched this feeding together, "that birds do not share juices the way humans do."

"Juices?"

"Yes. You see, the bird emerges from the mother in a shell casing, in an egg. Once born, the mother does not feed it milk from her body. She feeds it with food that she gathers. The child of a woman lives within the mother's liquids for ten moons. They share juices. The child emerges covered in the mother's blood and continues to feed off the milk of the mother's body. There is a liquid connection—a milk bond that seems to me important."

"You are quite right, Leida. Birds do not have breasts."

"Aureillia, how is it that eagle eats the snake without ingesting the venom? How is she able to feed it to her young without passing to them poison?"

"I am sure that I do not know. I would suspect, however, that it has something to do with the way the mother eats it herself first."

"I have come to believe that this is what we must learn to do—to digest the information but not the venom, to assimilate difficult information without allowing it to poison us or our young."

Eagle sat on the nest feeding her chick, the serpent moving from one mouth into another. As I observed them, the image assumed a different form, a gold surface—an engraved design.

"Danelle's rings," I said, all at once remembering the five rings he had carved for the women of the future. Together we had buried them at our meeting place at the hill overlooking the sea. I had seen this image before. It was one of the five scenes Danelle had carved onto the rings. The very question we were wondering over now—nourishing a child without passing to it poison. How had he known?

"I must take my leave," I said to Leida. I followed the path out of the forest, back to Knossos where I entered the Center, hurrying down the long, twisting hallway that leads to Danelle's workshop. I pushed open the door. A smell greeted me. The smell of Danelle, a piney, wooded smell. I walked over to his table, approached his shelves. I stood in the middle of the room and bowed in sacred gesture. "Please," I whispered. "I have come to see the oracle. I have come to request a stone."

Snake Eagle:

Ingests venom without becoming poisoned (Leida)

Strong, yellow feet
(we must strengthen our feet) (Aureillia)

Unlike birds, humans share a milk bond (Leida)
A liquid connection

Stories They Told Me

A Woman With Teeth and Claws

Once there were a man and a woman, created at the same time, in the same place, of the same materials. Their names were Adam and Lilith. They lived together peacefully for a long time.

After a time, Adam decided that he wanted to rule over Lilith. Lilith refused to submit to Adam. Being of equal origin, she saw no reason why she should. They began to argue, something they had never before done. Adam persisted. He even began to insist that she lie beneath him during intercourse. When she said "no," he tried to force her. Lilith would not tolerate this behavior. She left Adam.

Adam howled and raged so loudly that none of the animals in the shared environment could find peace, finally they approached Adam, inquiring about the howling. He reported to them that Lilith had abandoned him. Could they find her and bring her back?

The animals found Lilith swimming in the warm waters of the Red Sea. She explained to them that Adam had behaved in a manner unacceptable to her. They told her that Adam was lonely and his moaning was keeping the whole world awake. Would she please return to him?

Lilith stated to them that if he would accept her as his equal, she would return.

Adam refused her request.

Chapter 28

Danelle

"Birds are a symbol of the spirit of the soul," Rodin answered, when I asked him, "because they fly. Because the shaman is gifted in spirit flight, he is often depicted as a bird."

"The bird as the spirit of the soul?" I said. I had never considered the bird in this way but now that Rodin had said it, of course, it was clear. I had been pondering over the stone I had carved for Tolles, and that of Aureillia as a priestess of the Bird. But now, all the other frightful images I had created came rushing back at me. The images that had haunted and overwhelmed me. Images of men killing birds.

I became filled with the light of knowing—of understanding—a question had been answered. "Rodin," I said. "All this time, I thought those images of men killing birds were depictions of men killing women but now, I see that it is not so. I see that they are pictures of men killing themselves, murdering their very own souls."

"But your birds are clearly female," Rodin said. "Your birds have breasts."

"Most certainly they are female," I said. "The soul is a woman, of course." I was becoming excited. I knew that I had arrived at something. "Rodin, don't you see, this is not only about Aureillia. It is not only about women. It is not only about me becoming a detestable man. This is about a life disconnected from the soul."

"Why would the soul be a woman?"

"The soul is unquestionably female," I said. "How is it that you do not know this? It is creativity itself. It must be female."

"Are you telling me that you believe your soul to be a woman?"

"I know it to be. Your soul, too, is female."

"Nonsense," he said.

Though I had never before considered it, being loved by others, I now understood, is a blessing and a gift. Only when it became apparent to me that Rodin was not a man loved by many did I understand this to be true. He was respected, admired, listened to, and even revered—but there was something essential missing, the energy of life being passed back and forth, among and between, the liquid ebb and flow of giving and receiving—this did not occur with Rodin.

I began to wonder over this. I, myself, felt no love for him. I felt gratitude and respect, a friendliness, but these were all cool, metal feelings tinged with sharp edges and wrapped in protectiveness. My soul was not open to him.

What bothered me the most, however, was that it was clear that this was the way Rodin wanted it.

The energy of love thrives only in exchange. I had come to understand it as one of the strongest serpents among us. Rodin did not wish to be burdened with having to return love.

In the beginning, when I was coming to know him and the natural flow of love arose within me, I had the unpleasant experience of having him hand it back to me. Though no words passed between us, the message reverberated deep within me. "Take it back," it said. "I do not want this."

This was a cold, hard hurt.

At first, I thought it was only me, for I saw that he had relationships with others. I knew that he shared himself with women. I assumed that for them it was different. Then the time came that one of them took a strong liking to him and began to seek him out at my quarters.

The first few times, she was unsuccessful, having come at a time when Rodin was not there. She was a quiet woman, very well-mannered. When I invited her to come in or sit by the fire, she declined, humbly bowing and backing away. Finally she succeeded in finding him with me one day as we sat outside my hut in conversation.

"Do not bother me here," he said, before even offering her proper greeting. Her back curved to his comment.

"It is no bother, Rodin," I said, thinking his concerns were for me. "She is most welcome."

"No," he said, sternly. "She is not welcome here and she knows that. You know better than to come for me here," he said to her.

She said no words, nodded her head in agreement and walked away.

"I like people, Rodin," I said. "You do not need to protect me from them."

"I am not protecting you," he said. "That woman knows her place and it is not here."

"Her place?"

"Danelle, I am a Libyan man," he said, his voice was loud, eyebrows pushing together, "a son of the fathers."

"I too have a father," I said.

"You, Danelle," he said disdainfully, "are a son of the mothers."

"My dear Rodin," I said, matching his anger. "Would you pretend to forget that we are all born of women?"

"How can one live in separation from their soul?" I asked, rather to myself, for I knew Rodin would not come with me. "It is unthinkable, this disconnection. It is the disconnection that causes such horror." Something released within me. My being felt light and free. A smile passed over my face. "Rodin," I said, looking at him, for I could not contain myself.

"This is it. Do you see? This is part of the answer I have been searching for. Most certainly you hate that which you feel has abandoned you."

He looked at me and smiled but it was a smile forced through tight and pursed lips.

Aureillia

I had a suspicion that the fifth gold ring Danelle had carved would offer me a clue as to what I needed to do to help the people of the community as well as myself. Though I tried again and again, I could not recall what the image engraved on it had been.

So it was that I walked to our meeting place alone, with a shovel and began to dig. I dug, lifting shovels full of dirt. The deeper I dug, the darker the earth became (She holds the moisture within Her).

Eventually, nestled within this rich moisture, I saw the clay jar that contained the rings. I knelt down over the opening; the smell was deep and mossy. I pulled up the jar and emptied the rings out into the sand. Their gold glittered against the sun's light. I sifted through them until I found the one I had forgotten. Holding it within my fingers I examined it, lightly blowing on it to remove the sand from its crevices. "That's it!" I exclaimed. "That is exactly it! He's done it again. Oh Danelle!"

On the ring was the image of a group of people, men and women dancing. Their serpents rose from the earth beneath them, up through them, connecting to a larger serpent, surrounding and circling around them. The circle emanated out to encompass the local environment, which in turn lit up and emanated serpents back. (The trees too were dancing).

I looked out onto the gift of the sea stretching before me, the sun's nurturing light upon it. I looked up through the sheltering tree cover, the expansive blue sky beyond. "We must not dance alone," I said. "We must dance together." (The dance itself will set us aright).

I held the stone within my hand. It warmed to my touch. I slowly lifted the others, one at a time, admiring them, their fluid movement, the beauty, the grace of Danelle's hand revealed in the work.

As I did this, compassion poured into my being, compassion for Danelle, for his torment, for his pain, for his struggle. This feeling filled me so suddenly, so completely, that I could not imagine how I could have ever rejected him. "My dear, dear, friend," I said, bringing the rings into my heart. I knelt there over the opening in the earth, allowing it to happen: the compassion was melting the rock at my center.

Then it was that I remembered the words of my own prophecy:

Only in a world where the Goddess is murdered
Shall these things come to pass

I returned to Knossos and entered the Temple of the Snake Goddess. Approaching the leader silently and courteously, being respectful of the temple rules, I whispered, "I must be included in the next Snake Goddess festival. I must retell my prophecy."

She nodded her head in agreement, "I shall see to it."

I descended into the pit of the snakes and lifted one up. Her long, scaled body curled within my hands, filling my palms with a well known coarseness. Her eyes whitened as she looked at me. "Thank you," I said, "for all that you have given me. A dark wisdom I would not have acquired elsewhere."

Stories They Told Me

SUN

Giver of life!
Bursting ball of benediction
Unrivaled lover
From whose great carnal center
Passionately pours forth
Power.

Continuous circle of offering
Vast exploding flames
Giant furnace of allurement
Spinning suspended
Magnetically erected
Creating sustaining
Life in each moment.

Danelle

The boat eases along the moonlit surface of the water. The long, silent strokes from Jeftu's rowing behind me move us forward in a familiar rhythm. Stroke. Stroke. Stroke.

We stop. Make ourselves ready. He holds the torch. I sit with my hands upon the spear, watching the place of the light upon dark water. She swims once flat, once round, along the edge of the boat, her circling arms reaching, her bulging eyes wondering. My mouth tastes her succulence, her wet, juicy flesh. The deep, dense remains of what it is she has eaten, the crabs that have become her, whose flesh she has sucked out of their shells and used to form her tentacles, forming and reforming her being.

Into my mouth shall she be swallowed. From my center shall she grow into me; my arms, my legs. With her flesh shall I see. With her soft, pink tentacles shall I drink in the sun. From her body will I grow hair. Inside me shall she grow, flesh becoming flesh, always becoming.

Jeftu holds the torch steady. I lift my spear. I plunge it into her.

Aureillia

I had to find Danelle. I could hardly await the event of the new moon. It took all of my strength, this waiting. I did not know where to look for him except for the place I had last left him. That gray place. The place with no color. When the time finally arrived, I made my fire with Lilith and began to journey there. Deer appeared again in the path before me. This time I understood what it was she was trying to tell me for directly behind her stood Zula. Their eyes merged almost as one, until the deer vanished and Zula stood before me.

"Become like the deer," I whispered, then louder, "Zula, you must become like the deer. You must allow gentleness to be your teacher."

"How can I be gentle in the face of what has been done to me?" she snapped.

"Though you think they stole your power, you possess it still, only you squander it on Rodin. He is surely not worthy of it."

"They did steal it. They took it from us. Now only men have the power to be shamans in Libya."

"That's what they say, isn't it? And everyone believes it. But we, Zula, you and I, we know that not to be true. Why do we behave as though it were true? You and I, and all women, Zula, we must act in a way that shows it not to be true. We must tell a different story. Tell the women of Libya a new story, Zula. Awaken their memory. Remind them of what it is they already know. What they have always known."

A smile crossed her face. A smile with a touch of hope.

"Anything is better than this," I said. "Haunting a small man in the spirit world."

"Maybe," she said.

"Zula, can you teach me how to take a group?"

"I am afraid for this you will need a different teacher. Tolles will be able to help you. He will not return, however, until Danelle has."

"I must find Danelle," I said. "I must go now."

"I shall take you to him."

"No. I am most grateful, Zula, for all that you have done for me. This time, however, I need to find him on my own."

"Good-bye, Aureillia."

"Good-bye, Zula."

The space in front of me was, once again, clear. I regained my focus, placed my thought back to where I had last seen Danelle. I followed that thought. It carried me there.

Danelle

I knew I had to make things right with Promo. Since our incident, he came only with the group but remained silent. I did not want it to remain this way.

After asking around, I found him in a small inlet swimming with dolphins. This surprised me. I had expected to find him in many places, but this was not one of them. I sat on the beach observing.

It was a large group. They were having raucous fun with Promo. The waves crashed and foamed around their sleek gray bodies, his dark brown one among them. He yelped and hooted as he played with them, diving into the waves and attempting to outswim them. Being the faster animals, they caught him and held him between them, the speed of their movement forcing him along before sending him twirling helplessly up into the air.

When he noticed my presence, he called, "Come in, Danelle. Join us."

I hesitated, at first thinking it was not for us to have fun together. The play, however, was irresistible. I removed my clothing and swam out to where they were.

Two dolphins came to greet me, seizing me between them at once and propelling me forward through the waves. Liquid pressure pushed hard against my face, pressing down upon my head and shoulders. I held to their fins as they rushed me at high speed before lifting me to the surface and tossing me high into the above. Loud bursts of laughter escaped me as I twirled through the warm, clear air, filling myself with fresh breath before falling back into the waves, into the circle of their game where they waited for me, their delighted squeals and squeaks enlivening the atmosphere.

Promo and I were pushed into each other by the power of their movement. We rolled around within the moving web of water attempting to push away from each other. In spite of our best efforts, we continued to fall back together.

We were both giddy and quickly losing our will to resist going wherever the combined force of the water and dolphins directed us.

The dolphins eventually tired of us and swam away, leaving us standing weakened together in the water. I turned to Promo. The large smile across his face matched the one on mine.

"They are always so welcoming, and friendly," he said. "Magnificent creatures." he shook his head, dispersing the water that was clinging to his thick black curls, his long, dark eyelashes.

We waded together to the sand. I stepped into my shorts and sat down. Promo, remaining unclothed, lay down on his back upon the sun-warmed sand next to me and closed his eyes. I observed him, noticing for the first time that he was a beautiful man. It was amazing how mean-spirited language can make one unappealing. I could not understand where his cruel words had gone. I kept myself half-back, waiting for them to return. Was it the water or the dolphins or the combination of the two that had taken them away?

"Promo," I said, "I came to apologize for hurting you that evening a while back. I was not myself and I deeply regret it."

He sat up and regarded me. "Danelle," he said, in a kind, not at all antagonistic voice, "if only all men could be like you." He placed his hand upon mine. I could not believe this was Promo, the same Promo that I so disliked, that so irritated me.

"Your apology is gratefully accepted. You must know, however, that you were provoked. I provoked you."

"Why must you provoke so?" I asked.

"We all have our roles to play, Danelle. There are reasons for my provocations. I serve the community well in this way."

"Serve?" I repeated. "How could that possibly serve?"

He was shaking his head. "I can speak no more of this. No other can know."

"You mean to say that you provoked me to gain information? That you are a seeker?"

"Some people are extremely private. You were a closed jar. They sent me." He shifted his weight upon the sand. "It is I whom they reserve for the difficult ones."

"What did you tell them? Who is it that wanted to know?" I asked, angered.

"I was sent to make sure you were not in any danger, Danelle. There was great concern for your well-being."

I looked away from him, out toward the sea where the dolphins had gone. Behind us, birds sang within the thick, crowding trees.

"I have told them," he continued, "you have come through it. You shall soon return."

He stood up and stepped into his shorts. "My work is through here," he said. "I return to Knossos tomorrow. I shall bother you no longer."

"Promo," I said, standing and clutching his arm before he walked away. "How do you do this, have so many dislike you?"

"We all have our work to do," he said, shrugging his shoulders. His eyebrows were arched above his eyes. "There are not always choices. Most of the time, it does not bother me, but with you, with someone like you...," his voice trailed off.

"Yes?"

"I regretted having to torment you," he said. The water began to darken behind him in the afternoon sun.

"We can be friends now," I said.

"In here," he said, moving close to me and placing his hand upon my chest. "Only in here, you understand. My identity must not be known. I like my work. If we were to suddenly become friends. Well, we simply cannot," he said. "But, Danelle, it means everything to me," he took my hand into his and placed them both upon his chest. "You. Here."

I stood considering this man, doing work that made him unlikable to so many. I thought of Aureillia having to suffer both physically and emotionally in her work, yet they embraced their roles, bravely moving forward into whatever it was She would present to them. And me? No suffering was required of me, only to embrace the mystery, to say "yes" to the beauty. What was I waiting for?

Stories They Told Me

the birth of life

first there was water
a hot Precambrian sea floating, being, waiting
an ocean of expanding potential
sitting, frothing, shimmering
pulsing with the sound of anticipation

Snake moved through this water

She coiled and uncoiled
She stretched and slithered
She slipped out of Her skin
naked penetration
a jolting light of change
calling into being that which is present
only dormant
Creativity!

Danelle

On the beach, we clean our catch together. I stop working, having encountered a sight I have never seen before. Inside this octopus, this female, is an extra tentacle hanging from within her. It clearly does not belong to her.

"What is it?" Jeftu asks, noticing my sudden stillness.

I show him what it is I have found.

"Yes," he says, "sometimes it happens that he leaves it within her."

I hold it within my fingers, examining it.

"Don't worry," Jeftu says. "He grows a new one."

"Grows a new one?"

"Yes," Jeftu smiles, his top teeth pushing down on his lower lip. "A new one."

Aureillia

When I arrived to the place where I had last left Danelle, there she sat, that same woman, at a table with food on it, but there was a different man sitting across the table from her.

"Not you again," she said when she saw me.

"Danelle?" I asked.

"Who?"

"The man who was with you when I was here before."

"Up and left me, he did," she said, "after you showed up. Stopped drinking. Went all clean on me."

"Clean? Do you mean he changed?"

"He changed all right. Couldn't hardly recognize him."

I looked at the man sitting at the table. He smiled at me.

"You leave him alone," she said. "I like him just the way he is."

"I don't want him," I replied. "Forgive me," I said to the man. "I do not mean to offend. It's just that, who I want—the person I'm looking for, is Danelle. Could you tell me where he went?"

"Ah, moved to some cabin by the ocean, he did," she said, passing a look of disgust to the man across the table who nodded in agreement. "He lives there alone. Never talks to no one. A monk, he is."

She lifted a bone with some kind of meat on it off her plate, held it in two hands and began to eat it.

"A monk?" I asked.

"What's the matter with you?" she said, her mouth filled with half chewed meat. "Haven't you ever heard of a monk?"

"No. I haven't," I said.

"Of course you haven't," she said. "Just look at you."

I looked down at my white, sleeveless robe, so obviously unsuitable to this cold place.

"But where," I said, scrunching up my nose at the need to ask another question. "Where is the ocean?"

"Where is the ocean," she repeated, and let out a huge burst of a laugh. "You don't know where the ocean is either? Right crazy you are. Just like him, after he seen you."

"I am not from this place, it is true," I said. "If you could only point me to the direction of the ocean, I should be most grateful and I will bother you no longer."

She studied me for a moment, chewing again on her meat bone, then she lifted the hand holding the bone and pointed with it.

I turned to the direction she pointed. I closed my eyes and thought of Danelle as strongly as I could. When I opened my eyes, I stood before him. Inside a small, fenced in area, he stood, working the soil.

I was so delighted with myself for having accomplished it. I said, "I did it," out loud.

The sound of my voice startled him. "Aureillia," he said, when he saw me. "Is that you?"

"Yes. It's me," I said. This place was as she had described it. A small cabin on the edge of the land. I could hear the waves of a strong sea crashing against the rocks below us. I looked out upon the water, which was a brown color, not the blue green of the sea near Crete.

Around his cabin were patches of cultivated earth where many flowers bloomed. Most I had never seen before. The place was alive with color, pulsing with reds, pinks and purples, buzzing with the sound of busy insects. I looked at Danelle, aware that he had created this. I longed to touch him. "Danelle," I said, "I must apologize for the way I left last time. It was unfair."

"You have forgiven me then? I live everyday asking for your forgiveness."

"It is not forgiveness that you need," I said. "What is a monk?"

"A holy man."

"You are a monk?"

"No. What makes you ask that?"

"The woman, the one I saw you with last time. She told me."

"You spoke with her?"

"I was looking for you."

"She says it only because I live like a monk."

"If you live like a monk, then surely you are a monk."

"I am not a monk, I tell you. I have not been ordained into the church."

"What is a church?"

"Aureillia, must you?"

"It's just that, it's all so fascinating, don't you think?"

He smiled. It was a smile I had not seen since the time before. A most gentle and accepting smile. "You are a holy man," I said. "Only you do not know it."

He came toward me, reaching his arms out to embrace me but they went right through me. Disappointment filled his face.

"Danelle," I said, "you must come home, but first you must meet me back in the place where you murder me."

"No," he said. "I cannot. I could never go back there. I wish to put that behind me."

"There is no behind," I said. "And there is no ahead. There is only now. Because of this, you must meet me there."

"Your forgiveness. I need only your forgiveness."

"I do not forgive you. How can I forgive you for killing me? It is an unforgivable act."

Terror filled his face. He began to disappear, to change back into the other man. Danelle was leaving Danelle.

"You must trust me," I said. "As you once trusted me. Danelle, though you think that it is, this is not about forgiveness."

Danelle

Back at the village, I walk up the path from the river. This time, however, I carry no water. This time, I walk with intention straight to the courtyard where I find Afet sitting in a circle with other women weaving baskets.

Without delay, I approach her. She is surprised by my newfound boldness, even leans back a bit to receive it.

"I am ready," I say. "I hope I have not made you wait too long."

"Long," she smiles, "but not too long." She takes me by the hand and leads me to the clustered wombs of quarters. I follow her up the ladder, across the rooftops and down the ladder that leads into her shrine, the shrine of the Leopard. She walks through it, passing into a doorway on the far wall, which opens into another shrine. A new shrine adjoining hers.

I become aware of it the moment I enter it, the everywhere presence of bulls. Their sculpted heads with lifting, erect horns, suspended from the walls, their proud painted faces at the height of mine. Their horned presence curves gently and eloquently into this shrine. My being responds, feeling matched.

"Long have I waited for the right man to priest this shrine," she says.

"It would be my greatest honor."

We turn to the large sculpture which projects out from the west wall. It is a Goddess with the face of a leopard. A big cat with breasts, arms and legs open wide; giving and receiving. From between her legs emerges the head of a bull. The Goddess is giving birth to the bull.

"Only in this way many you return," she utters, upon seeing me notice it. "Through the Goddess. With the Goddess. In the Goddess."

Chapter 29

Danelle

Here, the dance is different. I sit and watch; an honored guest. Rodin has invited me to this celebration. It is him I sit beside. We are among the few to have seats. We sit in half-circle. We watch as others dance. Here the women and men dance separately. The drumming is faster. This is a first-fruits celebration.

I become filled with a longing for Minoa—remembering the dancing during celebrations there deep into the night, under the light of a rounded moon. Always after a festival I would step a little lighter, smile a little wider—cleansed and open—until the next one, when it was time to dance again. My feet felt it, and they were ready.

Here, after the ceremonial dance, there is food and music and dancing for all. I have not been in the company of this many people for a very long time. My knowledge of this language is not enough for the fast-pace that is a crowd. Rodin surprises me by introducing me to his sister. He has never mentioned a sister. One of the dancers, she is dressed in ritual attire, full length skirt, shell bracelets on her wrists and ankles. Her eyes sparkle with energy. Speaking, she reveals a mouth and accent similar to her brother.

She stays at my side, politely keeping me company. I assume he has asked her to do this so I will not feel isolated; I consider it a kind gesture.

She watches the crowd anxiously. It seems she wishes to do something else. I would like to release her but do not know how to without being offensive. Instead I decide to leave, bidding her farewell. She follows me, the shells around her ankles jingling against each other as she trails behind me down the grass-lined path that leads to my quarters.

"Thank you for your kindness," I say. "I can find my way back from here."

She does not respond, continues with me, hands clutching at the front of her skirt. It is very disconcerting. When we arrive at my dwelling, I am unsure what to do. She stands before me speaking no words but edging herself closer to me, the scent of flowers in her hair reaching me. It seems she is offering herself to me but I am not certain. In Minoa, a man may not touch a woman in a wanting way unless she has presented herself to him. There are clear signs. One is never in doubt. Here, not only are the customs different but there is an overall sense of hesitation from this woman.

"Are you offering yourself to me," I ask her finally.

She nods her head, moving closer so that the front of our bodies meet each other.

"Clearly something is not right," I say.

She puts her arms around my neck and kisses me on the mouth. She tastes good and the feeling of her warm body against mine fills me with a heat I had almost forgotten. I lean into the kiss, take another.

"Forgive me," I say, pulling myself away from her, "It is not that I do not desire you, I simply cannot allow myself this right now."

She releases me almost gladly and begins to walk away.

"Wait," I say. "Don't go. You've come this far. Let us at least come to know one another a bit."

She pauses and observes me from the corner of her eyes, as though questioning my intentions, before walking through the door I am holding open for her.

I light the lamp and pour us each a drink of water. She drinks the water thankfully. Glancing over at my worktable, she asks, "May I?"

"Yes, of course."

She walks over to it and begins lifting up the pieces I have been working on, examining them carefully. "Some say you are a shaman," she says.

"So I have heard," I answer. "But it is not so. I do not possess the talents of your brother. Do you know," I ask, "on Crete the women are the shamans?"

"So it was here once," she answers, her face lighting in excitement. "I can even remember them. How marvelous. But they took it. They stole it from us." Her eyes, fierce and burning, look toward some distant, other place. "We must pretend not to remember. There are times—many—when I really do forget. Last night," she whispers, "I had a dream of a woman. She was trying to tell me something, something about this very matter. It is not a clear memory, but what you have said has brought it back to me." She looks back down at the table and picks up an engraved sealstone.

"Why are you here?" she asks.

"I cannot say."

The stone she is holding is alabaster. On it is the image of a priestess—a priestess of the bird, but in local, Libyan attire. It is a female shaman.

"It's for you," I say. "I carved that for you."

"For me?" Her eyes widen in wonder. "But how?"

I fold my hands over hers, which holds the stone. "I am an oracle," I say.

* * *

The next morning, Rodin approached me. "What have you done with my sister?"

"Nothing," I said. "We only talked and became a bit familiar with each other. She is a remarkable woman."

"I did not send her to you for talking."

"Why does it matter to you what we did?"

"You have shamed my honor," he said. "I presented you with a gift in front of the entire community and you rejected it. This is an insult. She has always been difficult to control, and now you have given her a feeling of power."

"I apologize if I insulted you. I made a commitment to myself that I must keep. I thought you understood that. You will, of course, send my apologies to your sister."

"My sister is not angry. She thinks you showed her the greatest kindness. I forced her to go with you. She did not want to. She longs for another. One whom I do not approve of and now, thanks to you, she remains free for him."

"Why would you force her if she did not wish it?"

"You seem to keep forgetting," he said, "that I am not Minoan."

I stood looking at him, at how small he truly was, and the difference between us, the one that separated us in the now and the always became suddenly clear. It was only one difference, but now in the light of the morning I saw how it made all the difference—a simple and small thing. I was able to love women.

"Your work is through here, Danelle. If you remain now it is only because you choose to."

"I have not yet received my answer," I said.

"You have your instructions," he said.

"I wish not to return there, Rodin."

He looked at me from the side of the head as he so often did. "Has she ever given you any reason not to trust her, Danelle?"

"No. Never," I answered.

"Then go. Trust her and go. She is waiting for you. You and I both know," he said, smiling, "that here, as well as in Minoa, it is not nice to keep a woman waiting."

Chapter 30

Lilith

My mother had forbidden me to speak with the dolphins. So when we swam together, there were not human words. In this quiet, I began to hear.

That which had always been present—that which I had not before noticed now surrounded me in great waves of pounding sound. In the silence I came to hear that water is full of noise, vibrations. To these sounds I began to listen, gradually recognizing songs, stories, and music—a world of speech without words.

So it was that I said to the dolphins, "Teach me. Teach me the language with no words."

And they said. 

And I said, 

They said, 

I said, 

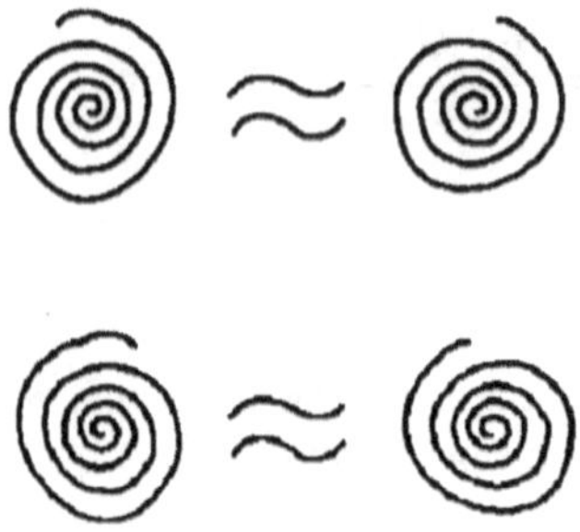

Chapter 31

Aureillia

I had been visiting the place of my final vision. I had been waiting for him in the underground caverns. I had been there many times. Danelle had not come.

Then there comes the time when I become aware of his presence. Though timid, though scared, he is there. I ask for help from all the beings that can offer it. I ask them to give me the strength I need to carry this out.

I stand in the underground chambers watching Barbara break the heads and arms off the Snake Goddess statuettes, preparing to hide them. They have already chased us out of our village into this chamber. Villagers are screaming in horror as they push their way past me. I turn to see him approaching me. I run, forcing him to follow me back to that place—the place where he murders me. When we arrive there, to the overhang, to the very spot where it always happens, instead of turning and offering my back to him, I face him directly, raise both arms high above me in protest and scream, in the loudest voice I can find within me, "No! I do not allow it!"

He is so stunned that his actions are interrupted. He backs up a bit, lowering his sword as he moves. I grab it into my hand and aim it at him. It is heavy and cold except for the place where he has been holding it. With it I feel strong, protected. All the anger within me holds that sword as I walk toward him.

He backs away from me and stumbles, falling back to the ground. I jump on top of him, sit on his chest, holding him down with my legs. I hold the sword close to his neck, wet with sweat, smeared with dust and dirt.

"Aureillia, no!" he shouts. "Don't do it!"

I hold it there for a moment, my hands shaking, pushing it against him, feeling its power. Then I see it. In his eyes, something flickers.

"Danelle," I say, dropping the sword.

* * *

From behind the wooden Goddess I speak, dressed in familiar Snake priestess attire. As both times before, the court is full. This time, however, I am not ashamed. I am not angry. This time, within me lies not bitterness.

Earlier, when I put my armbands on, I noticed that the sun had darkened my skin where the armbands had once been, making the bitemarks now barely visible. Without even having realized it, they had become yet another part of me. Simple exposure had been enough.

The large wooden statue of the Snake Goddess is on wheels. The court is silent, listening. I stand upon the tall steps within Her so that my mouth reaches the back of hers. Helena and Leida push me around the court. One bird, one butterfly, one snake.

Speaking I say:

> In a world where the Goddess is believed to be murdered
> These things may come to pass:
>
> In ceremonies of death
> The flesh of live women may burn
> The skies to our north

To thick black smoke may turn
The power of healing could be forgotten
Blood may flow
When in a woman
It should not flow
Mutilation!
Knives may come to know places
A knife should never know
The power of pleasure may be forbidden
Women!
To try to steal your power
This violence upon you they may shower
She may be shattered
Her images smashed and battered
There she could lie in many pieces
If worshiping of Her ever ceases
Do not believe it Minoans
You can make it not so
Provide a different ending to this show
Offer the Goddess a place to go

I descend the wooden woman. I stand in the middle of the court for all to see. The crowd of listeners cheers. I bow to them in sacred gesture.

Danelle

I was packing up my belongings. I had said my good-byes. There was a noise outside my door, a timid knock. I opened it to find Tolles standing on the other side of it.

"Father," I said, grabbing his frail body to mine and fully embracing him. "What are you doing here in Libya?"

"Danelle," he said, holding my hands firmly within his, tears of joy rolling down his cheeks. "I am so pleased to find you well. I have come to take you home."

"You come when I am ready," I said.

The fishing boats were returning to the cove below. Voices rose up to meet us. We walked to the edge of the hill and looked out at them. Jeftu and his companions looked up from their work and waved to us.

I put my arm around Tolles's shoulders. Together we faced the sun. "I have something for you," I said. "Something you requested before I left." I handed him the purple stone.

He observed it for some time before holding it into his chest and nodding his head. There was the smell of a new fire burning on the beach below.

"Shall we?" I said, motioning to the trail that would take us to the marina, to the ship ready to sail to Crete.

"Indeed we shall," Tolles said. We descended the hill together.

CHAPTER 32

Aureillia

Serpent Dance

It is not so much a dance as a remembering. It is not so much a union as a reconnecting. It is not so much an act as a way of being.

It is a way of engaging serpent energy, allowing it always to swirl, about moving with the energy that is present in a flowing, lucid dance.

Dance it together. Dance it often. See the serpent. Consider how it is that you hold Her within you.

Stories They Told Me

The Time of Which My Grandmother Foretold

We decided not to abandon the Center when the time came, the time of which my Grandmother had foretold...

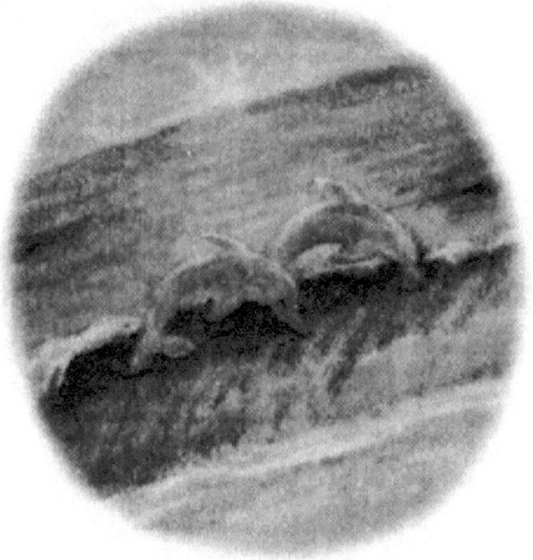

Part III

Chapter 33

The day had been long and busy. It was the festival of the Bees; a time of building and working together. We were building new walkways to new blocks of rooms. Minoa was growing. I had been assigned to plastering. It was not a difficult job, yet one grew weary of the repetitive movement and became quite covered in white dust.

I had returned to my room to wash and change before evening meal. As I entered the room, I noticed some new lettering upon the wall. I walked over to look at it.

Attachment is what makes us human, I had written a few days earlier.

Grounded, Thela wrote.

Connected, Leida wrote.

Lucky, Danelle wrote.

Danelle?

I put my fingers to the words and repeated them to myself as I traced them. Another hand appeared from behind and covered mine.

"Danelle," I said, turning to him, to his face, to his eyes, to his essence. "You're back."

"I'm back," he repeated.

I reached up and touched his face. The skin on my hand tingled. I couldn't believe the warm feel of him, Danelle, here in front of me, returned, restored to wholeness. His eyes looking into mine were clear and clean. He wrapped his arms around me, my breasts against his chest, his winged heart beating. My being filled with electric heat, my serpent rising, meeting his, our serpents combining, circling, swirling; transforming the air that surrounded us.

He took my hands into his and spread our arms out—two wings connected.

"Dance with me," he said. "Don't let go." I closed my eyes to savor him. "Never release me," he whispered, his voice quivering.

We danced. Our feet lifting in rhythm, our arms spread, rising and falling together. I thought of the eagles, how they dance together in the sky, no ground beneath them. I was glad to feel the ground beneath us. I was thankful for the earth every time my foot touched it, for the feel of Danelle, his strong, pulsing hands within my own, his smell, his look, for his unique Danelle presence, as our legs moved in sequence, as we sailed connected, through time.

About the Author

Theresa C. Dintino is an ancestral Strega (Italian wise woman), earth worker, and initiated diviner. For more than 20 years Theresa has studied and practiced an earth-based spirituality. In 2011, she was initiated as a diviner in a West African tradition. She currently helps others reclaim their personal lineages through her divination work.

Theresa is also the author of *The Strega and the Dreamer*, a work of historical fiction based on the true story of her great-grandparents immigrating from Italy to America and her great-grandmother who was a Strega, and *Ode to Minoa,* the odyssey of a Snake priestess in Bronze Age Crete. She is also the author of the nonfiction book *Welcoming Lilith: Awakening and Welcoming Pure Female Power.*

For more on Theresa and her work, visit **thestregaandthedreamer.com** and **ritualgoddess.com**.

Other Books by Theresa C. Dintino

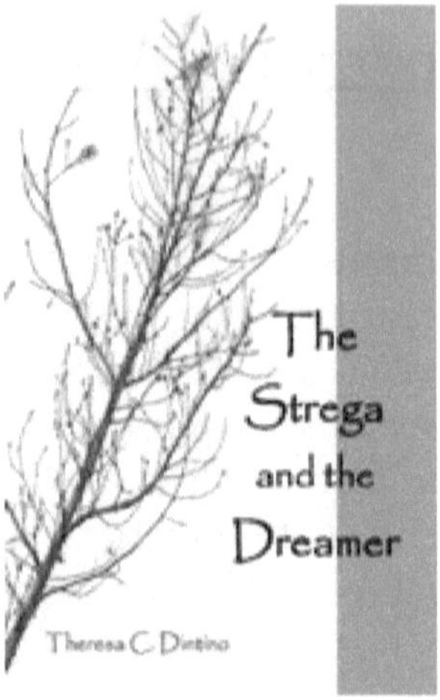

The Strega & the Dreamer
http://www.amazon.com/Strega-Dreamer-Theresa-C-Dintino-ebook/dp/B0095JXCD4

It is the story of a man who is willing to sacrifice everything for a dream, and a passionate woman questioning the confining roles allowed to 19th century women.

The Strega and the Dreamer is the tale of Italian immigrants coming to America from the Abruzzi region of Italy at the turn of the last century.

Eva is an Italian Strega, a midwife and healer, fully committed to her small hilltop village. Marcello is a man with a dream of America —a dream that Eva does not share. Famine comes to the Abruzzi & Marcello goes to America, leaving his family behind as he searches for a more prosperous life.

Eva dedicates herself to her Strega duties and the people of the village. Though it is taboo for a woman to do so, with the help of a doctor from the city she secretly learns of modern medicine. When Marcello finally calls for her, Eva has a decision to make. She must choose between staying in her beloved Abruzzi where she has her family and her Strega calling, or moving to America, where midwifery is considered barbaric and is being systematically eliminated.

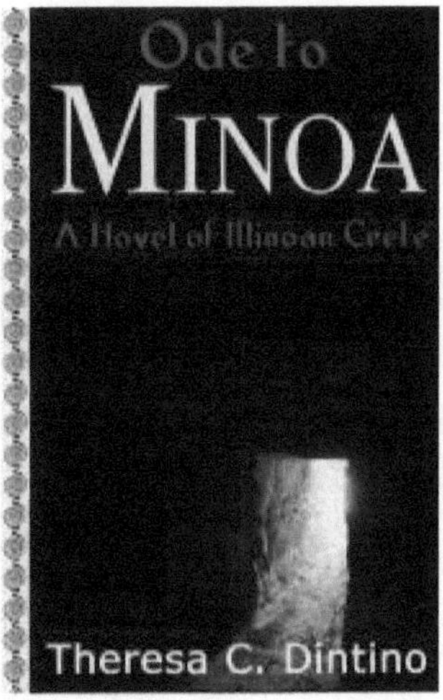

Ode to Minoa

http://www.amazon.com/Ode-Minoa-Theresa-Dintino/dp/156315143X

When Aureillia, the young Snake Priestess in Bronze Age Crete, begins having visions of an unspeakable evil, her simple life is thrown into turmoil.

As a member of a Goddess worshiping culture, her life is ruled by the cycles of the moon and deep connection to earth but soon will be affected by a far greater force. Visions of the future lead Aureillia to a loss of innocence and the discovery of her extraordinary power and the power in every woman.

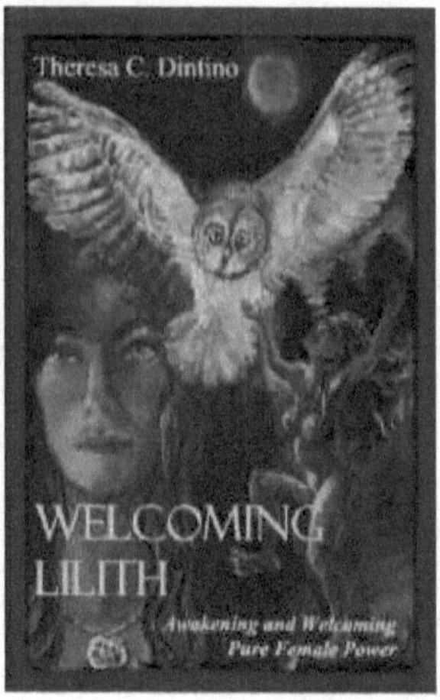

Welcoming Lilith
http://www.amazon.com/Welcoming-Lilith-Theresa-Dintino/dp/1937632768

Lilith is a Goddess and mythological figure who is misunderstood. She is reputed to be Adam's first wife before Eve, and she represents the first powerful and liberated female in history. Then why was she banished?

Through commentary and reflection on the multifaceted aspects of Lilith, Theresa C. Dintino guides the reader on an exciting inner journey to reclaim her own repressed parts. By examining how these Lilith energies may show up in her own life, the reader is encouraged to do the work to bring them back to life.

Rituals included in the book offer the opportunity to explore these powerful but often feared aspects. Reclaiming the lost fragments—her power, her anger, her shadow, her sexuality, her creativity and her deep inner truth—returns the female psyche to a state of wholeness and integration.

www.ingramcontent.com/pod-product-compliance
Lightning Source LLC
Chambersburg PA
CBHW020944260626
47169CB00006B/1803
* 9 7 8 1 9 3 9 8 1 2 5 2 0 *